Destructive Resonance

Book One
Theory of Collision

F. R. Kriegler

DESTRUCTIVE RESONANCE

Copyright © 2026 by F.R. Kriegler

All rights reserved.

This book is a work of fiction. Names, characters, places, businesses, events, incidents, locations, and dialogue are products of the author's imagination or are used fictitiously. Any resemblance to actual persons, living or dead, actual events, organizations, governmental or private institutions, or real judicial proceedings is entirely coincidental and unintentional.

While the narrative may reference real cities, institutions, corporations, professions, or governmental structures for purposes of realism, all characters, events, and circumstances are fictionalized and are not intended to represent any actual individual, organization, government, or legal case. References to corporations, workplaces, legal institutions, immigration systems, courts, or administrative processes are used solely as background context and do not imply endorsement, affiliation, criticism, or commentary regarding any real entity or authority.

The views and opinions expressed in this book are those of the author and do not necessarily reflect the official policy or position of any government, agency, or institution.

The emotional and psychological dynamics depicted in this story are literary explorations of human behaviour and are not allegations against any real person or institution.

This work contains mature themes and is intended for an adult audience. It should not be interpreted as factual reporting or legal commentary. The author and publisher disclaim liability for any consequences arising from interpretation of the content.

Content Advisory: This novel contains graphic depictions of emotional abuse, psychological trauma, self-harm, domestic violence, and explicit sexual content. These elements are integral to the psychological exploration of the characters and are not intended for exhilaration.

No part of this book may be reproduced or transmitted in any form or by any means without prior written permission of the copyright holder, except where permitted by law.

For information regarding rights, contact the publisher.

Published by:
Øresund Hunt & Press
Skindergade 7
1159 København K
Denmark

Website:
www.dresonance.com

First Edition: March 2026

ISBN (Paperback): 978-87-977011-7-1
ISBN (Hardcover): 978-87-977011-5-7
ISBN (eBook): 978-87-977011-1-9

Dedication

To God and the *few* who loved me fiercely enough to humble me —
your light was the compass.

To my son and my daughter —
I carry you with me, even in the silence of our distance.
May you inherit my resilience, but never my reasons for it.
You are my proof that something whole and gentle can grow from what was broken in me.

To my brother who stood by me in my most difficult time, who helped me navigate the darkness and showed me light.

To every person, good and bad, who left a fingerprint on my mind.
To those who taught me through care, and those who taught me through harm.
You all left marks. I learned to read them.

To the hatred, resentment, and quiet contempt I carried and received —
you sharpened my awareness, even when you tried to shrink me.

To the hardships that hardened me without hollowing me out.
To the years that demanded endurance before they offered understanding.
To the pressure that forced clarity.

To the stranger whose shadow I carry, whose example taught me what never to become — and in doing so, pushed me toward everything I am.
Who never allowed me to settle for less,
and to the darkness that accompanied that lesson,
both shaped me. I survived both.

To every figure of authority — lawyers, judges, bankers, police, supervisors,

and *keepers* of the gate — who handed me one truth wrapped in a thousand lies:
you taught me to read between the lines,
to question every surface,
and to find my own justice.

This book exists because I learned to listen closely —
to what was said,
to what was done,
and to what was never meant to be heard.

This book is my letter to you,
where words failed me in life.

This book is proof.
Forged in fire.
Written in strength,
for *you*.

Table of Contents

Preface

This is a work of fiction. The characters you will meet, the specific events that unfold in Stockholm apartments and strained silences, are creations of narrative. But the emotional and psychological terrain they inhabit is mapped from a place of stark familiarity.

The central question of this novel is not *whodunit*, but *how* — how does attachment become entanglement? How does recognition curdle into obsession? How do two people, seeking solace, architect their own captivity? These are not hypotheticals. They are the silent mechanics of relationships that turn toxic, the slow violence of emotional dependence, the prison of trauma bonding.

While the story is invented, its truth lies in the dynamics: conditional kindness, the erosion of boundaries, love spoken in the dialect of control. I have written these dynamics with a fidelity some may find uncomfortable, because comfort was never the point. Understanding is.

If you have ever felt the slow, chilling shift from being loved to being managed, or wondered how a sanctuary became a cage, you may find this story resonates with a terrible clarity. It is written for the part of us that recognises the pattern before we dare name it.

This book is my attempt to examine that pattern — to lay bare what happens when the deepest human need, to be seen and held, collides with our deepest flaws.

What follows is the testimony of that collision.

Acknowledgments

A book may be written in isolation, but it is never brought into the world alone. My deepest gratitude goes to those who stood as lights along this often-difficult path.

To my editors, Martin H. Bane, Erika Strömberg for your unwavering belief in this story and your surgical precision in helping me carve it into its final, sharpest form. Your insight was invaluable.

To my early readers and beta readers — thank you for your courage, your candour, and for walking through these emotional trenches with me to ensure the story rang true.

To the professionals who helped bring this book into the world: my copyeditor, the cover designer, and the entire team. Thank you for your expertise and care.

To my friends, who offered shelter, distraction, and unwavering support when the weight of this story grew heavy. You know who you are, and you know what you did. Thank you for the coffee, the silence, and the lifelines.

To my family — those bound by blood and those chosen by heart. Your love is the quiet foundation upon which everything else is built.

To this book, for restoring connections I thought had faded beyond reach.

And finally, to you, the reader. Thank you for allowing this story into your mind and heart. Writing is an act of faith in connection; you have fulfilled it.

Chapter 1

The Breach

The woman burst from her apartment in a violent, instinctive motion, flinging the heavy door open with a force that seemed impossible for her slender frame. She rushed through the threshold as if fleeing the scene of her own disappearance.

The quiet hallway reacted like a stage flooded by sudden light. Blinking, echoing, then freezing in shock. As the door yanked inward, it pulled a gust of stale corridor air into the apartment, stirring dust motes that drifted upward like forgotten memories. For a heartbeat, everything felt suspended.

The cold hit her bare shoulders. Still. Unmoving. A solid presence pressing against the skin. It carried the faint mustiness of old concrete and forgotten winters, a smell baked deeply into the structure. Mixed into it were traces of old paint, radiator dust, and the remnants of someone's overcooked meatballs drifting up from the ground floor. The building's age murmured through the walls. Water knocking in the pipes. The faint buzz of tired wiring. The low mechanical hum buried somewhere below. It was a winter that lived in the concrete rather than the sky, a chill born from decades of narrow corridors and neighbours who preferred not to hear too much.

Outside, the night of 17 January pressed in with its own heavy stillness. Cold. Dry. Bone-still. The temperature well below freezing.

At around 8:30 p.m., everything began to unravel.

Tonight, something in that stillness shifted. Shadows clung more tightly to the corners. The old pipes hummed faintly.

Chapter 1

Overhead, the fluorescent bulbs flickered with their familiar sickly hum. Their glow painted long, distorted shadows across the walls, shadows that stretched and recoiled as she ran.

Bursting through the threshold, her gaze swept past the door directly facing hers — **M. Karlsson** — without stopping, without recognition. Just a nameplate. She had never given it more than a passing glance. She did not know the people inside, only that it was a couple in their mid-thirties. She did not remember their faces or their voices. But before the night ended, the role they were about to play would overshadow everything else on this floor. For now, that door was just another face in the corridor. Another silent witness pretending not to see.

To her immediate right was another apartment door, belonging to a kind old couple from Argentina she had met a few times in the laundry room. Tonight, it stood as stiff and silent as ever. No movement. No curiosity. No salvation. Farther right, the elevator door sat adjacent to the old couple's flat. Silent. Just in front of it, about two metres ahead and just beyond the Karlssons' door, the staircase began its ascent to the upper floor, its green railing rising in a sharp, utilitarian line along the outer edge of the steps. It sat directly in her line of sight.

But she was not going up.

The soft grey slippers she had barely managed to put on scuffed against the floor. She did not hesitate. She veered left. Her palm slapped the doorframe for balance as momentum dragged her dangerously close to the green staircase railing. Her heartbeat thundered, hammering against her ribs. It pulsed in her ears, her wrists, the underside of her jaw. Each beat sharp enough to make her vision throb at the edges.

Behind her, the apartment door swung open with such sudden violence that its handle crashed into the interior wall. And it was not just an ordinary door. It was a hulking monolith. Its deceptive elegance masked its near-impenetrable strength. The kind of door that demanded respect. The kind that did not simply open, but yielded.

The impact sent a shock through the hallway like a gunshot. The shrill metallic crack of the loosened handle smashing into wall plaster ripped through the corridor. Vibration ran through the frame, along the white walls, and into the concrete floor. Dust shook loose from the upper moulding and drifted down in a thin, ghostly veil. The metal mail slot rattled violently, clanging against the door in a rapid metallic stutter.

Seconds earlier, as she had unlocked it, the reinforced multi-bolt mechanism had clicked and clacked like a machine designed for war rather than domestic peace. She had gripped the cold handle with her right hand and pulled, the hinges groaning in deep metallic protest, resentful at being forced open with such urgency. For one brief instant, it had felt almost unbelievable that she had managed to pull something so massive open at all.

Now it gaped behind her, wide open like a breached fortress gate. Then, with a slow, reluctant exhale, it drifted back towards the frame, not committing to the full embrace of the latch, but simply ajar, resting there lightly.

Like a brittle leaf collapsing after surviving a storm.

Her breath tore in sharp, ragged bursts, like someone gulping air after being held underwater too long. Cool hallway air cut into her lungs, burned her throat, scraped every inhale raw. She was hyperventilating without intending to, sucking in too much oxygen and not enough control.

The corridor unfolded around her in its familiar shape. As she ran, the thin seams in the dust-filmed concrete — faint lines mapping the building's history of quick fixes and long-delayed maintenance — passed beneath her. But her eyes were fixed on the stairs ahead.

At twenty-five, she should have been worrying about assignment deadlines, apartment rent, saving for a new winter coat. A life she had imagined when she first left Ukraine. Not tearing through a Swedish hallway with the same instinct she had grown up with back home. The instinct to move first and think later.

A burgundy silk nightdress clung to her damp skin, moulding itself to her body as if sensing the panic. Its surface shimmered faintly, clinging with the fragile loyalty of something never meant to face the world beyond a quiet bedroom. Thin straps trembled against sharply defined collarbones. Intricate lace quivered with her frantic breaths, delicate loops fluttering like insect wings caught in a storm. The open-shouldered top exposed goosebumps spreading across her upper arms. She was not cold. She was running on pure adrenaline. Fear mimicked cold.

Her breasts rose and fell beneath the trembling lace as the fabric slid over her narrow waist, accentuating the delicate taper of her torso with every frantic stride. Each hard breath pulled the material a fraction higher, revealing a glimpse of her midriff and the soft concavity of her navel. Her skin felt too exposed, as if the hallway itself could see through it. A pale, vulnerable contrast to the deep burgundy fabric clinging to her in all the wrong places.

Her legs felt heavy and electric at once. Shaking, but unstoppable. Each stride sent a shock up through her knees, her hips, her spine. There was a strange harmony in the way they moved, trained by years of walking, of fleeing, of never quite arriving.

Long brunette hair streamed behind her, catching the stale hallway air and thrashing as if trying to flee alongside her. Strands whipped and tangled in her wake while others clung stubbornly to her flushed cheeks. Her lips, naturally full, parted with each ragged, uneven breath. Her eyes were blown wide in raw, unfiltered terror.

A thin silver chain bounced against her neck as she ran — a simple Ukrainian piece her mother had given her on her twentieth birthday. At its centre hung a small silver heart, smoothed by years of anxious rubbing. Now, as she sprinted down the corridor, the pendant tapped against her collarbone in an uneven rhythm, each soft blow echoing the erratic beat of her heart.

She felt horribly out of place. Dressed for a dream. Running through a nightmare.

The corridor stretched ahead of her like a tunnel carved out of stale air and old secrets. Its walls were divided cleanly in half. The lower portion clad in pale, stone-textured slabs that trapped the night's cold. The upper portion painted sterile white, with a marching band of stencilled green leaves winding through the hall. Under the harsh ceiling lights, it looked absurd. Like a painted grin stretched across a dead face.

Slippers skimmed and smacked against the speckled floor. Each step landed soft yet echoed like a muffled slap, ricocheting off the corridor walls. The building's cold acoustics multiplied her footsteps, throwing them back at her too loud, too revealing. Reminding her she was not quiet, not hidden, not safe.

It felt like an eternity but took only seconds, not more than four long strides, for her to reach the far-left wing of the corridor, where the door marked **J. Brandholm** stood at the dead end. She almost crashed into it.

But she did not stop.

She could not.

Her mind had already torn itself away from thought, sprinting faster than her legs could carry her. The explosion behind her felt distant, muffled, irrelevant, like a memory collapsing into silence. The threat felt alive, swelling in the darkness she had just escaped.

She slowed for a fraction of a second. Her right hand reached out almost automatically, fingers curling around the cold staircase railing to her right, where the hallway met the first drop of the stairwell. The landing fell sharply here. The green metal bars angled downward along the outer edge of the steps. It was steady beneath her grip, something solid in the middle of everything spinning out of control.

Chapter 1

Using that railing, she pulled herself into a sharp right turn. Slow at first. Then tighter. More deliberate. A full 180-degree swing towards the stairs.

But as she pivoted, her head twisted, unwillingly, back towards where everything she was running from still waited.

Her own door.

A dark slice cut into the corridor.

She did not want to look at it.

Yet she could not look anywhere else.

She needed it to stay still. To stay harmless. Part of her begged for that. Another part, already knowing she was being chased, braced for the moment it would not.

Whatever she had left behind that door felt too close. Too real. Too alive. The fear was so total, so absolute, that everything inside her had collapsed into a single, primitive directive.

Run.

Her body tipped on to the stairwell landing, beginning the descent.

By the time her foot hit the first step, she heard it. The sound she had been dreading. Not a slam, but the deliberate, controlled pull of the apartment door being opened from the inside.

A raw, thin scream ripped from her throat.

Her whole body vibrated with an electric flicker beneath the skin.

Every muscle surged in rapid, uncontrollable bursts.

Her fingers numbed. Her legs prickled with sharp needling sensations from calf to thigh. Her stomach twisted violently mid-stride.

Her bones felt hollow. Her grip clamped around the railing, the exposed metal biting into her palm as she pulled herself downward.

Thc door was open.
Wide.

And in that opening, a figure filled the frame.

A man.
Tall.
Early thirties.

Broad-shouldered, moving with a rigid, unspoken masculinity. His skin was warm brown. His jaw clenched so hard the muscles jumped beneath it. His body was strong and coiled beneath striped red-and-blue checkered pyjamas, the fabric pulled tight.

His dark brown eyes locked on hers for a brief, searing moment. Intense. Conflicted. Burning with anger and fear. Then she disappeared into the stairwell.

His teeth ground together. Every breath came fast and ragged.

He was gasping, just as breathless as she was, shoulders rising and falling quickly, chest heaving as he sprinted after her. He was running towards her — one step, then another — trying to close the distance she had broken open between them. Fear lived in him too. Raw. Sharp. Unmistakable. The fear of a man who knew the situation had slipped beyond his control.

For a moment, the hallway seemed to brace itself, tightening around this chaos, shrinking down to nothing but the space between her fleeing body and his advancing one.

Nothing made sense. Her terror. His desperation. She ran as if fleeing for her life, and he followed with the urgency of a man afraid of losing everything all at once.

The scene carried all the signs of a nightmare beginning.

Chapter 1

She was terrified of him.

Of the man she already knew too well.

Chapter 2

A Spark in the Long Grass

To understand how two people arrive at a door they can never close, one must to go back. Back to when terror had not yet learned its name. When warning signs looked like gestures of care. Back to the moment he mistook her need for devotion, and she mistook his stability for sanctuary.

And if you trace it carefully, step by step, breath by breath, you will find that the ending was seeded in the beginning.

Not in cruelty.
Not in violence.
But in something far more dangerous.

Hope.

The day they met was *midsommardagen* — the Swedish celebration of the longest day of the year. The Stockholm sky looked too blue to be real, a painted canopy stretched wide above crowds that vibrated with heat, music, and the restless joy of a city fully released from winter's grip. The air was a thick, sweet perfume of grilled food, sun-warmed grass, and flower crowns still damp from the river. Between the picnic blankets, children ran barefoot through the clover, while couples sought the dappled shade of birch trees and a folk band played near the towering midsummer pole, its ribbons and blooms dancing in the breeze.

Hassan stood amid the celebration, weaving his own floral wreath with surprising, infectious enthusiasm. Sunlight warmed the sharp angles of his face, catching the quiet confidence he carried without effort. His dark hair, freshly trimmed, framed relaxed features that seemed built for the light. When he finally settled the finished wreath onto his head, it sat slightly crooked, lending an air of unstudied charm to his presence. Two women strolling past laughed softly, pausing to praise him for the prettiest crown they'd seen all day. He thanked them with an easy, warm grin, the kind of smile that wasn't meant to impress, but somehow did anyway.

A few minutes later, he settled onto the grass a short distance from the densest part of the crowd. He held his phone up, capturing the swirl of dancers on the stage and the rising cheer of his first true Swedish midsummer. There was a newfound looseness in his posture, a lightness born of the sun rather than the people around him. For once, life felt loud, bright, and undeniably alive.

And then, quietly, almost invisible against the backdrop of the festivities, there was her.

Anastasia.

She was sitting a few feet behind him to his right, her legs crossed and her fingers intertwined so tightly they looked locked in place. Her salmon-coloured hoodie hung loose on her slender frame, sleeves pulled halfway over her hands, as if offering a place to hide. Her brown running shoes pressed firmly into the grass, anchoring her as if letting go might cause the world to tilt on its axis. She sat like someone imitating calm while secretly stitching herself together beneath the fabric of her clothes.

Homesickness clung to her like a faint shadow. The echoes of war, the exhaustion of flight, and the memory of men who mistook her vulnerability for an invitation lingered behind her eyes. Yet she remained there in the heart of the crowd, trying to breathe in the joy of the day and let the summer heal the jagged edges inside her.

Hassan shifted to take another photo, and as his gaze swept back to the right, he noticed her. To him, she was just a stranger softened by the afternoon glow, the nearest person within asking distance. He leaned toward her without hesitation, unaware of the small tremor his gentleness sent through her.

"Hi," he said, his voice warm and effortless. "Could you please take a picture of me?"

He spoke with the calm of a man who never asked for too much. A tone people naturally agreed to, not out of pressure, but out of comfort. Anastasia looked up, startled out of her thoughts. Her greenish-hazel eyes, with warm brown flecks at the centre, lifted toward him in unguarded surprise. It was as if she hadn't expected the world to speak to her at all.

She nodded before she could find the words. "Yes," she whispered.

He caught the nod, smiled his gratitude, and extended the phone. She reached out with her left hand, closing the small gap between them, and lifted the device to frame him. He sat cross-legged on the grass, the floral wreath askew on his head as the breeze tugged at his hair. He flashed a relaxed half-smile that carried more confidence than he realised, and she clicked the shutter — once, twice.

"Maybe take a few while I'm standing, too?" he added, half-laughing at the slight foolishness of posing alone in a crowded park.

"Sure," she murmured.

He adjusted his rounded red sunglasses and straightened the wreath before standing, not really posing, but simply existing in the sunlight. He was naturally photogenic, the Microsoft lanyard around his neck swaying softly and his apartment key catching a glint of gold against his blue T-shirt and jeans. Anastasia took the photos, silent and focused.

When he stepped back toward her to retrieve the phone, their fingers brushed. It was a fleeting, warm contact that sent a faint twitch through her chest. He didn't seem to notice the spark at all.

"Thank you," he said softly.

In that moment, something shifted. It wasn't romance or fate. It was a sudden spark of safety in a world that had been too cold to her for far too long. She handed him the phone, and he didn't linger. He didn't notice the way her eyes held onto him for a heartbeat longer than necessary. He simply sat again, a little ahead of her, and turned his face back toward the stage.

Chapter 3

A Dance of Borrowed Light

Hassan was married. He had been waiting for his wife for more than a year and a half, checking his email the way someone checks for a pulse they're not sure they still have, hoping the next notification would finally say her visa had been approved. He lived between two worlds: the one he had built, and the one he was waiting to reclaim.

Anastasia carried a truth of her own, one carved far rougher, far newer. She had fled a war only to run into a man she met online, old enough to be her father: a fifty-two-year-old Swedish man of African descent who had lured her to Sweden with promises of safety, shelter, support. A place where she wouldn't have to be afraid. But promises can rot from the inside. When she arrived, desperate and disoriented, she saw what he had really wanted. Not companionship. Not compassion. Hunger. His intentions wrapped around her like a trap, and she escaped only by breaking a piece of herself free.

Both of them sat in that bright sun carrying wounds the world couldn't see, one built from waiting, the other from running. Neither expected their paths to cross, and yet, when they did, two very different kinds of loneliness quietly recognised each other. For her, the warmth of his palm was an unexpected shock, not desire, but something older and more elemental: a brief return to safety. His hand was steady without holding, firm without pressure, gentle in a way that didn't ask anything of her, grounding her in a way she hadn't felt since her world cracked open months ago.

For Hassan, it was a simple gesture. To him, she was just the girl who'd taken his picture, the quiet one in the salmon hoodie, eyes soft as dusk. He wasn't searching for connection, yet some faint part of him, buried under months of solitude and distance, reacted to the nearness of another human being. Just the unacknowledged ache of someone who hadn't felt another person's nearness in a long time.

For a few minutes, it seemed as though their interaction had already dissolved into the surrounding noise and colour. He returned to his recording, and she returned to the quiet pretence of not watching him. They sat apart like two strangers who had no reason to believe their lives were about to tangle, and every reason to believe they were never supposed to collide.

But then the music changed.

The band struck a louder, brighter tune. The crowd started swelling, forming circles around the midsummer pole. People took each other's hands. Laughing, spinning, dancing. A ripple of movement swept across the grass and passed right through them. Hassan stood too, brushing grass from his jeans. He adjusted his wreath, exhaled a content breath. Then, almost without intending to, he turned slightly toward Anastasia.

"You want to join the dance?" he asked gently.

Her lips parted in surprise, like she hadn't expected kindness to be aimed at her. Her eyes dropped for a beat, then lifted again, shy and unsure.

"I… yes," she said softly. "I can."

He extended his hand, neutral, polite, nothing more. She stared at it for an instant, as if the gesture itself was a language she'd forgotten. Then she placed hers in it with a careful, trembling touch. And when their hands curled together, something passed between them. Something much simpler: two lonely people finding a moment of comfort in a country that often felt cold. And for the first time since fleeing her home, she felt a small, steady warmth push back against the darkness she had carried.

She rose slowly from the grass, brushing green flecks from her trousers with a delicate sweep of her hand. Her long dark hair shifted over her shoulder in a gentle cascade. When she stepped closer, a faint floral scent reached him, not perfume, but the natural fragrance of a woman outdoors in summer. Clean. Soft. Familiar in the way unfamiliar things sometimes are.

He led her toward the circle forming around the midsummer pole. Children hopped. Couples spun. Old friends laughed as they linked arms and moved in unison. The entire crowd swayed together like one large, living organism, rhythmically shifting beneath the bright June sun. Hassan took his place in the circle, and she stepped beside him, shy at first, unsure how close she was meant to be. He kept a small distance. He softened the space around her, shifting slightly so she didn't feel crowded. A gesture so small, so unconscious, yet it landed inside her like a warm stone dropped into cold water.

The dance began. Simple steps, playful instructions shouted in English by the singer, the crowd hopping side to side like ripples moving through the circle. Hassan moved with easy confidence, blending into the rhythm. Anastasia tried to follow, but stumbled once, her shoe catching the soft, uneven grass.

He glanced back. "You, okay?" he asked, just loud enough for her to hear over the music.

She nodded quickly, embarrassed, but his smile was kind, disarming. "You'll get it." And something in the way he said it, not indulgent, just certain, made her believe, for one irrational moment, that maybe she could.

As the dance continued, they rotated through the circle, switching places with others. Each time the pattern brought them back together, she found him watching the crowd, not her, giving her space to simply exist beside him without performance. With every return, her shoulders dropped a little more, her eyes lifting from the ground to the people around her. At one point, when the steps required them to mimic a hopping motion, childish, silly. She hesitated, cheeks flushing pink. Hassan, noticing, leaned slightly toward her.

Chapter 3

"It's okay to look stupid. Everyone does," he murmured with a grin.

She laughed, quiet and surprised, almost shy. The kind of laugh she hadn't heard from herself in months. The sound escaped her like a small bird released from a tightening fist. She ducked her head as if trying to hide it, but he saw it anyway. Her hair caught beams of sunlight as she moved. Her eyes glimmered with a kind of vulnerability so honest it was hard to look at without feeling something. Her smile, timid but genuine, softened her whole face. There was a gentleness to her, a carefulness, that made her seem like she lived life half-bracing for impact. He didn't know why that affected him. But it did.

The dance shifted again, the circle changing direction. She stepped a little closer by mistake, their shoulders barely brushing as they moved. The contact was accidental. Her breath hitched. He felt it. He treated it as nothing, a wisp of air passing between bodies in a crowd. He didn't pull away dramatically. Didn't stiffen. Didn't react at all. And that unbothered ease, that quiet respect, made her trust him in a way she didn't understand.

When the dance ended, applause burst through the space. Families scattered back toward blankets; some lined up for food, others collapsed onto the grass with breathless laughter. Hassan stepped aside and lifted his wreath, adjusting the bend in one of the stems where someone had bumped him earlier. He didn't notice she was watching him until he lifted his head. Her gaze flicked away instantly. He smiled, softly amused by her attempt to hide her attention.

"You did great," he said.

She shook her head quickly. "No. I didn't."

"You didn't fall. That counts." A small smile tugged at her lips.

He extended his hand, not like before, just a simple introduction. "I'm Hassan, by the way."

She stared at his hand as if it were something fragile she wasn't sure she should touch. Then she placed her palm into his, lightly.

"Anastasia."

Her name carried a melody. Ukrainian softness, tempered by weariness.

"That's a beautiful name," he said without thinking.

She blinked, surprised, her gaze dipping away as if the compliment unsettled something delicate inside her.

Chapter 4

The Geometry of a Promise

Another silence gathered between them, filled with the kind of awareness that lingers after an unexpected dance with someone you never meant to notice. Minutes passed before either of them spoke again. The crowd around them shifted in waves, children darting between legs, teens laughing too loudly near the stands. The bright hum of midsummer wrapped the entire park in warmth.

Anastasia pulled her hoodie sleeves lower over her hands and looked toward the stage, not quite at him, but not away from him either. Her breath was steadier now, the jagged edges smoothed by distraction, by movement, by the rare gentleness she'd been shown. Hassan didn't rush her. He didn't fill the silence with chatter. He simply stood in it. Hands in his pockets, shoulders relaxed, gaze drifting across the crowd. He welcomed noise when it required nothing from him, when it let him breathe without thinking. He hadn't felt this light in months.

Eventually, she found the courage to break the quiet.

"Where are you from?" she asked, her voice small but steady.

"Pakistan," he said. "From Lahore." Then, returning the question gently: "You?"

Her eyes flickered, quick, guarded, but not closed off. "Ukraine," she said.

He nodded. "Beautiful country."

Her jaw tightened. "It was."

He didn't push, didn't pry. Only offered a quiet, sincere: "I'm sorry."

Chapter 4

She nodded once, the gratitude barely visible but deeply felt.

They stood there, letting the noise fill in the parts they weren't ready to talk over. A little while later, he asked politely, "Are you here with friends?"

Anastasia paused, only for a fraction of a second, but enough for a lie to shape itself on her tongue with the ease of a survival habit.

"Yes. She went to get food."

Hassan simply nodded, accepting it without pressing further.

"It's good to have someone to spend midsummer with."

Her expression flickered, just briefly. Loneliness, guilt, longing — some mix of the three that she hoped he didn't notice. But he wasn't watching her with the intensity of a man studying a woman; he saw people, not pretences. Her shift in expression went mostly unnoticed.

Before either of them could say anything else, the musicians struck the first notes of another song, fast, buoyant, almost too cheerful. The crowd stirred again, renewed excitement gathering like a tide. Hassan looked toward the forming circle. Then back at her.

"You want to dance again?" he asked.

This time her hesitation wasn't fear. It was something else. Something she weighed briefly, like a question she already knew the answer to. Her lashes lifted.

"Yes," she said. "I'd like that."

He offered his hand. Not lingering. Simply polite. She placed hers in his with more confidence than before — still soft, still cautious, but no longer trembling. They stepped into the circle.

The second dance was faster, looser. The kind of dance that didn't ask for grace, only willingness. People hopped and spun, the older crowd throwing themselves into exaggerated motions for comedy's sake, laughing at their own clumsiness. The air buzzed with pure midsummer energy. Hassan breathed it in deeply, and for a moment, the waiting didn't exist. There was only this: sun on his skin, music in his bones, and a stranger beside him who didn't know he was supposed to be somewhere else.

For the first time in months, he forgot to check his phone between songs. Forgot the waiting. Forgot the quiet apartment that felt like suspension. The relief unsettled him slightly. How easily it came, how quickly it erased the rest. He was usually stricter with himself than this.

He moved through the dance naturally. The small hops, the simple rotations, the clapping moments. His posture relaxed; his shoulders loosened. The wreath sat crooked on his head, half-wilted already, but he wore it without caring.

Anastasia tried to follow him again and this time, when she stumbled, she caught herself before he could notice. A small victory. One she kept to herself. There was a fragile grace to the way she moved, like someone who didn't yet believe she deserved space in the world, but was trying anyway.

When the song ended, Anastasia released his hand, slowly. Everyone clapped. They turned toward the stage as if the music still held their attention.

"You dance well," she said softly, surprising him.

He chuckled lightly. "I just try to keep up. That's all."

Again, her lips tugged into a small curve, still shy, still uncertain, but genuine. She pulled her sleeves further over her hands, fidgeting.

"You're enjoying today," she murmured.

He nodded.

"Yeah. Midsummer feels… good."

He didn't add why. Didn't explain the ache behind the need for warmth. Didn't explain what sunlight meant to someone waiting for a family that still lived far from him. Her gaze lingered on him, curious, steady, the kind of look people give when they're trying to understand something without asking.

She didn't know his story. He didn't know hers. But for the first time in weeks, she wasn't invisible. And for the first time in months, he wasn't alone.

They simply existed beside each other, breathing the same midsummer air, letting the noise settle around them. The park was alive in every direction. The kind of chaotic, honest life that made the world feel wide again. Hassan didn't fill the silence. He didn't feel the need to.

Anastasia sat with a kind of stillness that wasn't peace, more like someone holding their breath without realising it. The hoodie of her sweatshirt pooled loosely around her neck now; she'd pushed it back earlier, perhaps to feel the sun. Her hands rested lightly in her lap, one thumb brushing the opposite sleeve in small, nervous strokes. After a moment, she lifted her gaze.

"You live near here?" she asked, her voice still carrying a tint of caution.

"About twenty minutes' walk. I moved in a few weeks ago," he replied. "It's close to the city centre."

She nodded, letting that image settle. A man who walked through Stockholm neighbourhoods she didn't yet know how to pronounce, who probably navigated the city with ease while she still had to rely on apps and courage she didn't always have.

"You study?" she asked next.

He shook his head.

"I work. Software developer."

Something flickered through her expression, not admiration, but a quiet acknowledgement. Respect that didn't feel forced.

"Impressive."

Hassan huffed a small laugh. "Depends who you ask."

That earned a more visible smile from her.

Soft. Small. But real.

For a moment, she looked down at her hands again, thinking. Her fingers tightened once around the sleeve of her hoodie before she whispered, "You seem… kind."

He blinked, caught off guard, but not uncomfortable.

"I'm just trying to enjoy midsummer," he replied, his voice staying in that calm middle ground he always carried.

"Yes. But still."

The way she said *still* lingered. A quiet confession from someone who hadn't felt sincerity in too long. He didn't know how to respond, so he gave a small nod, honest, appreciative, without reading into it.

They went silent again, the weight of the moment balanced gently between them. The sound of new music drifted faintly from the stage as another band began setting up. But neither stood to dance this time. Hassan stretched his legs, brushing a bit of grass from his jeans.

"I should get going soon," he said simply.

Something in her posture stilled. Not visibly. Not dramatically. Just the faintest pause, the kind you only noticed if you were standing close enough.

She nodded. "Okay."

Chapter 4

He hesitated, only because she seemed unsure whether the moment was ending or simply shifting into a different shape.

"If you need anything in the city," he said gently, "or help with something… you can ask. I volunteer sometimes. So, if you ever need directions, advice, anything like that."

He kept his tone clean. Boundaried. Kind without implying more.

Her head lifted slowly. Her face softened, with gratitude, relief, the fragile trust of someone who had every reason not to trust anyone.

"That's very kind of you," she murmured.

He offered a small, polite smile. "Do you want to exchange numbers? Only if you're comfortable."

Her answer came immediately. "Yes."

She unlocked her phone with trembling fingers and handed it to him. He typed his name and number, then passed it back without looking at her screen or waiting for hers. She saved the contact quietly, held the device in her hands for a second too long, then whispered, "Thank you, Hassan."

He nodded once, then stood, adjusting the wreath on his head.

"Take care," he said, and the warmth in his voice was genuine, not performative.

He walked away, merging into the flow of families and groups leaving the park, becoming one more figure in the midsummer crowd. The sun cast a soft glow along his shoulders as he drifted farther toward the path.

Anastasia watched him go. The way you watch a door that had been locked for months suddenly shift open a crack.

She sat for a while after that, knees drawn in, hands still tucked under the sleeves of her hoodie, eyes following the movements of people who seemed to belong effortlessly to the moment. The memory of his palm against hers lingered, faint but undeniable. When she finally stood, the grass marked faint impressions on the backs of her trousers. She brushed them away gently, looked toward the direction he'd disappeared, and then toward the emptying crowd.

She didn't text him that day. Or the day after. Or the one after that. Not because she didn't want to, but because she didn't know how to speak first. Didn't know if she was allowed to. Didn't know if reaching out would break whatever quiet thing had settled between them. But still… the feeling didn't leave.

The memory of a stranger who treated her with respect, lingered in her chest like a warm ember, small but persistent. It was the way he had spoken to her without hunger or pity, without leaning in or stepping too close. The way he held her hand only because the dance required it, nothing more. The way he looked at her like a person and not a burden or an opportunity. That feeling stayed.

It followed her into the evenings when the room she didn't truly live in felt unfamiliar and temporary. When the silence pressed too tightly around her. When loneliness settled on her ribs with a heaviness she didn't know how to lift.

Days passed. And then one night, after sitting on the edge of a bed that wasn't hers, listening to a city outside that didn't know her name. She remembered the one person who had made her feel safe without asking anything in return.

Her thumb hovered over the phone for a long moment. Her breath trembled. She opened her messages and pulled up Hassan's number. And then she typed a single word:

Hi.

And hit send.

Chapter 5

The Architecture of Need

The days after midsummer slid by quietly. A week, then two, workdays that looked nearly identical to each other, stitched together by long commutes and longer hours at his desk. Hassan's life fell back into its usual rhythm.

Every morning he left his apartment near the city centre just before seven, stepping into the soft hum of Stockholm still waking up. The streets were calm, the air cool, the sunlight bouncing gently off the windows of old buildings. He walked five minutes to the nearest metro station, passing familiar corners: the bakery with the cardamom scent, the narrow alley that always carried a draft, the newsstand run by the silent man who nodded instead of speaking.

From the metro to the train, then from the train to the bus. Three changes, sometimes four. He didn't mind. Not really. He owned a car, a modest sedan parked in a nearby lot close to his building, but he rarely used it. Because his work was far away, he preferred working on the train. The commute gave him time to code, to think, to prepare for the day ahead.

His office at Microsoft was a world of glass walls, quiet hallways, soft clicking keyboards, and screens glowing with code. Hassan spent hours buried in it, debugging, building, rewriting, explaining, fixing. It was demanding work, but predictable: the kind of structure he'd grown used to, the kind of structure he needed. Colleagues greeted him with polite smiles and light conversations about sprint deadlines or weekend plans. He smiled back, answered what he had to, and returned to his tasks. His mind stayed anchored in the work, steady and disciplined. That was how he preferred it. He was exceptionally good at what he did, and he loved doing it.

Chapter 5

Every evening, when the office began to empty and the sky shifted into its long Swedish twilight, he gathered his things and retraced the same route home: bus, train, metro, walk. Then the door of his apartment closed behind him, leaving him in a silence that was clean and manageable, but undeniably empty.

He made simple dinners. Watched a little TV. Read. Sometimes video-called family back home. He checked his email often, hoping for news about his wife's pending visa. Nothing came. It never did. He slept lightly, woke early, repeated everything again.

Midsummer felt far away already. A brief, bright interruption in a life lived mostly indoors, mostly in quiet. He didn't think about the girl in the salmon hoodie. Not consciously. She had simply folded into the blur of that day, the wreath, the music, the sun, the laughter. Life moved on.

And then, on a quiet Wednesday morning, half-dressed, half-awake, one sock on and the other in his hand, he saw the message waiting on his phone. A number he didn't recognise. A single word:

Hi.

He frowned slightly, thumb hovering for a moment before opening the thread.

Hassan: *Hello, who's this?*

He didn't expect to know the answer. His mind was already drifting toward the day ahead. The meetings stacked on his calendar, the deadlines creeping closer like they always did. But the reply came minutes later, quickly, almost as if she had been waiting for him to be awake.

Anastasia: *Anastasia. We met in Skansen on midsummer day. Remember?*

He paused. And then the image clicked into place, the salmon-coloured hoodie, the soft eyes, the quietness in her voice when she told him her name. *Of course.*

Hassan: *Yes, of course. It's been a while. How are you doing?*

There was a longer pause this time. Not too long, but long enough to reveal hesitation.

Anastasia: *I'm doing ok… I need your help. Is it okay if we can meet?*

He straightened a little, the tone of the message tightening something in his chest. People rarely asked for help unless they truly needed it. He typed slowly, carefully.

Hassan: *Everything okay? I work until Friday, but we can meet on Saturday, if you like.*

Another pause.

Anastasia: *Yes… all good. Saturday would be great.*

He exhaled quietly, relieved she hadn't said something worse. He glanced at his week, mentally shifting tasks, imagining what time would make sense.

Hassan: *We can meet at Espresso House. 11:00?*

Anastasia: *Yes. That's perfect.*

Hassan placed his phone on the side table and stood to get ready for work. He didn't think much of it. Didn't read between the lines. Didn't imagine anything beyond a simple conversation over coffee.

But somewhere across the city, in a room that didn't belong to her, Anastasia sat with the phone still in her hand long after the messages stopped. Her heartbeat had slowed. Just a little. Just enough. Saturday felt far away. But it was something to wait for and she hadn't had something to wait for in a long time.

Chapter 5

Espresso House near Stockholm Central was warm and softly lit, a blend of Edison bulbs and hanging greenery, all framed by the café's signature dark wood furniture. The red-brick walls gave the place a familiar hum, the kind that felt safe regardless of the weather outside, and a faint aroma of roasted beans filled the air.

Hassan arrived a few minutes early, punctual as always. He wore a short-sleeved purple dress shirt, the kind with neat cuffs ending just above the biceps, paired with dark blue jeans and his comfortable brown Sketchers. His hair was combed neatly to the side, the light catching the smooth line of his fresh trim. He stepped up to the counter, ordered a latte for himself, then chose a table near the window, bright but not too exposed. He sat, relaxed, waiting without expectation.

Then the café door opened. Anastasia stepped inside, and for a moment, the ambient café noise softened.

She wore a floral dress, soft colours, intricate pattern. A V-neck that framed her collarbones with gentle elegance. The fabric floated lightly around her waist and thighs as she walked. Her slender arms were bare, delicate, the summer light catching the soft undertone of her skin. Her hair flowed down naturally, brushed neatly, and her posture, though a little hesitant, held a graceful femininity that drew the eye without trying.

Hassan stood immediately, polite and warm. "Hi," he said, offering his hand.

She smiled — small, shy, but genuine. "Hi."

Her handshake was light, almost cautious, but not cold.

"Please," he said, gesturing to the chair across from him. "Have a seat. You look very nice today."

Her cheeks coloured faintly. "Thank you."

"What would you like to drink?"

"Cappuccino," she said softly.

He nodded and walked back to the counter, adding her order to his. When he returned, he settled back into his seat with easy composure.

"So," he began gently, "how have you been? Is Sweden treating you well so far?"

She folded her hands in her lap. A familiar gesture he remembered from midsummer. "Yes. All is good. Still new. Still learning. But… I am okay."

They spoke lightly about Ukraine, about the war, about how the days since midsummer had passed. Their coffees arrived; warm cups placed delicately between them.

"My family is safe," her voice soft but steady. "They live near Ivano-Frankivsk. Western Ukraine. So… as safe as it could be."

"That's good. That must be a relief."

She nodded, though the heaviness behind the motion said it was a complicated kind of relief. After a moment, he leaned slightly forward.

"So… what do you need help with?"

She hesitated only a second. "I'm looking for a place to live. The friend I was staying with… she is moving to another city."

He absorbed the information with calm empathy. "Okay. I can check with the volunteer group I know. They usually find accommodation for people who need it. I'll put in a word."

Her relief was immediate, visible. "Thank you," she said quietly, sincerely. "Really. Thank you."

They finished their coffee slowly, conversation drifting into gentler terrain. What her hobbies were, what she had studied back in Ukraine. Linguistics. Journalism. Her voice warmed slightly when she spoke about it, revealing a depth he hadn't seen before.

And then the question she hoped wouldn't come.

Chapter 5

"Where are you staying, by the way?"

She hesitated. Just a fraction too long.

"I'm staying with a friend," she said carefully. "It's temporary."

Technically true. The safest kind of lie.

She didn't mention the apartment, the one where she lived like prey. The way she timed her returns for late evening. After long walks through parks, after hours spent sitting on public benches scrolling her phone with nowhere to be, just to minimise the minutes she would have to share under the same ceiling with *that man*. She had stopped thinking of him by name. He was just a presence now. A shadow in the hallway. A door she avoided.

She didn't mention how she waited for the bathroom light to turn off before leaving her room to get some food. How she learned the rhythm of another person's breathing through thin walls. How every locked door still felt like it could open.

"It's not ideal," she added softly, eyes lowering to her cup. "But it's fine for now."

Hassan nodded, taking her words at face value. He didn't interrogate the details. Didn't ask about the landlord, the address, the neighbourhood. His restraint wasn't ignorance, it was respect. If she wanted to expand, she would.

"How do you spend your days?" he asked instead.

"Outside," she said too fast. She forced her shoulders to relax. "Mostly walking. Libraries. Parks."

He listened, not to impress her, but simply because he respected stories, especially the ones people rarely got the chance to tell.

When they finally stepped out of the café, sunlight spilled across the pavement. He walked beside her toward the bus stop, pace steady, conversation light. She spoke more openly than she expected to about learning Swedish, about how strange it felt to be in a new country, about adjusting to a place that looked peaceful yet never quite felt reachable. He listened. He shared just enough, nothing too deep, nothing too closed off, just enough to make the walk feel natural.

At the bus stop, she turned to him. "Thank you again," she said.

"Of course," he replied. "If anything comes up, I'll let you know."

The bus pulled up. She stepped toward it, then paused… just for a heartbeat.

"Goodbye, Hassan."

"Take care, Anastasia."

She boarded. The doors closed. The bus pulled away. And he walked back toward the station, unaware that this quiet Saturday morning would be the second hinge in a story neither of them had planned for.

Chapter 6

A Room of One's Own Making

Two days after their meeting at Espresso House, Hassan was sitting at his desk in his office, the evening light slanting across his keyboard, when his phone buzzed. A message from a volunteer coordinator.

We found a room. Single occupancy. Safe host. Needs basic documents.

He exhaled, relieved on her behalf in a way that surprised even him. He didn't hesitate. He dialled her number. The line rang twice.

"Hello?" Her voice was softer than he remembered, calm, careful, but with a tremor beneath it, as if she had been alone for too many hours.

"Hey," he said, leaning back in his chair. "How are you?"

"I am doing fine… how about you?" More composed now, but still fragile around the edges.

"All good," he replied. "Actually, I have good news for you."

He could almost hear her straighten, breath catching slightly. "Oh? What happened?"

"There's a volunteer. He has a spare room in his apartment. He's willing to help. All I need is some documents from you, and you can move in as soon as you want."

There was silence, one heartbeat, two, and then she breathed in sharply. "Oh my God…" The relief in her voice cracked through the words. "Thank you so much. You have no idea… how much this means to me."

He smiled without realising it. "Happy to help."

She hesitated, and for the first time her voice warmed. "No… really. Thank you."

After they ended the call, she sent her documents within the hour. He forwarded them to the coordinator, exchanged a few messages, and by evening everything was arranged. She packed what little she had. She sneaked out of the apartment in *his* absence. By night, she had moved.

A simple room. Clean bed. White curtains. A window overlooking the street, but to her it felt like the first real breath she'd taken since crossing the border into Sweden.

That night, a message lit up Hassan's phone.

Anastasia: *I moved. Thank you so much.*

He typed back quickly.

Hassan: *Good to hear. No worries at all.*

A pause. Then:

Anastasia: *It means a lot… I would like to take you out.*

He blinked. *Out?* He hesitated; fingers stilled above the keyboard. It felt strange to accept gratitude this way. Strange to imagine sitting with a woman he barely knew. Strange… because a small part of him noticed the energy in her message, the eagerness, the softness.

Alone in her new room that evening, she nearly cried, not from sadness, but from the relief of not having to perform. In Sweden, her accent marked her as a refugee before she could finish a sentence. Her Ukrainian softness, ordinary in Kyiv, felt exposed here, too open, too melodic, too willing to trust. Hassan's measured English, his quiet corporate composure, the weight of belonging he wore without effort, these were codes she could not yet decipher. His kindness had felt like a bridge between two foreign languages: his loneliness and hers.

He typed slowly.

Hassan: *There's no need for that.*

Seconds passed.

Anastasia: *Please. Just a coffee and a sandwich. I want to thank you properly.*

He exhaled, long and resigned.

Hassan: *Okay. Saturday? Afternoon?*

Anastasia: *Yes. 13:00?*

Hassan: *Works for me.*

She sent a little *thank you* a moment later, shy, careful, sincere. He set the phone down and stared at it longer than he meant to. Just coffee, he reminded himself. Just gratitude. Nothing more.

A few days later, the city centre buzzed with the usual weekend energy, tourists drifting through the narrow streets, locals chasing sunlight between the buildings, buses humming past the central station.

Café D'Abramo carried a restrained elegance: beige walls, deep green velvet chairs, marble-topped tables that glowed under golden sconces shaped like tiny lanterns. Behind the counter, dark walnut framed the espresso bar. The air held roasted beans and a trace of caramel. A row of tiny potted rosemary plants lined the windowsill, giving the café a fresh, rustic charm that blended beautifully with the coffee. It felt warm without being crowded, a place you could sit for hours without realising it.

Hassan arrived early, as he always did. He wore an off-white polo shirt, black jeans, and white trainers, neat, simple. His hair, combed to the side, caught the café light in soft brown tones. A trace of cologne stayed close to him. Clean, controlled. He looked like a man who took care of himself without fussing over it. He found a seat near the middle, back straight, eyes watchful.

Chapter 6

Another Saturday. Another café.

At 13:01, the door chimed. He looked up.

And there she was.

Not the girl from the midsummer field. Not the fragile figure in a salmon hoodie crushed by the weight of her life. This woman… she was dressed in an olive-green open-shoulder top that framed her collarbones beautifully, high-rise ankle-length jeans, black ankle boots, and soft brown sunglasses resting in her hair. The sunlight behind her made her silhouette glow faintly as she stepped inside.

She looked revived. Alive. A woman stepping into her own life again.

He stood immediately.

She approached and before he could extend a hand, she leaned in and hugged him. A soft, grateful embrace. He froze for a fraction of a second, surprised, then returned the embrace lightly, respectfully.

"Hi," she said, smiling as she pulled back.

"Hey," he replied, smiling too. "You look… really nice."

A soft flush touched her cheeks. "Thank you. You look really nice yourself." Her eyes were bright, a small light flickering behind them that hadn't been there before. She let her gaze settle on him for a second longer than necessary.

"You're really happy," he said gently, almost amused.

"I am," she admitted, tucking a loose strand of hair behind her ear. "Because of you."

He shook his head. "You really didn't have to do this."

"You helped me. This is how I thank someone for their kindness."

Her tone was firm, like the invitation wasn't meant to be declined.

She sat, reached for the menu, then glanced at him with quiet anticipation.

"What would you like?"

"We can order together," he said.

So, they did. Two coffees. Two sandwiches. And, at her suggestion, chocolate muffins. A small indulgence, but something about it made her smile like a child allowed dessert after dinner.

After a few minutes, the barista set their order down.

Anastasia sat with her elbows propped on the table, hands gently folded, chin resting on them as she looked at Hassan with complete attention while he explained his work on artificial intelligence, teaching computers to understand not just words, but intention.

"One day," he said, gesturing with his coffee cup, "you'll be able to talk to a computer the way you're talking to me. It'll understand context, tone, emotions, even what you didn't say." He laughed softly, almost embarrassed. "Sounds like science fiction, I know. But that's where we're heading."

She didn't respond right away. She just watched him, straw hovering near her lips.

Then: "You're building the future."

He shrugged. "Trying to."

The rest of the café faded for her, cups clinked, conversations rose and fell, Edison bulbs glowed overhead, but her focus didn't shift.

Hassan talked easily, naturally. He had a way of making even small subjects interesting, history, politics, random pieces of information, stories from his commutes, little observations about life in Sweden. He spoke with the quiet confidence of someone who carried knowledge gently, not arrogantly. Every time he said something insightful or unexpectedly funny, her eyes brightened just a little more, and a soft dimple flickered in her left cheek like a hidden secret surfacing only when she was truly delighted. She studied him as if trying to memorise the way he occupied the world.

He didn't examine the way she was looking at him. He just talked like he always did, warm, open, lightly humorous, enjoying the company, not reading deeper. They ate. Coffee warmed their hands. Chocolate muffins softened the conversation. Lunch became easy, fluid, natural.

At some point, she asked softly, "Do you have anything to do today?"

He shook his head. "Nothing in particular."

A small breath escaped her, something like relief. "Would you like to walk?" she asked. "Around *Gamla stan* — the old town? It's close."

He considered it for half a second, not because he doubted, but because he was careful with himself, and then nodded. "Sure. I need to burn some calories."

Outside, the weather was forgiving, mild sun, soft breeze, the city alive with weekend energy. They walked side by side through the narrow cobblestone streets of the old town. Souvenir shops spilled onto the walkways with postcards, wooden *Dala* horses, and tiny Swedish flags. Musicians played violins near the church steps. Tourists drifted in rivers of colour.

She walked close enough to listen, respecting space, yet drawn to it. Their conversation deepened almost without them noticing. She told him more about her studies, the stories she wanted to write someday. He spoke more about his work, coding, long commutes, the quiet way he built his life in Sweden.

There was no flirting. Just the gentle unfolding of two people who didn't feel threatened by each other.

At one point, by the water near Slussen, she asked in a quiet, curious voice, "Do you have a girlfriend?"

He didn't break stride, though the question caught him off guard. "No," he said simply.

The word settled between them, small, clean, finished.

He saw it register in her: the way her shoulders loosened, the way something in her face opened.

He didn't mention his wife. Didn't mention the long wait. Didn't mention the life already attached to his name. Her face flickered through his mind, not as accusation, just as presence. A fact he'd chosen to erase for three seconds.

He walked on. The lie followed.

He felt an anchor drop somewhere deep inside him, but he didn't correct it. She nodded, absorbing the answer. Something quiet and hopeful began to take shape behind her expression, something he refused to examine.

They continued walking for nearly three hours, drifting through alleys and across bridges, slipping into small shops where handmade jewellery and tiny sculptures crowded the windows. She laughed more easily now, clear, unguarded, genuine laughs that came from safety rather than nerves. He noticed the change. It made him happy. That's all.

By the time they reached her bus stop, the sun had lowered into amber. They paused. She looked at him as though committing the moment to memory.

"Thank you," she whispered. Not for the walk. Not for the coffee. Not even for the room. For everything.

He nodded, warm. "Take care, Anastasia."

Chapter 6

She stepped forward and hugged him again, lighter, shorter, but sincere. Then she boarded the bus. He watched her sit by the window, adjusting her hair, tucking one leg beneath the other as if steadying something inside her. The bus pulled away.

Later that night, Hassan lay in bed staring at the ceiling. The apartment felt larger than usual. The silence heavier. He replayed one moment, one question:

"Do you have a girlfriend?"

And his answer:

"No."

He pressed the heel of his hand to his forehead. *Why didn't I tell her? Why didn't I tell the truth — that I had a wife in another country, waiting?* He didn't know. He didn't understand himself. But the unease lingered.

A thought slipped in, uninvited:

Maybe I like her.
No.

He shut it down fast, like slamming a door on smoke.

I can't. I don't have the right. I am married. I must tell her.

Guilt settled into its place, familiar, almost comforting in its certainty. He exhaled slowly, forcing his hand back to his side.

Meanwhile, across the city, in her small new room, Anastasia sat on her bed, smiling softly at the memory of him.

Already feeling something she wasn't ready to name.

Chapter 7

Confessions in a Minor Key

The days after their last meeting unfolded strangely, quiet in a way that felt less like peace and more like holding your breath. Hassan saw her name appear on his phone twice that week.

Anastasia: *Hope you're doing well.*

He read it on the metro, thumb hovering, then locked the screen.

Anastasia: *How was your week?*

That one came on a Thursday evening, alone in his apartment, the silence pressing in. He set the phone face-down on the kitchen table and stared at the wall for a long time.

He wasn't avoiding her, at least that's what he told himself. He was avoiding everything. Work felt heavier than usual. Long hours. Endless debugging sessions. Meetings that stretched late into the evenings. By the time he got home, he barely had energy left to speak.

And then there was home, the real one, the one across oceans. Even there, distance had begun to press into his wife's voice. Frustrated. Lonely. Suspicious.

The calls became smaller. Not shorter, they still stretched for forty minutes, sometimes an hour, but the space inside them kept shrinking.

He'd ask about Sara's day. She'd tell him in small sentences. He'd tell her about his. Silence.

Then: "You sound different."

He didn't know how to answer that.

Different how?
Different tired?
Different distant?

Different like a man slowly becoming a stranger?

"I'm just tired," he said.

"You're always tired."

A statement of fact, not sympathy. He wanted to explain. The commute, the deadlines, the apartment that never felt like home, the loneliness that pressed against his chest every night. But explaining would sound like complaining, and complaining would sound like blame, and blame was the last thing she wanted to hear.

Still, it came. More and more.

They argued more than they talked. Little things, why he sounded distracted, why he was outside instead of resting at home. Each question small on its own. Together, heavy. Distance didn't just stretch their marriage; it thinned it, strained it, made every silence feel like a threat.

Hassan felt himself shrinking under the weight, pulled between two worlds, belonging fully to neither. So, when Anastasia's messages arrived — gentle, simple, undeserving of coldness — he let them sit unread on purpose. He didn't want to drag her into the storm that was gathering around him. She deserved better than being another person waiting for his attention.

But the silence lingered longer than he expected. Days passed. Three? Four? He wasn't counting. Work bled into home, home bled into stress, and his evenings became nothing but headaches and unanswered calls. Yet somewhere between exhaustion and restlessness, he remembered her voice, light, warm, grateful. He remembered her smile at the café. The way she listened to him without judgement, without demands, without knowing anything about the chaos inside him.

And one evening, when the apartment lights felt too dim, and his thoughts felt too crowded. He opened her chat. His fingers hovered for a moment. Then he typed.

Hassan: *Hi, sorry… been a bit busy lately. Work stress. Wasn't able to respond. How are you?*

He hit send before he could second-guess it. He didn't expect a reply right away. And he didn't get one.

Hours later, when he'd already convinced himself she must be upset, his phone lit up.

Anastasia: *I was a little worried about you. I'm glad you're okay.*

Her message was warm. Soft. A quiet relief wrapped in two simple lines. He replied with a small *thank-you*, nothing heavy. She didn't push for more. She never did. Hours drifted into the next day before her next message appeared.

Anastasia: *Can I ask you something…? If you have time.*

He paused. Something in those dots felt delicate.

Hassan: *Sure. What do you need?*

The answer came slowly; each line typed with visible hesitation.

Anastasia: *I've been looking for a laptop for some days… just something simple so I can work, study, write… I don't understand computers well. Maybe you can help me find one? If it's not too much. No pressure.*

That part made him smile quietly. Even in need, she apologised for taking up space. He leaned back in his chair at work, rubbing a hand over his face. Helping someone with tech, that he could do. That required no emotional exposure, no messy conversations, no self-explanations. It was simple. Clean. Straightforward. And he liked helping. Always had.

So, he asked around. A colleague mentioned an internal Microsoft group that coordinated donated electronics for refugees. He reached out. They connected him with a woman, a teacher. Who had an old but functional laptop sitting in her basement, gathering dust. He wanted to pay for it, but she just wanted it to go to someone who needed it. Hassan arranged everything in less than an hour.

When he texted Anastasia, his message was almost casual:

Hassan: *Found you a laptop. Someone is willing to donate it. Here's the address. You can pick it up today if you want.*

The reply came almost instantly.

Anastasia: *What? Really?? Hassan… thank you. Thank you so, so much. I can't believe… you did this for me.*

He stared at those lines longer than he intended. She wasn't just grateful, she sounded relieved. Like someone who had been walking with a weight in her hands and suddenly had it lifted.

Later that evening, she went to retrieve it. The woman had already placed the laptop in a small tote bag. It wasn't new. But it looked unused, clean, ready. When Anastasia stepped outside with it pressed to her chest, she snapped a picture of the bag and sent it to Hassan.

Anastasia: *I got it. Thank you… you have no idea what this means to me.*

He was sitting at his kitchen table when the message arrived, dinner untouched, stress thick in the room. For a moment, just a moment, the heaviness in his chest eased. Not because she idolised him. Not because she praised him. But because helping her was the first thing in weeks that made sense. No arguments. No silence. No complicated expectations. Just a small human need, and a simple solution.

Hassan: *I'm glad it worked out. Use it well.*

She didn't reply right away, and he didn't expect her to. But when her message finally came, it was shorter and softer than before:

Anastasia: *You're a good person, Hassan.*

That sentence stayed with him longer than anything else she had ever sent. Because lately, between the fights with his wife, the loneliness of the apartment, and the quiet exhaustion settling under his skin, he wasn't sure he believed that anymore.

He locked his phone and sat still in the silence of his flat. But her words lingered.

A few days passed. Just the ordinary distance of two lives running parallel. He worked. She studied. The city carried on around them both.

Then, on an evening soft with the last light of summer, her name appeared again.

Anastasia: *I'm sorry to bother you… but would you maybe have time to help me with something? My laptop is acting strange. I don't know who else to ask.*

He read it twice. Simple. Practical. No pressure.

He typed back before he could overthink it.

Hassan: *Sure. I can come by after work tomorrow, if that works.*

Her reply came quickly — relieved, grateful, warm.

Anastasia: *Yes. Thank you, Hassan.*

So, the next day, on a quiet evening, he found himself outside her door. She opened it before he could knock, as if she'd been waiting. A small smile. A soft *"hi."* Then she stepped aside and let him in.

Nothing unusual. Nothing suggesting where the night would end.

Chapter 7

Hassan spent an hour walking her through settings and updates, his tone patient, steady, the familiar warmth she'd begun to crave without meaning to. She listened with her full attention, as always. Eyes focused, chin resting lightly on her laced fingers, elbows near the edge of the table.

When he finished, Hassan closed the laptop with a soft click. "That should fix it," he said with a smile. "It'll work better now."

"Thank you," she whispered.

But her voice was different. Softer. Thinner.

He looked up. She wasn't smiling. She wasn't nervous. She wasn't distracted. She was gathering courage the way someone gathers breath before going underwater. Her fingers tightened slightly, knuckles paling.

"Hassan…" she began, then stopped. Her throat worked around a breath that didn't fully form. She tried again. "Hassan… can I tell you something?"

He nodded slowly, unaware of the ground shifting beneath both of them. "Yes, of course."

She exhaled shakily, then looked directly at him. Not at his hands. Not at the table. Not at the laptop. At him.

"I… like you," she said, her voice trembling at its edges. The words weren't bold. They weren't dramatic. They were heartbreakingly sincere. "I like you very much."

Silence pressed between them, thick, immediate, unyielding. She swallowed hard, eyes shining but not crying. Not yet.

"I did not plan this," she continued, barely audible. "I did not want to feel this way. But every time you help me… every time you speak to me kindly… I feel safe. I feel… seen. And I haven't felt that in a very long time."

Hassan's breath caught. She didn't notice. She was too busy trying to steady herself, trying not to break in front of him.

"You don't have to feel anything back," she whispered quickly. "I just… I needed to tell you. I needed to be honest, even if it's stupid. Even if it ruins everything." Her voice cracked. "I like you, Hassan. More than I should."

And that was when he finally breathed, slow and heavy.

"Anastasia…"

His voice came out rougher than he intended. She looked up at him with hope she was trying so hard to hide. He closed his eyes for a second. And the truth he had been avoiding finally broke through.

"I'm married," he said.

Her face went still.
Not surprised or shocked.

Just wounded — quietly. Deeply.

"I have a wife. I wanted to tell you that day when you asked me if I have a girlfriend. I don't know why I didn't say it," he said, forcing himself to meet her eyes. "She's in Pakistan. Waiting for her visa. I've been waiting for her for almost two years."

Anastasia's breath left her in a tiny, trembling rush. She looked down at her hands, fingers curling inward as if trying to protect the softest parts of herself.

"Oh…" she whispered.

The single syllable held worlds. He watched her swallow the pain, pull it inward, hide it, bury it behind a composed, fragile stillness that only made it hurt more. A long moment passed before she nodded.

"I understand," she said, forcing a tight, small smile. "Of course I do."

"Anastasia —" he tried.

But she shook her head gently, cutting him off, not wanting pity.

"You don't have to explain," she murmured, voice steadying through sheer force of will.

Hassan's chest tightened painfully. He wanted to tell her she hadn't done anything wrong. He wanted to tell her she was kind, and strong, and deserving of love not built on fear or escape. He wanted to tell her she mattered. But he couldn't. Not without crossing lines he had no right to cross.

He looked down.

"So…" she tried, her voice thinning despite the effort to steady it. "If you ever need a friend. Or someone to talk to. I'm here. I won't ask for anything."

He opened his mouth.

Nothing came.

The silence stretched. She watched him, waiting, hoping for something he couldn't give.

He stood, carefully, heavily, like the truth had weight.

"I should go," he said quietly.

She nodded, not trusting her voice. Her eyes glistened, but she blinked the wetness away before it could form into tears.

"And I won't make things difficult for you," she said. "I promise."

At the door, he paused. Turned around.

"Anastasia —"

"Thank you," she said. "For everything."

She stood slowly, dignity intact, pain barely hidden. At the door, she added softly, "Thank you for being honest. Even if it took time."

He couldn't meet her eyes. He just nodded and stepped out.

She followed him, pausing at the entrance. In the dim light, he could just make out her profile as she turned her head.

"You're a good man, Hassan," she said quietly. "I hope you know that."

He walked away. He didn't look back. He couldn't. Her words followed him.

Across the city, in her small room, Anastasia sat on her bed, staring at the door he'd walked through. She didn't cry. She just sat, hands folded in her lap, his words moving through her again. *I'm married.* They sat inside her like stones.

She pulled her knees to her chest and rested her chin on them. The city hummed outside her window. Somewhere out there, he was walking home, carrying her confession with him. She didn't know if he would ever speak to her again. She didn't know if she wanted him to.

Later that night, Hassan lay in bed. He replayed every moment, her confession, her face. *And I won't make things difficult for you. I promise.* He shouldn't have been affected. He shouldn't have felt anything.

But he did.

Because deep down, beneath duty, beneath distance, beneath the years of emotional corrosion he'd endured, he had liked her, in the quiet, dangerous way that changes things. More than he should admit. More than he dared let himself feel.

And now the truth sat between them like a locked door — close enough to touch, impossible to open.

Chapter 8

A Cracked Vessel Seeks Harbor

August 23rd, 15:37

Hassan's laptop chimed with a new email during a meeting at work, a technical session with senior engineers that required his full focus. He ignored the first notification… then the second… then the third. But the fourth drew his eyes.

Migration Board – Decision Notification.

His heart lurched. He clicked. Read. Then read again. *"Your spouse's residence permit has been approved."*

The sentence struck like voltage along his spine.

For one suspended heartbeat, he forgot how to breathe. Heat surged through his chest, relief, shock, a happiness so sharp it felt unfamiliar after two years of waiting. He stood too quickly. A colleague stopped mid-sentence.

"Everything okay?"

"Yeah — yes, I just need… one moment."

He stepped out of the meeting room, pulse hammering, and walked quickly down the hallway to the empty balcony area where he could breathe. His fingers shook as he dialled his wife. She picked up after the second ring.

"Hello?" Her voice, Sara's voice — familiar yet distant.

"Hi…" He swallowed, unable to contain the smile pressing at his lips. "I have amazing news for you."

A pause. Then softly, cautiously: "What is it?"

Chapter 8

"Your visa," he said breathlessly. "It's approved. Sara — your visa is approved. Congratulations."

For a moment there was silence, shocked, suspended, weightless. Then — "Oh my God…" Her exhale trembled through the phone. "Thank God. It took so long… I can't believe it. I'm so happy, Hassan."

He closed his eyes, letting that relief wash through him. Almost two years of waiting. Two years of stress, distance, calls that felt like duties. Two years of carrying a marriage alone. Finally, movement.

"Listen," he said, shifting into problem-solving mode, "now please talk to my cousin. She and her husband run the ticketing agency. Give them the money I gave you for the ticket. Book it as soon as possible."

The money he'd handed her during his last trip to Pakistan months ago. Savings scraped together from overtime and restraint. Money meant for this exact moment.

But instead of agreement… instead of excitement… instead of relief… her voice wavered, not with gratitude, but with panic.

"How can I book it?" She sounded overwhelmed. "I don't know what to ask them. How do I book a ticket? I don't understand!"

It didn't sound like confusion. It sounded like fear wearing confusion as a mask.

Hassan straightened. "It's simple. Tell them your dates. They'll handle everything."

"I don't even know them!" her tone sharpened. "Why are you asking me to do this?"

He felt the joy drain out of him like water through loose fingers. "Sara," he said, voice tightening, "you're a doctor. Booking a ticket should not be hard —"

"It is!" she shouted over him, frustrated, emotional. "I don't know how to do it!"

A few heads turned in the hallway as Hassan rubbed his forehead. He glanced at the clock. The meeting he had left was still running. His manager would be expecting him back. Her panic had risen into rigid anger. He felt his own patience finally snap.

"Are you a child who doesn't know how to book a ticket?!" His tone was sharper than he intended, frustrated, exhausted, drained.

"YES!" she fired back. "YES, I don't know! I don't know how to do it!"

Silence dropped between them.

"Okay, fine then." Not yelling. Just flat.

He closed his eyes, jaw clenched. He didn't have time for this, not after the one piece of good news they had waited nearly two years for. And before she could say anything else, he hung up. Not out of cruelty. Out of necessity. His hand tightened around the phone. He stared at the dark screen, emotions tangled and heavy.

He went back to his meeting like nothing had happened. A slide glowed on the screen. Someone was explaining superposition of quantum particles — how matter could exist in two states at once.

As he sat in the meeting, mind elsewhere, phone cooling in his pocket, he understood something he didn't want to admit: even the happiest news couldn't escape the storm their marriage had become.

For the next three days, Hassan didn't speak to Sara. He needed to breathe before stepping back into the storm.

Chapter 8

On the second night, he found himself standing at the fridge at 2 a.m., eating cold leftovers straight from the container, not tasting anything.

He worked long hours. Returned to an empty apartment. Slept poorly, waking at 3 a.m. from half-formed nightmares of arguments that replayed themselves in unfinished loops.

He wanted to call her. To mend things. To celebrate her visa properly. But every time he picked up the phone, his chest tightened, and the joy he had felt that day dimmed beneath the shadow of their fight.

August 26th.

Hassan's birthday eve. And she still hadn't called.

On the late afternoon of the third day, the thought slipped in quietly, almost against his will: *Maybe I should apologise. I shouldn't have called her a child. It's my birthday tomorrow. Let's make peace.*

He stared at the phone in his hand for a long moment, thumb hovering.

Then he pressed call.

The line rang once.
Twice.

Each ring stretched thin and brittle, like breath held too long.

Then — a click.

"Hello?"

But it wasn't Sara. It was her father. A man Hassan respected deeply. A man who had once embraced him like a son, or performed it convincingly enough.

There had always been something in their gaze: polite, controlled, faintly contemptuous. The kind of respect that never quite forgets you are not their equal.

"Dad?" Hassan said cautiously. "Assalamu alaikum… is Sara there?"

The response was immediate. Cold. "What exactly is happening between you and my daughter?"

His spine stiffened. "What do you mean, what's happening? I —"

"You should be ashamed." The voice that had once been warm was now edged with steel. "You don't know what you have done? Or do you think we don't know how you speak to her? How do you treat her? She has told us everything."

Hassan's mind blanked. "What everything?" he said, losing his breath.

"You shout at her. You treat her poorly. You humiliate her, blame her for things she cannot control. She told us" — the pause burned — "that you treat her like she's stupid. Throughout your relationship we've seen how you don't spend on her, don't give her money, neglect her, dominate her. You are a bad husband."

The verdict was already delivered.

His breath hitched. "Dad… I — I never… I didn't mean to —"

"How could you? We trusted you with our daughter. And this is how you treated her? And don't you forget that she's not alone here."

The words hit him like blows. He pressed a hand to the wall to steady himself. "No… no, that's not… she misunderstood. It wasn't like that —"

But her father wasn't listening. Or couldn't. Or simply didn't want to. And behind him, others emerged. Her mother, her brothers, her uncles, voices layered into one collective barrage, humiliating him, attacking him. The call went on for thirty minutes, then an hour. Hassan stood in his apartment, phone to his ear, absorbing accusation after accusation, crying desperately.

Every private moment of marriage — fights, disagreements, insecurities, every one of them — had been spilled. Exposed. Thrown into the open. Sara had shared everything with her family. His flaws. His worst moments. His weaknesses. Things meant to remain sealed between husband and wife now stood like wounds on display.

The walls felt thinner.

"And we are recording you," her father said. "We won't let this go. Not only were you a bad son, now you are also a bad husband!"

Hassan flinched. *Bad son.* Not to them, to his own blood. *So, she'd told them that too.* The fights with his parents. The distance. The resentment. Things he had never said aloud outside the marriage were now being recited like evidence.

Hassan's mouth went dry. He became aware of his own breathing.

"Why are you recording this?" he said, crying. "I never… I am so naive that I didn't even think to record anything."

By the end of the call, his chest felt like it had collapsed inward. "Dad," he said, tears breaking through restraint, "I love her. I've been waiting for her for two years. I worked day and night to bring her here. You know that."

But her father's tone remained cold. "You haven't fixed anything," came the reply. "Your behaviour is terrible. We don't want to send her to you anymore. This marriage is over."

The line went silent.

Hassan closed his eyes. He felt small. Stripped. Humiliated. Like someone had reached inside him and twisted everything he was trying to hold together. He didn't even recognise his own voice anymore. The silence afterward was suffocating.

His knees nearly buckled. For several minutes he could not move. He felt something he had not felt in years, the urge to disappear.

To step out of himself.

Out of this life.

Out of the heaviness pressing on his ribs.

The city felt distant. Indifferent. He stared at the dark window, Stockholm lights reflecting faintly on the glass. He took a step toward it. Then another. His hand reached for the latch.

And stopped.

Some last, stubborn thread of the man he used to be held him there, trembling. Standing at a door inside himself he hadn't touched in a long time.

He didn't know if that thread was strength or cowardice.

His breathing grew shallow. For minutes, long, painful minutes, he wondered whether anything he did mattered. Whether all the sacrifices, all the waiting, all the love… had been for nothing. Whether he had failed as a husband before his marriage had even begun.

He pressed the heels of his palms against his eyes until colours bloomed. When he lowered them, the apartment was still there. Still empty. Still waiting.

Islamabad. The word surfaced without permission. Gated houses. Polished marble. A world he'd never quite entered.

Sara wasn't just his wife. She was also a closed book he had never been able to fully open. A doctor in white corridors, uncertain in ordinary rooms. She spoke of feminism at university, equality in theory, symmetry in principle. But theory did not cook dinner. Theory did not clean the apartment. Theory did not sit alone in a foreign winter waiting for a life to begin.

When Hassan spoke of sacrifice, she heard complaint. When he spoke of struggle, she heard inadequacy. Her love felt conditional, not on who he was, but on how well he performed as the flawless provider, the man who could mirror her father's success. But Hassan was not a mirror. He was a prism, refracting every expectation into unrecognizable colours. He brought her to Sweden in winter, to a small apartment, to a life of waiting. And waiting, for a woman raised to be received, felt like erasure.

He remembered the moment he realised their love spoke different grammars. It was during her visit, that Gothenburg winter when he was still a student, still chasing a master's degree like it could save him. They were walking by the frozen river and she had asked, casually, almost kindly: "When will you buy a proper car?"

Not a car. A proper car.

As if the bicycle he rode to work was a childish affectation, not a necessity. He had tried to explain, rent, insurance, the arithmetic of survival. But her expression settled into a polite, impenetrable disappointment. That was the wall: his reality was, to her, a negotiable condition. Hers, to him, was a language of unspoken entitlements he could never afford.

Raised with comfort. Raised with everything done for her. A doctor who could hold a patient's life steady, yet panicked over a plane ticket. A woman who believed equality meant sameness, and sameness meant his failure to become what she had been promised.

Hassan had always believed something different. Not that women were lesser, but that men and women were not the same. In his house growing up, men were taught to provide. To steer. Worth measured by what they could give, not what they felt. Women were taught to nurture, to tend, to turn a house into a home. Equality meant both were essential, but their roles were not interchangeable.

His belief system left no room for his own emotional needs. Men endured. Men absorbed. Men carried the weight so others didn't have to. But endurance is not infinite. It fractures. It splinters under pressure that never lets up and when it does, the break is clean and irreversible.

Sara wanted partnership without hierarchy, and he wanted harmony within it. Neither could see that they were speaking different languages entirely.

He loved her once. Maybe he still did. But the distance had turned them into strangers who only met at the fault lines. Brief, jagged collisions that left cracks neither could repair.

He sat there in the dark, breathing through his mouth, tasting salt from tears he hadn't realised were falling. The silence of the apartment pressed against him like a second skin. No one to call. No one who would understand. Just the low hum of the refrigerator and the distant traffic outside, indifferent sounds that reminded him the world kept moving while his had stopped.

He felt broken. His birthday had become a cruel joke. He wished he had never been born. He sank onto the edge of his bed, elbows on his knees, palms pressed against his eyes until colours burst behind the lids. He felt utterly, unbearably alone.

Tomorrow was supposed to be his day.

Instead, it felt like the first day of the slow death of the person he used to be.

He needed someone. Someone who listened, who did not judge, who asked for nothing but presence. And in that raw, cracked moment, one name surfaced without effort.

Anastasia.

Her quiet attentiveness. Her gentleness. The way she listened without correcting.

And before doubt could intervene, he typed.

Hassan: *Hey… are you free?*

The reply came within seconds, as if she'd been holding the phone.

Anastasia: *Yes. Is everything okay?*

He stared at the message for a long moment. *No. Nothing is okay.* But he typed:

Hassan: *Can you please come over? I… I need someone to talk to.*

A pause. Then:

Anastasia: *Send me the address. I'm coming.*

He hesitated only once.

Then sent it.

And that night, broken, defeated, unravelling. Hassan opened the door.

To her.

For the first time.

Chapter 9

Borscht and Ghosts

Hassan and Sara had been married five years. An arranged marriage, ordinary on paper, hopeful in the beginning, a junction of two families more than two hearts. Back then, Hassan worked as a junior engineer at a firm in Lahore, still assembling a future piece by piece, still believing marriage meant partnership, trust, and a quiet kind of companionship that grew with time. Deprived of love for most of his life, he wanted someone to understand him and love him for who he was. Sara seemed gentle before the wedding. Soft-spoken, polite, the kind of woman who appeared composed and respectful. Hassan thought she would be a calm presence beside him. He thought they would learn each other as life unfolded.

But marriage reveals character the way pressure reveals metal. She was from Islamabad. Reserved, polished, distant in the way people survive by containment. He was from Lahore. A city of warm hearts and loud welcomes, where kindness was instinctive and conversation was medicine. They were opposites in every direction. Hassan was a man whose presence could light a room, whose laughter could settle nerves, who solved problems by talking them through.

To him, love was honesty. Respect was oxygen. Silence was rot. If something hurt him, he said it. If something hurt her, he expected the same.

Sara had learned differently. In her world, honesty was dangerous. Words, once spoken, could never be taken back. So, she collected her hurts like arrows. Quietly, patiently, secretly. Waiting for a time that never came to release them safely. Until it did: safe in her parents' home, when he was far away. When Hassan offered guidance, she heard judgement. When he tried to lead, she felt herself disappearing. She didn't know how to tell him that his certainties felt like cages. So, she said nothing. And the nothing became a language of its own.

Hassan wasn't a perfect man. But he was sincere and open-hearted. A man who would give everything if he understood what was needed. A man who wanted one simple thing from the woman he loved: to feel respected. He believed men were simple that way. They didn't need flowers or poetry. They needed to be heard. They needed to know the woman beside them believed in the direction they were walking.

But Sara had stopped believing in directions anyone else chose long ago. She had her own fears. Fears he never learned to reach, fears that made silence feel safer than honesty. She hoarded every internal scar and misunderstanding, letting them ferment until they became a toxic, collective resentment. Even when she said, "It's okay," she never forgave him. She never let anything go. And slowly, inch by inch, she began to see the worst in him, even when he was giving his best.

Hassan kept trying. He tried explaining the role of harmony in a home, the balance, the give and take. But she heard accusation in every explanation. She took guidance as oppression. She saw leadership as control.

The distance began as quiet space. Then it sharpened. Then it hardened. She visited him only once before remaining in Pakistan, waiting for her visa. The gap between them had turned into something colder, something that started to eat away at him slowly. What was meant to be a partnership had become a battlefield of misunderstandings.

They were two people speaking different languages, both convinced the other was refusing to listen.

Later that evening, Anastasia went to him. She pressed his name on the intercom panel. The call went through to his apartment, and without much thought, he pressed the button to release the main building door. She stepped inside, climbed the short entry stairs, and emerged into the main hallway. A space that immediately impressed its history upon her.

It was a seven-storey Stockholm block, constructed in 1967, and it wore its decades with stubborn, quiet endurance. The air held the faint, pervasive mustiness of old concrete and forgotten winters. A smell baked so deeply into the structure that the building itself seemed to exhale it. The corridor was bathed in the sickly, intermittent glow of a motion-activated fluorescent light, its cold gleam catching the outdated band of stencilled green leaves that wrapped the upper half of the walls. The floor was off-white, grainy concrete, webbed with tiny branching cracks. To her right, the main staircase ascended, a zig-zagging column with institutional green metal railings, its mustard-toned wooden handrail worn smooth by countless hands. It was the building's spine, cutting through the structure as a continuous vertical channel.

The air here was still, held together by habit more than care, carrying that particular Swedish blend of domesticity and melancholy. It was the kind of place where you could scream and no one would open a door, not out of cruelty, but out of a cool, disciplined instinct not to intrude. Don't interfere. Don't notice more than you must.

She went up to the first floor, took a left, walked straight ahead, and saw the nameplate: **H. Khan**. She knocked.

He opened the door.

He didn't look at her. He couldn't. His gaze stayed fixed on the floor, the way a man looks when he's fighting a pain that has no words. Like his eyes were holding the last thread of control he had.

Anastasia closed the apartment door softly behind her, as though loudness alone might break him further. She moved slowly, taking in the space. The off-white wardrobes lined neatly by the entrance along the narrow hallway, on her right, leading to the bathroom, the hint of a kitchen in the corner. The bedroom door straight ahead, closed like a sealed memory. And to her left, the living room, where he sat on a sofa.

The furniture was modern, expensive, carefully arranged. The 65-inch TV sat centred on a sleek black console. The grey L-shaped sofa curved elegantly. The small chandelier above them cast warm, muted light.

But the room felt hollow. Everything looked lived-in but unlived-with. A space waiting for a life that never arrived. It carried a careful restraint, the same quiet discipline that held the man sitting inside it.

She stepped toward him. He didn't move. He didn't speak. His hands hung between his knees, fingers interlaced so tightly the knuckles blanched. His shoulders shook once. Then again. When he finally spoke, the voice wasn't his usual one; it was thin, scraped raw.

"I… lost everything today."

Anastasia's breath caught.

He swallowed hard, eyes still fixed on the floor as if lifting them might crack him open. "I don't even know where to start." His voice trembled. "I just… I need a friend tonight. Someone who can listen. Someone to calm me down without judging." A pause. A breath. A collapse. "I stood at the window and… I understood how someone could want to jump," he whispered, voice cracking. "I just… wanted everything to stop."

Her heart lurched.

He shook his head, tears clinging to his lashes. "My wife ruined my reputation. She told all our secrets. Every fight. Every mistake. Things no one should know. And tonight —" his voice fractured again "— tonight was supposed to be my birthday eve, and I called her to make peace. Instead her father picked up and her whole family gathered behind him. They humiliated me — all of them. I don't have anyone else here. Before you came… I spoke to my parents." He covered his face with both hands. "They also blamed me."

His shoulders trembled violently. "No one wants to hear my side. No one cares. She told so many lies… I don't even know how to defend myself. Even my own family believes her. I… I don't know what to do anymore."

A tear hit the floor between his shoes. Then another. And another.

For a moment, Anastasia simply stood there. Stunned, breath caught in her throat. She had seen him thoughtful, gentle, polite, patient… but never broken. And now he sat before her like a man stripped of everything — dignity, strength, certainty, hope.

She moved, quietly. Softly. She walked around the coffee table and sat beside him, not touching him, giving him space to pull away if he needed to.

He didn't.

So she reached out. Gently, carefully, she wrapped her arms around his shoulders. He didn't cling. He didn't lean. He simply stopped resisting gravity.

"It's okay," she whispered. "You're safe. I'm here. Everything will be okay."

She rubbed her hand slowly along his back, steady, soothing strokes. He didn't sob loudly. He broke quietly. The kind of breaking that fractures breathing rather than walls. When his tears slowed, she took out her handkerchief and dabbed gently at his face, her movements soft, respectful.

"Tell me," she said. "Tell me what happened."

He drew a shuddering breath and began.

"It started with the ticket. Her visa got approved… and I told her to book it. She just needed to call my cousin's ticketing agency and give them the money I already gave her." Another breath. "Then she said she didn't know how. That she couldn't talk to them. That she didn't know what to ask." He closed his eyes tightly. "I said, 'Are you a child?' I was stressed. It was stupid. I shouldn't have said it that way."

A pause.

"But she told her family I insulted her. That I belittled her. That I treat her badly." He swallowed. "Two years ago, when she visited me in Sweden… she said I called her blind." His brow furrowed with confusion. "I didn't even remember. And then it came back. Maybe once, when we were crossing the road. The light turned red and she stepped onto the street and a car honked. I said, 'Are you blind? Can't you see the light is red?' It slipped out. I didn't mean it. Just worry."

He shook his head. "That one sentence became a weapon." Another breath. "Then she said I didn't buy her water once." His eyes looked haunted. "Anastasia… I was a student back then. In Gothenburg. This is one of the most expensive countries in the world. I worked three jobs: one as a shop assistant at a store, the other washing dishes in the afternoon, then delivering food on a bicycle in freezing winter nights." A tremor passed through him. "My eyelashes would freeze. My beard would turn white with snow. But I kept going. I had to. I needed to save for her. For our future."

His voice thickened. "One afternoon, after walking around in the city centre, she asked for water. I told her to wait five minutes until we got home. Five minutes. And that became proof that I don't care about her." His hands clenched into fists.

Anastasia listened, and in the spaces between his words, she began to understand the shape of the woman she was hearing about. A woman from Islamabad, from a world where waiting five minutes for water was not inconvenience but proof of neglect.

"Then… the ticket." He let out a hollow laugh. "The one I bought for her when she was returning to Pakistan. It was from

Copenhagen because it was cheaper. One train ride from Gothenburg. That's all she had to take. But her parents bought another ticket from Gothenburg instead, which was expensive. Undermining me. Insulting me. And I had to cancel my ticket. That too was a huge loss."

His voice dropped lower, more defeated. "And the phone... Last time I visited Pakistan, I brought her an iPhone from Sweden. But there, imported phones need taxes to be paid before they can be used. She was coming to Sweden anyway. I told her it wasn't necessary. Now it's claimed the phone was stolen, that's why it doesn't work." His hands loosened, then went limp. "There were so many accusations," he whispered. "So many blames. I didn't even understand what kind of monster they think I am."

He looked up, not at her, but past her. "I worked so hard," he said softly. "I loved her. I waited two years. And she told them everything. Every private detail. Every word. And they believed everything." His eyes brimmed again, but the tears didn't fall. "And no one... not one person... wanted to hear my side."

Anastasia remained beside him. Quiet. Still. Present.

The refugee had become the refuge.

She didn't interrupt. Didn't judge. Didn't instruct. She listened. The way no one else in his life seemed willing to. And for the first time that night, something in him loosened. Not much. Just enough.

They spoke for hours. His voice broke, steadied, broke again. Hers remained soft, steady, an anchor in water too deep to touch bottom. The apartment, once cold and hollow, filled with low murmurs. Two people sharing a night heavy enough to bend ceilings.

Exhaustion overtook him, not as collapse but as release.

Eventually, sometime past dawn, his breaths grew slower. He leaned back against the sofa, eyes half-closed. Sleep didn't arrive gently. It shut him down. The collapse of a man who had held too much for too long.

Anastasia watched him for a moment. She brushed her fingers softly through his hair. Comforting. Humane. She pulled the blanket over him. Then she quietly stood, wrote a small note — *I'll come back soon* — and slipped out of the apartment, closing the door with tender care.

Outside, the cold August morning air stung her cheeks. She walked home quickly, slept two hours, then woke up again with purpose. In her kitchen, she made *borscht* — deep red, aromatic. A Ukrainian inheritance, a bowl of memory and survival. She quickly baked a small cake and wrote a card for him. She carried everything back to Hassan's apartment, cake in a small container and borscht in a glass bottle, before he could wake. He didn't go to work that day. He couldn't.

He woke to warmth first. Not the room, but the smell. Something earthy. Comforting in a way that caught him off guard. The light had shifted while he slept. Morning had crept in without asking permission.

For a moment, he didn't know where he was, or why his chest still felt crushed. Then he saw her. Anastasia stood near the small table, carefully placing a bowl in front of him, steam curling upward like breath in cold air. The first act of care he had received in a very, very long time.

"I'm sorry," he said immediately, his voice rough, embarrassed. "I fell asleep in the middle of… everything."

She looked at him gently. "It's okay. You needed rest."

He rubbed his face with both hands, shame washing through him. "You didn't have to do this."

She gave a small, matter-of-fact smile. The kind that didn't reach her eyes but still held steady. "You said I was your friend," she replied softly. "You have done so much for me, and this is the least I can do. It's just what friends do. They take care. It was your birthday. I thought this would cheer you up."

The words landed gently, but they cut deeper than any accusation could have. Because she still believed, or wanted to believe, that he was worth caring for.

And he no longer did.

No one had taken care of him like this in a long time. Not without conditions. Not without judgement. Not without keeping score. He watched her as she sat across from him, the soup between them. The cake. The small handwritten card. She wasn't trying to fix him. She was simply there. Present, steady, unafraid of his brokenness.

He cut the cake. A small piece, eaten in silence. He read the card that said: *Happy birthday, Hassan. Thank you for being there.* Her handwriting mesmerized him.

He tasted the soup. Borscht. Rich. Savory. Warm.

This was the first meal she had ever made for him. Before, their meetings were cafés and sandwiches. A relationship conducted in neutral, public territory. This was different. This was her crossing into his private space, and leaving a mark of her own.

She wasn't just feeding him; she was translating a piece of her home into his. For a man whose own home had become a site of betrayal, the act felt perilously intimate. He looked at her, really looked this time, and for the first time since everything had collapsed, he felt something unfamiliar bloom beneath the pain. Gratitude. And something gentler. Something dangerous.

They talked slowly after that. Carefully. As if both of them were afraid that speaking too loudly might shatter what little balance remained.

She told him about the war, not in headlines, but in fragments. The sound of sirens at three in the morning. The weight of leaving. The way fear becomes routine until it stops feeling dramatic and starts feeling permanent.

He listened, fully present, his own pain momentarily suspended as he realised how much she had endured without complaint. But while Anastasia sat beside him, grounding him in the present, his mind kept dragging him back to Pakistan. Back to humiliation. Back to voices raised over the phone.

Two people, wounded differently, sitting at the same table. Needing, without naming it, the same thing. Not rescue. Not answers. Just someone who saw.

He wanted someone to understand him. And accept him for who he was.

She wanted the same.

Chapter 10

The Trial Without a Jury

Sara had stopped responding completely. No calls. No messages. Nothing. Just silence, weaponised and deliberate. And then his family began. Calls filled with accusation. With disappointment. With shame. They told him to fix it. To make it right. To apologise. Even when he didn't know what he was apologising for.

He tried explaining. Tried defending himself. No one listened. Her father's words echoed in his head on a loop, sharper each time: *You humiliated her. You are the problem.*

And then came the worst of it. Her relatives. From Islamabad. They came to his parents' house like a tribunal. Faces hard, voices loud, honour dripping from every accusation. They spoke of him as if he were a criminal. A failure. A disgrace. And his family, his own blood, stood there and said nothing.

Even worse: they joined in. They humiliated him in front of them.

"We will fix him," they said.

As if he were broken machinery. As if five years of patience, sacrifice, and loyalty meant nothing. As if the nights he spent freezing on a bicycle delivering food, studying by day and working by night, waiting for a woman he loved — meant nothing.

He was thousands of kilometres away when this happened. Abroad. Powerless. Unable to stand in the room and speak for himself. Unable to defend his name, his intentions, his heart.

But the worst part wasn't the accusation. It was not being believed.

Chapter 10

Every time he thought of it, his chest seized. His hands shook. Tears came without warning. On the train, at his desk, in the bathroom at work where he locked himself in and stared at his reflection, unrecognisable. He couldn't focus. Code blurred on the screen. Meetings passed without meaning. Colleagues spoke, and he nodded automatically, present only in body. Inside, he was unravelling. He cried alone at night. Cried quietly. Cried like a man who had lost not just a relationship, but his dignity.

Sara had exposed every private moment. Every argument. Every weakness. She had stripped their marriage bare and laid it before others to judge. The breach of trust was complete. Irreversible. Whatever love had existed, whatever hope remained, was gone. He didn't want her back. Not anymore.

But in Pakistan, honour is everything. And his had been dragged through the dirt.

So, he booked a ticket. Five days later. Not to bring her back. Not to beg. But to stand in front of them and speak. To reclaim himself. To expose the lies. To look people in the eye and say: *This is who I am — and this is not what you've been told.*

The decision brought something unexpected: clarity. He would clear his name, and in the same breath, he would leave her. The two were inseparable now. The man who walked off that plane would not be the same one who'd been dragged through the mud.

For the first time in weeks, he felt light. Confident. Almost himself again.

He left for Pakistan carrying that weight. But also, strangely, a sense of release. He boarded the flight from Stockholm without ceremony.

The layover in Rome stretched longer than it should have, hours thinning into something airless. Hassan drifted through the terminal without direction, the last weeks pressing against his ribs like a second skeleton. Around him, the airport pulsed with unfamiliar languages, departures and arrivals crossing paths without ever touching. Lives brushing shoulders, then dissolving into separate skies.

Then he saw the piano.

Black. Polished. Waiting.

It stood slightly off to the side of the concourse, exposed under white terminal lights, as if daring someone to sit down and declare themselves.

He did.

For a moment his fingers hovered above the keys, suspended between impulse and restraint. Then they lowered.

The first notes of "Bella Ciao" rose into the open space. Soft, almost careful, as though testing whether the air would accept them. Then steadier. Firmer. A melody born of resistance. Of farewell. Of leaving without permission.

As he played, his thoughts narrowed to a single point.

Sara.

Not anger. That had burned out.
Not love. That had thinned into something unrecognisable.
Not even grief.

Finality.

Each note felt deliberate, measured. Like closing a door slowly and pressing it shut with the palm of his hand to make sure the latch caught. Years of effort. Compromise. Apology. Containment. He felt them move through his wrists into the keys. This was not nostalgia. There was no ache in it. Only severance.

The melody carried through the terminal and dissolved into the mechanical hum of announcements and rolling luggage. No one stopped. No one applauded. The world continued, indifferent.

Chapter 10

When the final note thinned into silence, he did not linger.

He stood. Adjusted his jacket. Flexed his fingers once, as if testing circulation. Then he walked away without looking back. Leaving the song suspended in the air behind him, leaving the marriage inside it, leaving whatever hope once occupied that space sealed within the echo.

Lahore struck him the moment he stepped outside the airport. It smelled like dust, fuel, familiarity, and judgement.

At home, his mother didn't wait.

"You ruined us," she said, the words sharp and unfiltered. "Do you know what people are saying? I wish —" The sentence fractured under its own weight "I wish I had never had a son like you."

Hassan stood still. "Ammi," he said quietly, "please listen —"

"Listen?" his father cut in, stepping forward. His jaw was tight, hands clasped behind his back as if restraining something physical. "We are the ones listening — to insults. To accusations. To your wife's family telling us how their daughter suffered with you."

The word suffered lingered in the air like a stain.

He swallowed. "She is lying," he said. "I swear on everything I have. Every accusation — I can explain."

They didn't want explanations. Still, he tried. The phone. The water. The ticket from Copenhagen. The years he worked two jobs while studying. The winters on a bicycle when his eyelashes froze.

"I did everything with intention," he said, his voice steady but hollow. "Not cruelty. Never cruelty."

Silence followed.

But something thinner than certainty. A doubt that did not want to exist.

A meeting was arranged with several of Sara's relatives at a neighbour's house. Neutral ground that quickly turned into a battleground.

The neighbours, who had once proposed the match between Sara and Hassan years earlier, were meant to act as mediators. Instead, they arrived already aligned. They were relatives of Sara's maternal family. Distant enough to call themselves neutral. Close enough to feel obligated.

Neutral ground had already tilted.

And he had walked into it knowingly.

The air in the room was thick, heavy with monsoon humidity and heavier still with judgement. Ceiling fans pushed the heat from one corner to another without relief.

Eight people sat across from Hassan and his parents. Uncles, aunts, extended relatives. Sara didn't come. Nor did her parents. They had sent representatives.

Proxies.

They circled him and his ageing parents like vultures, pressing shame into every corner of the house.

When the meeting formally convened, Hassan sat flanked only by his mother and father, facing a wall of hostility. At first, the room was filled with their accusations.

"You raised him wrong," one of Sara's uncles sneered at his father with a precision meant to wound. His father's jaw tightened.

"He is arrogant," another added, piling weight onto his parents' disgrace.

Chapter 10

They blamed him for suppressing her, for humiliating her. Each charge was delivered as fact, not allegation. No one asked him whether it was true.

Hassan did not raise his voice.

He did not interrupt.

His hands rested flat against his knees to keep them from shaking.

And then he started.

He explained every single accusation: the water, the ticket, the phone. Everything.

He spoke with the quiet, desperate clarity of a man who knows the truth is his only shield. When he finished, no one moved.

Silence did not fall all at once.

It crept.

Then one of the aunts shifted in her seat. Her eyes, which had been hard, began to flicker. Not with sympathy, but with calculation. The narrative she had rehearsed no longer fit cleanly.

Then she began to weep.

Not theatrically. Not loudly.

Just a hand rising to her mouth as something inside her realigned.

"We have seen you, Hassan," she said, her voice uneven. "You could be strict. Yes. But I knew you couldn't do what they were accusing you of."

The realisation of what they had done to him hit the room like a physical blow.

"This man is not lying," someone whispered into the sudden quiet. "He is being crushed."

No one repeated the accusations.

Instead, questions began turning outward.

"What exactly did she say?"

"Why was this told differently to us?"

The pressure shifted.

Not loudly. Not dramatically.

It pivoted.

The certainty that had filled the room thinned. Sara's relatives from Lahore began questioning the version they had been given. The tone changed. Defence turned into scrutiny. The representatives who had arrived prepared to condemn him now found themselves explaining inconsistencies.

But truth, in the face of pride, does not heal.

It humiliates.

Later, at home:
"We are sorry, we didn't know," Hassan's parents murmured.

"I told you they are lying. And even you all stood against me. You should have trusted your son," he fired back, angry that they hadn't defended him from the beginning.

But Sara's parents did not accept the shift. They demanded another meeting. A final reckoning on their own soil. This time, it was at her parents' house in Islamabad.

Hassan went. He entered their house flanked only by his parents, stepping into a room filled with her entire extended clan. Men standing along the walls. Women seated in tight rows. No empty space anywhere.

Chapter 10

The atmosphere was not one of reconciliation. It was a hunt.

Ten people circled him like wolves around a wounded lion, tightening the perimeter. The meeting stretched on for gruelling hours, the air turning stale as the interrogation cycled through the same accusations again and again.

"You humiliated her," someone shouted. "You think education makes you better than us? You think you can control our daughter?"

Hassan sat in the centre with his spine straight, hands clasped between his knees, elbows braced against his thighs. Anchoring himself against the pressure.

"I never controlled her," he said. "I asked for respect."

Laughter — short, disbelieving.

"We gave you money. We made you who you are," they threw at him.

His hands separated. His right fist clenched. "I am a self-made man," he said, and this time there was no tremor. Only steel.

"Everything I have, I earned. I never knelt before anyone. What you gave has already been returned in full. You think your money can buy me?"

That was the problem.

All their wealth, all their connections, all their carefully curated power. None of it could force him to bend.

They owned the room, the voices, the verdict. But not the man sitting inside it.

A man who held his honour and self-respect like a blade. A man who could never be bought, and therefore could never be controlled.

Scoffs rose. Bodies shifted uneasily. The room recoiled, not from weakness, but from defiance that refused to yield. Explanations dissolved before they could land. Context had no purchase here. Nuance was treated as evasion.

"You are judging shadows," he said. "Not facts."

And then they played their final card.

They brought her.

Sara stepped into the room and sat directly in front of him.

No words at first. Just her presence.

The strategy was clear: break him in front of her. Force confession through spectacle.

The sight of her, sitting there, prepared to dismantle him publicly, was more than he could bear.

He stood up immediately.

The chair legs scraped sharply against tile as he pushed it back. Turned his back on them, and walked out of the house. Down the corridor. Through the front door. He stormed into the lawn.

The night air was cold and stale, heavy with the smell of damp soil and exhaust drifting from the road. He kept walking until the house noise dulled behind him, and looked up at the dark sky.

"Why are You putting me through this?" he yelled, his voice cracking, a raw plea thrown against the silence of the night sky. "This is too much!"

He stood there, chest heaving, tears streaming down his face, vibrating with the injustice of it all.

Moments later, his father came out. He simply placed a hand on Hassan's shoulder, calming him down, asking him softly to come back inside.

Chapter 10

Hassan wiped his face with the back of his hand. Drew in a slow breath and held it until the tremor steadied.

If this is how it is going to be, then be it. Let's see how low she wants to fall.

He went back in.

Sara held the memory of her grievances that spanned years like a ledger. Not literally, but the precision was the same. Pages aligned. Columns balanced. Nothing forgiven. Nothing misplaced.

"You remember the airport?" she began, looking straight at him, her voice level, almost clinical. "When I first landed in Sweden? You didn't bring flowers. Not even a single rose. My father always brought my mother orchids. You just took my suitcase and said, 'The train is this way,' as if I were a colleague arriving for a conference."

A murmur moved through the room.

She didn't pause for breath.

"That winter in Gothenburg. The day I wore the emerald shawl my mother gave me. I'd dressed for you." Her jaw tightened. "You came home from work, looked right through me, and said, 'Let's go, we are getting late for the movie.'"

Hassan inhaled to respond.

She cut across him.

"And the crossing. That first week. The light was red. I stepped off to cross the road, a car honked. You grabbed my arm so hard it bruised. You shouted, 'Are you blind? Can't you see?' in the middle of the street. People turned. I wanted the ground to swallow me."

"There was no one there!" Hassan interjected, his voice strained. "I was scared you'd get hurt —"

"You called me blind," she stated, as if reading a charge from a police report. "Does a husband call his wife blind?"

No answer was acceptable.

She continued, a relentless prosecutor.

"The *Eid* dinner with your manager. Your old job as a shop assistant in Gothenburg." She didn't look at him now; she looked past him, addressing the room. "I wore the blue silk dress. He didn't even tell me I looked nice. Not once. He kept joking and laughing with his manager and his colleagues, while I sat there, invisible."

A brief pause. Controlled. Returning to him: "Afterward, in the taxi, you said, 'You were very quiet.' You didn't ask why."

Her eyes were dry. Focused. Not wounded. Precise.

She leaned forward slightly.

"And the water. After that long walk through the city centre. I was thirsty. You said, 'Wait five minutes, we're almost home.' Five minutes." Her voice thinned but did not break. "You couldn't buy your wife a bottle of water. My brother heard that story. He asked me, 'Does he think you're not worth twenty kronor?'"

The room absorbed it as indictment.

He listened, a cold clarity cutting through the humiliation. Something in him shifted. Not defensiveness, not even anger.

Recognition.

Almost all the accusations were from Gothenburg, from the years he was a student, working three jobs, counting every krona, living on instant noodles and frozen dreams. A time when survival was the only luxury he could afford.

She continued.

Each memory was chambered before it was spoken.

Moments he barely remembered, small frictions long dissolved in his mind, were drawn out, aimed, and fired into the room.

Every accusation struck clean. No warning. No hesitation.

He felt them land one by one, precise and deliberate, punching through whatever remained of his composure. Not explosive or dramatic. Just impact. Then another. Then another.

She lifted private moments out of the dark and set them under public light. Each one stripped of tone, stripped of context, stripped of the quiet negotiations that make up a marriage. Until he stood exposed as the villain in his own story.

"The phone — I told them not to say that it was stolen." She dismissed it with a wave, as if it were a small human error, nothing worth defending.

"And your cousin's wedding in Lahore," she continued, turning back to him. "Do you remember that?"

He said nothing.

"You wanted me to dance with you in front of everyone. I told you I didn't want to." Her voice remained steady. "Yes, we had rehearsed. Yes, you were excited. But I was uncomfortable."

A faint shift moved through the room.

"You kept insisting. You said it would look bad if I refused." Her fingers curled against her thigh. "When I hesitated, you leaned close and said, 'Don't make a scene.'"

She held his gaze now.

"And when I still didn't move, you whispered, 'I want to slap you so hard right now.'"

"I danced," she said. "Not because I wanted to. Because I didn't want to be humiliated in front of your entire family."

Silence.

"And everyone clapped. They thought we were happy. Huh."

A long pause.

"The examples you've given," Hassan said, his voice low but clear, "are from when I was a student. When I had nothing."

He looked around the room.

"The last one. She knows I apologised for that. Several times."

His gaze returned to her.

"The twenty kronor for water was an hour of my life on a bicycle in the freezing dark. The flowers, the compliments you wanted, they weren't withheld out of neglect. They were luxuries I couldn't afford."

He paused.

"My love was not in display. It was in work. It was in sacrifice. You're judging a starving man for not setting a beautiful table."

She stared at him, unmoved.

Context did not soften anything. It simply added another entry to the ledger.

She continued.

"You have everything now. Stability. Status. You can provide. But I want to leave when you are at your peak in life. So, no one can say I stayed with you for your success or your money. Not even you."

He did not argue anymore.

There is a point, in sustained fire, when the body stops reacting to individual wounds. It only registers loss.

Hassan looked at her. The woman he had loved, the woman he had waited for and felt the futility settle in him like a physical weight. With a clarity that felt like death, he understood what had been lost.

There was no explanation for the private language of a marriage. No way for anyone outside it to understand the meanings that lived in silence, in habit, in endurance. He was offering nuance to a room that had already chosen clarity.

And clarity, once chosen, has no patience for complexity.

He looked at his parents. His mother was weeping. His father seemed smaller somehow, shoulders folded inward, as if the weight in the room had settled directly onto his spine. The pressure broke him not from the outside, but from within.

Justice had no place here. And soon he was going to realise that it had no place anywhere.

"No one outside a marriage understands what happens between two people," he said quietly.

The words fell without impact.

In a system built on power rather than truth, the world made the weak kneel, regardless of who is right or wrong.

So, he gave in.

Under the crushing weight of his parents' desperation and his own exhaustion, Hassan swallowed his dignity.

"I apologise for everything," he said, the words tasting like ash in his mouth. "I ask you… to send my wife back to me."

Agreement came, but not freely.

Terms were dictated for his surrender. Conditions followed. Submission. Silence. Subordination.

He was to correct himself and to avoid repetition.

He accepted each demand with a nod.

Not because he believed in them. But because walking away meant losing his family and in Pakistan, losing family is a death of another kind.

Hands were shaken.

Voices softened.

Peace was declared, but it was a peace forged in chains. He was, in essence, agreeing to become a slave in his own marriage.

And in doing so, he saved his family's honour. But he left the last shred of himself on that floor in Islamabad.

Sara would never understand what that moment cost him. Men in his world didn't explain, they provided, they protected, they endured. She saw patriarchy; he saw duty. She saw control; he saw responsibility. They were both right. They were both wrong. And between those two truths, there was no room for either of them to breathe.

September 15th.

Four days after the meeting in Islamabad, he returned to Sweden alone. Sara was still not talking to him. When he called her father to let her join him, the answer came cold and calculated: "She is receiving psychological treatment. She will come later."

Later. Always later. Hassan hung up and stared at the wall. The apartment felt unchanged. That was the worst part. He had sacrificed his ego. His peace. His truth. To save a marriage already hollowed out.

Hollow things sometimes feel light. He mistook the emptiness for relief.

He thought this was the end of the suffering.

It was only the beginning.

Chapter 11
A Silent Archive

After the cold, final reply from Sara's father, something inside Hassan loosened and something else began to ache. He stopped waiting for messages that never came. Stopped rehearsing explanations no one wanted to hear. And only then did he realise how long he'd been suffocating.

Instead, he found himself walking more often toward Anastasia.

They didn't plan it at first. It simply happened. A bench in a park that had begun to recognise them. A café where the barista no longer asked for their order. Long walks through streets that changed colour with the hour, conversations stretching past dusk and into that quiet Scandinavian blue that never quite turned into night.

Sometimes they talked for hours.

Sometimes they sat in silence, close enough to feel each other's presence without needing words.

And slowly, almost imperceptibly, Hassan began to breathe again.

With Anastasia, there was no tension in his chest. No need to defend himself. No careful measuring of words. She listened the way people do when they are not waiting to reply, only to understand. When he stopped speaking, she let the silence rest between them.

She let him be.

One evening, they sat on the grass near the water, the city glowing behind them, reflections breaking apart on the surface like scattered light. Anastasia leaned back on her palms, face tilted toward the sky, her hair catching the last warmth of the day.

"You know," she said softly, "when I first met you, I didn't think you'd become… this."

He smiled faintly. "This how?"

She turned her head toward him. "Someone I look forward to seeing. Someone who feels… familiar."

He smiled.

By then, he had told her everything.

About his childhood.

About the years of responsibility.

About the marriage that had broken him quietly, piece by piece.

About the waiting. The humiliation. The shame that wasn't truly his but had been placed on his shoulders anyway.

He told her the truth. Not as a confession, but as a laying down of arms.

And Anastasia had listened.

She didn't flinch.
Didn't recoil.

Didn't ask him to be less complicated.

She accepted him. Not the version of him that survived, but the one that still wanted to live.

Weeks passed like this. Almost a month of regular meetings, of shared meals and borrowed time, of laughter that came easier with each passing day. Hassan found himself reaching for his phone without thinking, wanting to tell her small things. A joke from work. A song he'd heard. A memory that surfaced unexpectedly.

He began to realise something that frightened him in its clarity.

He was falling in love.

Not in the loud, reckless way people talk about. But deeply. Quietly. With the kind of certainty that doesn't ask permission.

One afternoon, in the same park where so many of their conversations had unfolded, Hassan stopped walking.

Anastasia took a few steps ahead before noticing. She turned back, puzzled.

"What is it?"

He looked at her the way a man looks when he has already decided and now must speak.

"I need to say something." His voice was steady, but his hands betrayed him, fingers curling once before relaxing again.

She waited. Didn't rush him.

"I didn't plan this," he continued. "I wasn't looking for it. I wasn't ready for it." He let out a breath. "But I can't pretend anymore."

She felt her heart begin to race.

"I love you," he said simply. "Very much."

The words hung between them — not dramatic, not even desperate. Honest.

For a moment, Anastasia didn't speak. She stepped closer instead, closing the small distance between them.

"I love you too," she said, her voice quiet, but unwavering. "I think… I've loved you for a while."

Chapter 11

He didn't speak. He didn't need to.

He reached for her hand, moving slower than urgency, careful with reverence.

"There is nothing in my life I haven't told you. Nothing I want to hide from you. This is who I am. Flawed, tired, still standing."

She squeezed his hand. "I know. And I choose you anyway."

Happiness felt fragile. Temporary. Exposed. He did not want this to drift.

The decision came to him fully formed, without doubt.

"Then marry me."

Her breath caught, not in shock, but in recognition.

"Yes," she answered. "I will."

From that moment, they were almost inseparable.

The weeks that followed had a quality Hassan couldn't name. Something between discovery and return, as if he were finding a version of himself he'd forgotten existed. They met when they could, which was often. She'd appear at the café near his office, and he'd look up from his laptop to find her already settled across from him, a book in her hands, as if she'd always been there. He started leaving work earlier without deciding to.

One afternoon, they walked through Gamla stan as the light turned amber, and she stopped to stare at a window display of handmade candles. She didn't say she wanted one. She just looked. The next day, he placed a small box on the table between them. A candle the colour of late autumn, wrapped in brown paper. She didn't thank him with words. She just looked at him the way she'd looked at the candle, and he understood.

They moved through the city like two people finally walking at the same pace. Hassan found himself lighter, more open, laughing the way he once had years ago. With Anastasia, there was harmony. Agreement. A softness that didn't require explanation. She met him where he was, not where she wished he'd been.

And Hassan, deeply, madly in love, let himself forget, if only for moments at a time, that there was still a life behind him he had not yet escaped.

Days passed by.

It almost felt like happiness was possible. But soon, small things started surfacing. Things he wouldn't have noticed a week earlier or would have noticed and dismissed.

They'd be sitting in a café, and her phone would light up with a message. She'd glance at it, then at him, then back at the screen. Her thumbs would move, once, twice, and she'd set the phone face-down on the table.

"Anyone important?" he asked once, lightly.

"No one." The answer came too fast.

Another afternoon, her phone buzzed while they were walking. She glanced at it, silenced it, and kept talking without missing a beat. But her hand stayed in her pocket, wrapped around it, long after it should have been forgotten.

Later, walking by the water, her phone chimed in her pocket. She didn't take it out. Didn't check it. But her pace slowed, just slightly, and her eyes drifted to the side, not at the view, but inward, as if calculating something. When he asked if she was okay, she smiled and said yes. The smile reached her eyes. Almost.

Then there was the evening she excused herself to the bathroom and left her phone on the table. It buzzed. He didn't look, didn't want to look, but his eyes caught the screen. A name he didn't recognise. A message preview he couldn't read fast enough before the screen went dark. When she came back, she picked up the phone, glanced at it, and slipped it into her pocket without a word.

Chapter 11

At first, Hassan told himself he was imagining it.

The way her attention kept slipping away.

The way her fingers curled tighter around her phone than around his hand.

The way her shoulders tensed whenever the screen lit up.

Anastasia had always been present. When she was with him, she was *with* him. Or so he thought. But over the weeks, something changed. She smiled, she laughed, she said all the right things. Yet there was a thin, restless edge beneath it all, pulling her somewhere else.

He didn't question it at first.

On the evening of October 11th, the silence between them grew heavy enough that he could no longer ignore it.

They sat across from each other, the room dim, winter pressing against the windows. Anastasia sat curled slightly inward, phone in her hands, thumbs moving faster than her breath.

Hassan watched her for a long moment before speaking.

"What are you always doing on your phone?" he asked quietly.

She looked up too fast.

"What?" A pause. "Nothing. Just… talking to friends."

Something about the speed of her answer unsettled him.

"Friends? The ones you're always with?"

She hesitated, just a fraction too long.

"Yes. Friends from Ukraine."

He nodded slowly, though unease crept deeper into his chest.

"And you're still staying at the volunteer's place, right?"

"Yes," she said quickly. Too quickly. "Of course."

The words landed wrong.

Hassan leaned forward, elbows on his knees, his voice lowering, not accusatory, but concerned.

"Anastasia… whenever we're together, you seem stressed. Distracted. I can see it. If something's wrong, tell me. Let me help you."

"There's nothing," her eyes dropping back to the screen.

He waited.

She didn't look up.

"Please," more firmly now. "Talk to me."

She shook her head. "You're overthinking."

He exhaled slowly. "Then show me."

Her fingers froze.

She looked at him as if he had struck her.

"What? Why would you ask that?"

"Because I care, and because I feel like you're slipping away from me."

Her voice rose. "Don't you trust me?"

"I want to, but I can't if you won't let me."

She straightened her back, defiant.

"You don't understand. You won't like what you'll see."

He opened his palm between them, steady, open.

Chapter 11

"Nothing can separate us. If something's wrong, we'll face it together."

Her eyes filled with fear.

"We probably won't be together after this," she whispered.

"Let me be the judge of that," he said.

For a long moment, she didn't move.
Then, slowly, reluctantly, she placed the phone into his hand.

The phone felt heavier than it should have.

Hassan unlocked the screen.

At first, he didn't understand what he was seeing.

Names he didn't recognise.
Conversations stretching back weeks, months.
Messages filled with intimacy that was not his.

His chest tightened.

He scrolled.

And the world collapsed.

Men from Ukraine.
Men from Sweden.

Promises. Flirtation. Hope offered generously, to all of them.

Photos. Selfies. Late-night messages. Words, nicknames she had once spoken to *him* now repeated elsewhere, diluted, meaningless.

His breathing grew shallow.

He scrolled further.

Her ex. Still there. Still present. Money issues.

Then something colder surfaced.

Trips. Gifts. Money transfers. Conversations about places she had never mentioned.

Bali.

An older man. Swedish. Paying for everything.

And then the truth that cut deepest of all — she was no longer living at the volunteer's place.

She was living with *him*.

Hassan's vision blurred.

It felt like standing on a mountain peak and suddenly discovering there was no ground beneath his feet, only empty air.

He said nothing.

And kept scrolling.

Every message was a blow. Every smile she had given him rewrote itself into something false.

All this time, while he had been opening his life to her, proposing marriage, imagining a future, she had been living several others.

Scrolling continues.

Then he found a folder labeled simply "Recordings."

Dozens of files. Hours and hours. Dates stretching back months. The first week she arrived in Sweden. Every day since. The last recording had stopped moments ago.

He opened one. His own voice filled his ears. A conversation he didn't remember, from a day he'd long forgotten. Just ordinary. Just life. And she had recorded it.

Chapter 11

She had been documenting everything. Every moment. Every word. Every vulnerability he'd ever shown her, stored like evidence.

He opened another. Another man's voice filled his ears.

He stopped scrolling.

He handed the phone back to her.

She took it cautiously, watching his face.

"Are you okay?" she asked.

He didn't look at her.

A long pause. Too long. Too much information to absorb. Then finally:

"Nothing," he said, his voice breaking, "is okay."

Chapter 12

The Secret Vow

Hassan leaned forward, elbows on his knees, both hands buried in his hair, fingers twisting hard, as if he could pull the pain out of his skull. His breath came in short, uneven bursts.

Again.
Again, I trusted.
Again, I had believed in the version of love I have been searching for my entire life.

And again, it had shattered in my hands.

He felt rage — hot, blinding.
He felt betrayal — sharp, precise.

But beneath it all was something worse.

Humiliation.

The realisation that while he had been rebuilding himself piece by piece, she had been dismantling him without his knowing.

He just sat there, broken, feeling the familiar weight of collapse settle over him once more. He stayed seated, staring at the floor, hoping it might open and take him with it.

"Please leave," he said quietly. "I can't even look at you right now."

Anastasia froze.

"Please… talk to me," she said, panic rising. "Hassan, please."

"I said leave."

She stepped closer instead, breath shallow, hands clenched together. "I didn't mean to hurt you. I swear. I just —"

He lifted his head. Whatever she saw in his eyes made her stop mid-sentence.

"You destroyed me." The restraint snapped. His voice rose, cracked. "You destroyed me."

She flinched.

"I trusted you," he went on, chest heaving. "I let you into my life when everything in me was already broken. I told you everything. Everything."

Tears ran freely down his face now. Unashamed, furious, disbelieving.

"You let me say I love you. You let me propose to you —" his voice broke, "— while you were doing this behind my back. When I confessed my love to you, that was your moment to come clean. Like I did."

"I was wrong." Her words tumbled out, desperate. "I know I was wrong. But you have to understand —"

"I don't understand," his voice rose. "I don't understand how someone can look me in the eyes and lie like that."

She shook her head violently. "I never loved them. Any of them. I swear. I was just — afraid. I was alone. I didn't know where I would end up."

He turned away from her, walked into the living room, and collapsed onto a chair. His elbows rested on his knees, his head buried in his hands again.

She followed him.

"I gave you my heart," his voice muffled. "And you treated it like something disposable."

Slowly, carefully, she lowered herself to her knees in front of him, fingers clasped.

"I was a refugee," she begged through tears. "I needed safety. I didn't know how to survive here. I didn't know who would stay. I didn't know who to trust."

He didn't respond.

She reached for him, hesitated, then placed her hands lightly on his knee.

"I met him once. Not too long ago. He offered help. A place to stay. I didn't plan any of this. I didn't think. I made a huge mistake."

"You lived with him." Hassan lifted his head. His eyes were red and hollow. "You took money from him. You went on trips with him."

Her lips trembled. "Yes, I'm sorry. When you told me that night, that you have a wife — it broke me."

He shook his head slowly, sharp disapproval in his eyes.

"And you've been recording. Every single day." His voice cracked on the last word. "That's insane."

Her lips parted. "The recordings were just for my safety. I started when I first came to Sweden. I was scared."

She grabbed his hands, fingers desperate. "But I'll cut everyone off now," she rushed to say. "Everyone. I swear. It's only you. It was always you."

He laughed then. A short, broken sound that held no humour at all.

"You want me to understand? I don't even recognise what I'm looking at anymore."

Chapter 12

She leaned closer, desperation pouring out of her. "Please forgive me. I'll do anything. I'll disappear from everyone else's life. I promise. I am sorry I have been spoiled."

He closed his eyes.

For a moment, just a moment, he wanted to understand her. Wanted to believe there was a version of this that didn't end in ruin.

But the images wouldn't leave him.

The messages.

The lies.

The ease with which she had lived two lives.

"I can't. I can't do this again."

She broke completely then, sobbing into her hands. "I love you — please!"

The words came too late.

He stood, walked to the entrance door, opened it.

She rose slowly, her face soaked, her body shaking. "Please don't do this," she whispered.

He stood there like a corpse.

Finally, she gave in.

"I never meant to break you." She looked at him like she was memorising him.

Hassan said nothing.

She stepped out of the apartment. The door closed behind her with a soft, final click.

He slid down against the door, sitting on the floor, his back pressed to the wood.

The apartment felt hollow now, stripped of sound and warmth. Even the city outside seemed to have withdrawn, leaving him alone with the echo of his own breathing.

When the silence came, it was absolute.

And for the third time in his life — he was alone once again in the wreckage of love.

Two days passed.

Then three.

During that time, messages began to arrive.

At first, he didn't open them. He couldn't. The screen lit up with her name again and again, and each time his chest tightened.

On the morning of the third day, he finally read them. He sat on the train to work, elbows resting on his knees. They had come in fragments — broken, raw.

Anastasia: *I am so sad about how I became this version of myself.*

Anastasia: *I hate who I am.*

Anastasia: *I can't live with myself anymore.*

Anastasia: *It's a big pity for me that you met me. I regret appearing in your life. Before I met you, my life made me the way I appear in front of you. The bad way. And I don't have anywhere to go to be fixed by someone. My family can't fix me and I can't even go to them. But you gave me more than anyone in my life to help me fix myself now. I will do this. I did it already in my mind. But it didn't help me forgive myself. Who I am. I am thankful to God that he gave me a good heart. But the person who I am, or was, doesn't deserve you at all. I really hope that you'll take the best from knowing me all this time. I got you, and then I destroyed everything. That was my chance.*

Anastasia: *I don't see any purpose in my life.*

Chapter 12

Anastasia: *I want you, but I won't forgive myself. How disgusted I became. The longer I lived, the more I became who I am now. And this is too much. I knew it. Thank you for stopping it. I am really very sorry for you that you were a part of my life. Please remember my heart. I love you, my Krolik. Only God knows how much. Maybe we'll meet in heaven.*

The words didn't feel manipulative. They felt terrified. Fragile, like someone standing at the edge of themselves with nowhere left to go.

After reading the last one, Hassan closed his eyes.

He had always been this way, unable to turn away from pain when it asked to be seen. He was a man raised to fix things. To shoulder weight quietly. To step forward when something was broken, even if the cost was never fully measured.

And when he saw her unravelling, the anger that had once burned so hot began to cool into something heavier.

Understanding.

Justification.

Maybe she had done what she thought she had to do to survive.
A foreign country. No family. No roof over her head.
Maybe I judged her too quickly.

And then he started typing:

You should…

A pause.

He stared at the screen until his vision blurred.

He had seen this before.

He knew what saving someone cost him.

If he answered, something would reopen.

If he stayed silent, she might unravel.

Mercy felt like weakness. But loneliness felt worse.

He imagined ignoring her. Imagined sleeping alone. Imagined her with someone else.

He knew what he was doing, and did it anyway.

Hassan: *You should forgive yourself. What's done is done.*

Hassan: *When I come home today, I'd like to see you there.*

He looked at the messages for a long moment after sending them.

It felt like mercy.

It felt like hope.

But it was also the first step into something he hadn't fully thought through.

That evening, she stood in his doorway again, eyes red-rimmed, shoulders drawn inward, wearing the same clothes as the last time he saw her.

They went inside.

She fell to her knees again. Crying. Apologising until her voice gave out. Saying his name like a prayer. He watched her unravel, wearing the mask of mercy.

When the tears slowed, he wiped her face, pulled her up from the floor, and made her sit beside him.

For a long moment, he just held her hand. Then he spoke.

"I know you've made mistakes," he said quietly. "And it's very hard to forget. But I understand you."

He paused, feeling her trembling beside him.

"You thought you needed many doors open. Many options. Because you were afraid of being abandoned again." He swallowed. "I get that. When someone has no ground beneath their feet, they grab whatever keeps them from drowning. I don't condemn you for that."

She looked down, but he lifted her chin gently.

"But that's not how you build a life. Fear is not a foundation. You can't build anything real on it. A life built on escape will always feel temporary. Always unstable."

Her eyes filled again.

"You don't need more," he said softly. "You need one decision. One direction. One truth."

Their eyes met.

"People aren't what they do when they're afraid. They're what they do when they're safe. You weren't safe. I can see why you did what you did to survive."

He paused.

"And understanding leaves no room for judgement. Not because what you did was right, but because I've been afraid too. I've done things I'm not proud of. Things I needed someone to understand. But no one ever did."

He took both her hands in his.

"I'd rather be broken with you than whole without you."

She stared at him, disbelief and hope warring in her eyes.

He leaned back slightly, studying her. Not with rage, but with something heavier.

Conviction.

"I don't want you there anymore," he said quietly. "Where you're staying."

She looked up at him, startled. "What… what do you mean?"

"I mean," he said, choosing his words carefully, "you can't keep living like that. Depending on men who take advantage of your situation."

Her lips parted. "I didn't know where else to go."

"I do," he replied.

She hesitated. "Hassan…"

"You'll move here," he said, not commanding, but certain. "With me."

Relief flickered through him as he said it. Quiet. Possessive.

The word steadied him more than it should have.

Her breath caught. "Are you sure?"

He nodded once. "Yes."

The decision set something irreversible in motion.

"And you'll give me all your data and recordings from the past. I'll destroy them all."

"Destroy?" she asked.

"Yes." He held her gaze. "You need to let go of the past. You need to forgive yourself. And you'll never record again. I think that's the least you can do for me."

She hesitated, then nodded. "Okay. I'll listen to you. Once we get all my stuff back, I'll give you everything."

Two days later, when they went to collect her belongings, the air in the old man's apartment felt stale, heavy with unspoken things. The man stood to the side, watching silently as she packed her clothes into bags.

Hassan met his gaze once.
Long enough.

There were no words. But the message was unmistakable.

You are sick.
And you know it.

The man looked away.

Anastasia said nothing. She didn't thank him. She didn't explain herself. She gathered what little she owned, zipped the last bag closed, and followed Hassan out without a backward glance.

They loaded the car in silence.

The door shut, the engine started, and they began driving back home.

This would end the overlap. Close the doors. Remove the other men from reach.

As they drove away, Hassan felt both relief and dread coil together in his chest. Two forces moving in opposite directions, bound by the same choice.

On the way back, he told her they would perform the *nikah* ceremony the next day, allowing them to live together religiously as husband and wife.

She agreed.

He told himself he was saving her. She told herself she finally belonged somewhere.

But somewhere beneath that, something else was already calculating.

Once they were back at the apartment, she collected all her electronics. Two laptops, an old Samsung phone, three memory cards with all the recordings and handed them over to Hassan. He put everything in an old laptop bag and told her he'd destroy it.

They were the same devices she'd carried from Ukraine when she fled. The only proof she existed before him, now surrendered.

Then he left, without ever checking what was inside. *He should have.* When he came back, he told her he'd thrown it all in the recycling bin.

She nodded in acceptance, almost in disbelief. As if it were that simple.

Later, he took her to the local market run by Arabs and asked her to choose a dress for the nikah. She picked a burgundy modest dress with an *abaya* — a flowing garment that covers the head, for herself. She liked it very much.

October 17th.

The very next morning, they sat across from an imam in a small, quiet mosque. No family, no celebration. Just hushed voices, trembling hands, and words spoken with the weight of permanence.

"Hassan Khan, son of Shehryar Khan, do you accept Anastasia Kovalenko, daughter of Volodymyr Kovalenko, as your wife?" the imam asked.

"I do," Hassan said.

"And you, Anastasia Kovalenko, daughter of Volodymyr Kovalenko, do you accept Hassan Khan, son of Shehryar Khan, as your husband?" the imam turned to her.

"Yes," she whispered, looking at him. "I do." Tears filled her eyes.

It was done.

Chapter 12

In the eyes of God, they were husband and wife.

But the world outside those walls remained unchanged.

On paper, in records, legally, Hassan was still bound to Sara. Sweden did not allow two wives. This marriage existed in secrecy, suspended between faith and fear.

He did not ask himself what would happen when Sara came.

He did not imagine the collision waiting ahead.

He only knew this: he could not endure another night alone, nor could he let Anastasia face another night on her own.

All of it happened in a short span of time. Hassan did what he thought was best, given the situation he was in.

And Anastasia?

She was no longer drifting.
She was no longer borrowed.
She was, now, his.

Religiously. Secretly. Dangerously.

The days after the nikah carried a strange, suspended lightness. Not happiness exactly, happiness felt too fragile a word for what moved between them. Something quieter. A mutual astonishment that they had, against all evidence, chosen each other anyway.

That astonishment lived in small ways. In how she reached for his hand before he could reach for hers. In how he watched her sleep and didn't look away when she woke.

Sometimes they spent long afternoons on the wooden bench outside their building. His head resting in her lap while she combed her fingers through his hair. The late-October sun, when it appeared, was pale and weak, but they sat in it anyway, breath fogging the cooling air.

She spoke of existence as though it were a riddle deliberately obscured. Not the familiar chaos of wars and borders, but the world itself: the planets, the cosmos.

One day she asked, "Do you ever feel that everything we've been told is just the surface? Because I don't believe the earth is what they say it is."

"What do you mean?" he asked.

"Do you think it's flat?"

"Perhaps," he said. "I've always kept that door open."

"I think it is." She leaned forward, elbows on her knees. "They hide it from us. The governments. The scientists."

He nodded slowly.

Her profile cut sharp against the grey sky, her eyes fixed on something distant he couldn't see. She was beautiful in her certainty.

"You've thought a lot about this," he murmured.

"A lot," she admitted. "Sometimes I imagine the hollow earth. What might be inside, how anyone could reach it."

He took her hand instead of answering.

"And what about you?" she asked. "What do you believe?"

After a pause: "I think there is a lot that has been concealed from us. The Antarctic wall that seals our realm from whatever lies beyond. There are even portals over there. Doorways between this world and the others."

She inclined her head in quiet agreement. "I have also thought about it."

Then she turned fully toward him, her green-hazel eyes softer than he'd ever seen.

"You know… you're extremely smart, Hassan. My sage."

Something cracked open in his chest, like a long-sealed window pried loose.

"You're so…" She searched for the word. "Extraordinary."

"Extraordinary?"

"Yes." Pure conviction, no hesitation. "Sometimes I want to do *this* to you." She raised her palms facing him, fingers pointing upward, and inclined her head slightly in a bow toward him.

The universe hung between them, heavy and somehow exactly right. Not because he craved worship, but because she'd found a way to name the quiet awe she felt when she looked at him. He recognised its echo whenever his gaze met hers.

"You don't need to bow," he said softly. "Just stay."

"I will. I'm here."

They lingered until the cold drove them inside, her head on his shoulder, his arm around her. Two souls who had found someone willing to embrace any possibility, not from desperation, but from deep recognition.

The earth could be flat, hollow, surrounded by ice walls patrolled by beings who would never understand them. None of it mattered.

They were perfect for each other.

That was enough.

Chapter 13

The Dose of Mutual Annihilation

For the first few weeks, they had a fever to them. When their bodies joined, something in them synchronised. A resonance so complete it felt like healing. They were starving. They couldn't keep their hands off each other: on the kitchen counter, in the bathtub, on the beach where the ocean drowned every sound, in the forest where no one could hear her moans. They were everywhere.

When he was inside her, the world narrowed to heat and the beat of the rhythm they built together. For those moments, nothing else existed.

Just this.
Just them.

Just the fierce, desperate belief that if they held on tight enough, they could fuck the past out of each other.

When they weren't touching, the silence returned. Not the comfortable kind, the kind that reminded them why they needed to touch in the first place.

Anastasia tried to make the apartment liveable. She unpacked quietly, methodically, as if structure itself might keep something from collapsing. Clothes were folded with care, then reorganised again — this time by colour. Reds together. Oranges fading into yellow. Greens, blues, violets. A spectrum stitched into the wardrobe like an attempt at control over a life that had none.

She was good at it.

Too good.

Hassan watched sometimes from the doorway, struck by the precision of her movements. There was something almost desperate in the way she needed everything to align. As if chaos, once exposed, could only be fought with symmetry. It calmed something in him.

During the day, he worked. Code scrolled. Meetings blurred. Commutes passed in a fog.

But the fog didn't silence his mind.

He understood her. Yet understanding didn't stop his own fears from driving him insane. His mind refused to stay where his body was.

What if she was lying again?
What if this, too, is a performance?
What if the truth I've seen is only one layer deeper than another lie?

The thoughts arrived uninvited, spiralling into darker corners he didn't recognise in himself. At work, he caught himself imagining things that made no sense. Criminal stories, secret lives, hidden phones, conspiracies built from fear rather than fact.

He hated himself for it.

He loved her.
And yet, he trusted nothing.

Every evening, when he returned home, he found her changed.

Quieter. Slower. Withdrawn.

The woman who once moved through the world with fragile confidence now carried herself like someone exposed. As if being seen fully had stripped her of her skin.

Demons only feel powerful when they are hidden. Once exposed, they leave you naked beneath another's gaze.

She sat more. Spoke less.

And when she did speak, her voice carried a caution that hadn't been there before.

They were both depressed.

Just differently.

Hassan lived ahead of the moment. Imagining consequences, disasters, betrayals yet to come. Anastasia lived behind it. Replaying mistakes, re-feeling shame, bracing for judgement that never needed words.

Whenever they couldn't bear it, they joined, which was often.

The first real rupture arrived quietly.

It was one of those days that collapsed without announcing itself. Hassan came home in the late afternoon to the stillness of the apartment. Curtains half-drawn, air stale, quite thick enough to feel intentional. Anastasia was in bed, wrapped in the sheets, phone glowing inches from her face. She didn't look up when he entered. She didn't ask how his day had been. She didn't say anything at all.

He stood there for a moment, waiting for acknowledgement, then retreated to the living room. Hours passed. The light shifted. His hunger sharpened into something meaner. The kitchen remained untouched. No food, no movement, no trace that time had been acknowledged by anyone but him.

She stayed in the bedroom. The phone never left her hands.

He told himself to wait. He sat on the couch, hands clasped, jaw tight, counting nothing. Each minute felt like proof of a fracture widening beneath the floorboards.

Eventually, the silence became unbearable.

He stood and walked back to the bedroom. "Can we please eat something?" His voice came out flatter than he intended.

She didn't look at him. "Sure," she said, eyes still on the screen. "Can you order something? I don't feel very good."

He laughed once, short and sharp. "Of course you don't. You've been on your phone all day."

She finally turned her head toward him. "I was sleeping. I just started using it now."

"That's all you've been doing since I got home. What are you even doing on it?"

"Nothing." She sat up slightly, her back pressing against the headboard, phone clutched closer to her chest. "I'm not doing anything wrong."

Her tone shifted, defensive now, brittle. "I'm so tired of being checked all the time."

"Checked?" He stepped closer. "You haven't spoken to me since I walked in."

"You could have talked to me too. You didn't."

"Why do you think we have to be equals?" he said, the words coming out sharper than he intended. "I'm the one who's tired. You should at least ask me how I am."

She stared at him, something hard and exhausted flickering behind her eyes. "And I'm the one who's broken."

The room felt suddenly too small. His chest tightened, panic curdling into anger. He gestured toward the phone. "That thing is making you crazy. I'm done with this shit."

She exhaled sharply. "Oh my God — here you go," and flung the phone across the bed toward him with a sudden, reckless motion. It landed near his feet. "Check it. Go ahead."

For a second, neither of them moved.

He picked it up. The weight of it surprised him. Not physically, but symbolically. He didn't look at the screen. He didn't unlock it. Instead, he lifted his eyes to her face.

They held each other's gaze.

Something passed between them. Recognition, challenge, permission. She didn't tell him to stop. She didn't look away. There was a flicker in her expression that he would later replay again and again, trying to decide whether it had been resignation or consent.

He lifted the phone in both hands, tightened his grip and snapped it in two. The sound was dry and final. Plastic cracked. Glass split.

Anastasia flinched, then went still.

For a moment, neither of them spoke. The broken halves lay on the bed between them like evidence of something irreversible.

"What the fuck did you do?"

Her voice broke the silence like glass underfoot. She scrambled across the bed, tears already spilling as she gathered the two halves into her hands, thumbs trembling uselessly over dead edges.

"All my pictures," she said, breath hitching. "Everything. My data. My life was on this." Her words came apart as she spoke them. "Why would you do that? Why?"

She raised her eyes to him then, disbelief overtaking anger, as if she were still waiting for him to laugh and admit it was a joke, that he hadn't actually crossed that line.

"You've gone insane," she cried.

The word landed harder than any accusation before it.

Hassan turned away.

Chapter 13

He walked out into the hallway, his body moving before his thoughts could catch up. He leaned against the wardrobe behind him. His hands shook. His chest felt hollowed out, like something essential had been ripped loose and left behind in the bedroom with her tears. He saw his reflection in the hallway hanging mirror.

What the fuck is wrong with me?

The question looped relentlessly. He dragged a hand down his face.

I broke it. I actually broke it. Over nothing. Over fear.

His mind raced ahead, as it always did. The familiar spiral tightened its grip.

This is getting out of hand. You're losing control. You're becoming someone you swore you'd never be.

He breathed hard. He saw a *face* smiling back at him.

He closed his eyes. Guilt arrived late but heavy, sinking inside with nauseating clarity.

He went back.

She was on the bed still, shoulders folded inward, curled into herself, the broken phone resting uselessly near the same corner of the sheets. Her crying had softened into something quieter, more dangerous. Small, exhausted sounds that came from deep in her chest.

"I'm sorry," he said. The words felt inadequate the moment they left his mouth. "I shouldn't have done that. I don't know what came over me."

She didn't look at him at first.

"I scared myself," he continued, voice lower now. "I don't want to be like this. I don't want to hurt you. Please forgive me."

She wiped her face with the back of her hand, then finally met his eyes.

"I understand," she said quietly.

The simplicity of it stunned him.

"I think..." She hesitated, swallowing. "I think I needed that."

He froze.

The admission hung between them. Disturbing, intimate, undeniable. Her expression wasn't accusatory. It was stripped bare. There was relief there. Shame too. Something else, darker and harder to name.

He looked at her. Really looked.

She had just admitted she needed what he'd done. Needed him to break something in her so she could breathe.

This woman took my worst moment and said she understood. Said she needed that.

Something shifted in his chest — something precious. Awe, maybe, or the terrible weight of being seen and not abandoned.

She had seen him at his most broken and chose to stay.

He would move worlds for her.

"I'll give you my spare phone," he said quietly. "The one from work. It's an iPhone — I think you'll like it."

She didn't answer at first. Just let the words settle. Then she nodded against his shoulder. A small movement. Acceptance, or exhaustion, or both.

He tightened his arms around her, and they stayed like that, not speaking, not fixing anything, just existing in the aftermath.

Chapter 13

The anger didn't disappear; it transformed. Guilt and need tangled together, each feeding the other. The closeness felt overwhelming, almost violent in its intensity, as if their bodies were trying to overwrite what their words had broken.

Being together was always like this for them. Consuming, blinding, a suspension of every fear they carried. In those moments, everything else dissolved to the way her need sharpened and turned demanding. How she pushed him past hesitation and into a version of himself he had never tested before.

The silence that followed his apology was not empty; it was charged. A live wire strung between their bodies. It hummed with the residue of shattered plastic and shattered calm. When she leaned into him, it was not a retreat, but an advance into a different kind of confrontation.

Her breath hitched against his neck, and the plea slipped out like a confession she could no longer hold.

Their kisses were not soft. They were admissions. Her mouth was salty with tears, his tasted of panic. Every touch was a question and an accusation. His hands, which had snapped her phone, now cradled her face, and the contrast made her shudder, terror and thrill indistinguishable

Clothes were not removed so much as breached. Fabric gave way like a boundary collapsing. She pulled him down with her. The air grew thick with the heat of their breath and the scent of their sweat. He was inside her, and it felt less like love and more like a claiming. A desperate attempt to occupy the same space, to fuse the broken parts.

Her eyes, dark and wide, locked onto his. They were not the eyes of someone seeking pleasure, but of someone seeking obliteration.

"Choke me," she whispered, the words a hot breath against his lips. "Please."

He hesitated, his hands on her hips stalling. The fracture of the phone was still vivid in his mind.

"I beg you!" The plea was raw, stripped of pride, a direct line to the part of her that wanted to feel anything but the hollow ache inside.

His thumb brushed her jawline, then his hand settled around the column of her throat. Not squeezing, just holding. The pulse beneath his palm hammered against his skin, a frantic bird.

"Harder," she gasped, her hips arching up to meet his thrust.

He complied, pressure increasing, watching her face. Her eyes fluttered shut, not in distress, but in ecstasy. A low moan tore from her throat, vibration buzzing against his palm. The power of it, the trust and the terror of it, surged through him. A dark, unfamiliar current. He *enjoyed* it. The control. The surrender. The way her pleasure became his.

"Slap me," she breathed, her voice ragged.

This time, his question was a hoarse whisper. "Are you sure?"

Her answer was a litany, a spell cast in the tongue of their shared history. "Yes, please! Call me *moya malenkaya shalushka.*" *My little naughty one.*

The old endearment, twisted here in the heat, shattered his last restraint. His hand left her throat, the air rushing back into her lungs with a sharp gasp, and then his palm landed on her cheek. The sound was crisp. A bloom of red appeared on her skin. A tear escaped the corner of her eye, but her smile was wild, triumphant.

"*Moya malenkaya shalushka,*" he whispered into her ear, the words guttural, as he drove into her.

"Fuck me harder," she commanded, nails scoring his back, anchoring herself to the pain.

And he did. It was a storm they were building together. Each slap was a punctuation to a thrust, each gasp for air a hymn. The choking was careful, calculated, released just as her eyes began to lose focus, only to return her to the brink again. It was a dance on the edge of a cliff, and they were both daring the other to jump.

She guided him not with gentleness but with insistence. Wordless at first, then unmistakable. Asking for pressure, for control, for a closeness that hovered at the edge of harm and felt, to her, like proof of being wanted.

The world narrowed to the points where they connected: his hand on her throat, her legs around his waist, the fierce, joining heat between them.

It was not lovemaking. It was mutual annihilation, a desperate attempt to burn out the rot inside them. She was not a victim; she was a co-conspirator in her own dismantling. He was not a monster; he was the perfect, willing instrument of her release.

He felt the shock of it. How easily desire slid into authority, how intoxicating it was to be trusted with someone else's edge, with the exact point where pleasure and fear blurred into the same sensation.

What unsettled him most was not that he complied, but how natural it began to feel to take, to hold, to command. His body understood before his conscience could object. Their movements lost any pretence of tenderness and became a private language of hunger and permission, negotiated breath by breath, squeeze by squeeze. Comfort and danger collapsed into each other until there was no clean boundary left. Only intensity, only the fierce clarity of being necessary to her.

The room felt suddenly unfamiliar, as if they had returned to it from a lucid dream.

And that was the most dangerous part.

But it felt majestic. A terrible, beautiful lie they forged with their bodies, that this was closeness, that this violence was intimacy, that in hurting and being hurt, they could finally, for one blinding moment, feel completely real. The rupture wasn't healed, it was buried beneath tenderness and silence, waiting to resurface.

Their entanglement tightened.

Not because the damage had been undone. But because, for a brief moment, being together made it feel worth it.

Later, in the dark, she whispered:

"You didn't break my phone. You broke my archive."

He thought she meant photos. She meant the only proof she existed outside this apartment. Messages from her mother, calls from *babusya* — her grandmother, a digital trail that said, *I was someone before you.* Most of it was already gone. Weeks ago, when she'd handed over all her electronics.

This phone was all she had left. And now he'd broken that too.

By breaking it, he hadn't just punished her. He had erased her. Again.

And part of her had wanted that. To be so thoroughly owned there was no past left to haunt her. But another part, quieter and darker, still hoped. Hoped something survived. Hoped she wasn't entirely gone.

That was when the small things truly began to crack.

At the beach one afternoon, the sea flat and grey beneath a low winter sky, Hassan tried to do something practical.

"I'll send you money every month," he said, pulling out his phone. "For groceries. For yourself."

She frowned. "Why?"

"So, you don't have to ask," he replied, already opening the app store. "Install this. I'll set it up."

She hesitated. "I don't like these apps."

He looked at her. "Why?"

"The government tracks everything," she said. "Banks. Phones. People."

Something snapped — not loudly, but sharply.

"Why won't you just listen to me?" he said, his voice rising despite himself. "I'm trying to help you."

She stiffened. "I didn't say no."

"I asked you to do one simple thing," he said, frustration spilling over. "Is it really that hard?"

The wind carried the silence that followed. The sea didn't care.

A few days later, in the kitchen, it was an apple.

Just an apple.

"Cut it like this," he said absently, demonstrating.

Her hand stopped mid-motion. "You think I don't know how to cut an apple?"

"That's not what I said," he replied.

"That's what you meant."

"No," he said, already tired. "You're hearing something else."

She set the knife down too hard. "You always think I don't know anything."

He stared at the counter, realising with dread how quickly everything turned into something else.

For nearly a month after the nikah, she barely left the apartment while Hassan was at work.

Some days she didn't leave at all, only when she was with him.

The outside world felt hostile to her now — full of eyes, of judgement, of reminders of who she'd been exposed as. Hassan felt it too: the pressure closing in, the walls tightening.

They loved each other.
But they were both suffocating.

Then, one afternoon, his phone rang.

Sara's father.
Hassan stared at the screen, his heart dropping into his stomach.

The past, it seemed, was not done with him yet.

Chapter 14

A Prison of Two Keys

Anastasia had begun to watch him. Not openly. But with the quiet vigilance of someone who no longer trusted the ground beneath her feet. She noticed how long he stayed on his phone. The way his expression changed when a message came in. The pauses. The silences. The moments when he drifted somewhere she couldn't follow.

Maybe he has secrets too.

It wasn't just suspicion anymore. It was a desperate, clawing need for equilibrium. He had seen her fully, in all her flawed, deceptive glory, and the power imbalance was a stone on her chest. *He* was the wronged one, the patient one, the one on the moral high ground. The thought was suffocating. So her mind, in its twisted, survivalist logic, began to dig.

Maybe he isn't so perfect. Maybe he has demons too. Maybe I can find them. If he falls, we can be level. Equal in the mud.

Instead of striving to rise, her wounded soul sought to drag him down. It was the only form of balance she could conceive.

The thought crept in slowly, then rooted itself deep:

If he wasn't perfect, then maybe she wouldn't feel so small standing beside him.

It wasn't that she wanted to hurt him.

It was that her subconscious mind needed balance.

If she could find a flaw, any flaw, then the weight pressing on her chest might ease. She wouldn't be the only broken one. She wouldn't be the only one exposed.

Chapter 14

So, she watched.

Measured. Compared.

And every time she came up empty-handed, the unease inside her sharpened.

December 12th.

The excavation found its moment.

Hassan's phone rang while they were both in the living room. He glanced at the screen and his face changed instantly. The colour drained from it, as if the blade of honour he had once carried had slipped in his grip and found his own throat.

Anastasia's gaze snapped to the phone, then to his face. She saw the blood drain from his complexion. She noticed the way his thumb hesitated over the screen, the flicker in his jaw before he swiped to answer. He brought the phone to his ear, his voice emerging as brittle, professional courtesy.

"Assalamu alaikum," he said quietly.

She didn't understand the words, but she recognised the language.

Urdu.

She sat still, heart beginning to race.

"Hassan, how are you?" Sara's father's voice came through, warm on the surface. "Sara is ready to come to you now."

The room seemed to tilt.

His free hand gripped his knee, knuckles bleaching to bone-white. Then the formal posture cracked. His shoulders slumped. He leaned forward, elbow on his knee, his hand cradling his forehead as if trying to hold his skull together.

"I… I don't know what to do," he said, his voice broke.

Tears came suddenly, uninvited. The kind that arrives when a man has been holding himself together by will alone.

"I don't know what to do anymore," he repeated, quieter now.

Anastasia's breath caught.

She understood nothing of the language, but she grasped the gist of everything. The name. The tears. The abject helplessness in his posture. The pieces snapped together with a cold, definitive click.

Sara.
Ready.
Coming.

This was the past.

And it was walking back into the room.

The threat was no longer abstract. It was being discussed in warm, familial tones on the other side of the world. And Hassan, her anchor, her fortress, was weeping because he was trapped.

He can't tell them about me.

The fear that lived in her chest burst into full, blinding bloom. It wasn't just jealousy. It was existential terror. Her support, her shelter, her everything in this cold country was all tied to him. A man legally and culturally bound to another woman. A woman whose arrival would render Anastasia a ghost. An illegal secret, a problem to be disposed of.

Hassan listened in silence as arrangements were implied, expectations laid out. He murmured vague replies, non-answers disguised as politeness.

"I'll… I'll let you know," he said finally.

He ended the call and let the phone slip from his hand onto the cushion. It was the gesture of a man laying down a weapon he could no longer carry.

Chapter 14

For a moment, neither of them spoke.

He didn't look at her. He stared at the window, seeing the impossible geometry of his future.

Anastasia's eyes were wide, searching. Fear rising fast, sharp, uncontrollable.

Hassan's expression was something else entirely.

It was the look of a man standing at the centre of a burning house, calculating exits that no longer existed.

Anastasia stared at him. Her breath came in short, shallow sips. The question she had carried for weeks now clawed its way out, thin and sharp.

"Are you going to leave me?" she asked.

Her voice trembled, but there was accusation in it too. Desperation twisting fear into something sharp.

He turned his head slowly. His eyes met hers. The eyes of a man drowning in deep water, looking at a person clinging to the same piece of wreckage. A look of shared, panicked claustrophobia.

"No," he said immediately. "Of course not."

"You're going to bring her here," she said. Her voice gained strength, edged with rising hysteria. "And then you'll kick me out."

"That's not true. Listen to me."

"She is coming. You will have her back. And you will throw me away like I am nothing!" She stood up, her body trembling. "I have *nothing*, Hassan! I have no one! You took everything from me — my safety, my place, my memories! You even broke my phone. You made me rely on you, and now you will make me disappear!"

"Anastasia, stop —"

"Where will I go? Tell me! Back to that monster? Back to men like *him*? Is that your solution?"

"I said I will *not* make you go!" His voice rose, fraying at the edges — a mix of desperation and utter exhaustion. "I will figure something out!"

He stepped toward her. "I don't want you to go anywhere."

"I know how this ends. I'll be gone. You'll fix your life. And I'll disappear."

"That's not happening," he said, voice firm now. Not commanding, but pleading.

"Figure *what* out?" She threw her arms wide. "How to have two wives in this country? How to hide me in the basement? How to choose which one of us gets your bed and which one gets the street?"

"I don't know!" he roared back, finally breaking, surging to his feet. "But I will. Give me time. Trust me!"

He said it again, smaller now, like a prayer he was trying to believe in.

"I always do."

She looked at him. Her sanctuary and her prison. Her love and her impending ruin. She saw no grand plan in his anguished face.

Hassan had built his entire life on solving impossible problems.

But this one wasn't code.

Wasn't logic.

Wasn't something that could be optimised or debugged.

It was human.

And humans don't resolve cleanly.

Anastasia sank back onto the couch, shaking. He stood there, torn between two lives, two truths, two women. Neither of whom he could fully let go of, neither of whom he could fully keep.

He didn't yet understand this wasn't a problem to be solved.

It was a reckoning.

And it had already begun.

Chapter 15

The Devil's Dance

Sex had stopped being solace. It had become something older, less forgiving. Every argument, every ricochet of accusation and counter-accusation, every silence stretched thinner and more brittle than the last, narrowed inevitably toward the same fevered corridor: the bedroom. The wall he pinned her against. The floor she dragged him down to.

They fought with their mouths and negotiated with their skin.

And it worked. For a time, it worked spectacularly. The collision of their bodies was so fierce, so total, it incinerated minor grievances like paper dropped into flame. What language failed to resolve was drowned in sweat, breath, and the obliterating rhythm of flesh striking flesh. They were not making love. They were performing maintenance. Wiping the system clean with the only solvent strong enough to dissolve the residue of accumulated resentment.

The cruelty was this: it was transcendent.

Not gentle. Gentleness belonged to people who had not yet drawn blood. Their bodies carried too much history; tenderness was a dialect they no longer remembered how to speak. What remained was hunger. Impatient, unfiltered, almost violent in its urgency. He took her with a force born not of anger but of terror: the terror of a man trying to prove, one more time, that they were not already ghosts. She answered with equal ferocity, nails carving down his back, teeth closing on his shoulder, marking him the way a prisoner marks a cell wall: *I was here. I still am.*

Even in its brutality, it was beautiful.

There was a synchronicity that mocked the chaos of their waking hours. His body knew hers the way a musician knows his instrument. Without thought, only instinct. The precise arch that opened her. The fractional shift in pressure that made her gasp. The rhythm that dismantled her entirely. He had memorised her with scholarly obsession. And she had charted him just as thoroughly: the locked tension in his shoulders that yielded only beneath her hands, the broken sounds he surrendered when she took him deep. The way his composure, that curated fortress, collapsed the moment her thighs locked around him.

In this one arena, they were flawless.

It was the devil's dance, and neither pretended otherwise. A dance without exit, without curtain call. They moved because stopping meant turning toward the silence waiting beyond the music. They moved because the rhythm had entered their bloodstream, because abstinence would require naming what this was, and neither possessed that kind of courage.

Afterward, they lay among the ruins and told themselves this time had altered something fundamental. This time the surrender had been complete enough. This time the communion had penetrated deep enough to rewire what had shorted between them. The pleasure was real. The release was real. Those suspended heartbeats, when thought disintegrated and they existed only as heat and pulse. That was real.

Morning was the lie.

Morning returned them to themselves. The slow reconstruction of ego. The familiar angles of resentment sliding back into place. The crawl of identity reasserting its borders.

So, they dosed again.

More often. Longer. Harder. What once erased now only blurred. The recovery took longer; the silence returned faster. Bruises darkened. Sleep thinned. The edge sharpened.

Each time they promised restraint. Each time they circled back to the same altar.

Round and round. An embrace indistinguishable from a stranglehold. Spinning toward an edge neither could see clearly, but both felt in the tremor beneath their feet.

Still, they danced. Twice a day. Sometimes three.

Waiting for the music to die on its own because neither of them had the nerve to be the one who walked off the floor first.

But the music began to warp.

It was a Sunday.

Not night, when darkness might have offered its familiar mercy, draping their rituals in shadow and plausible deniability. The light outside had already begun to fade; late December days in Stockholm were cruelly short, dusk by three. But what remained slipped through the half-drawn blinds in long, weakening stripes, as if the light itself was surrendering.

This was the third time she had wanted him that day.

The first had been morning, urgent and wordless, her body finding his in that hazy border between sleep and waking. The second had been early afternoon, quick and hard against the kitchen counter, his hands gripping the cold steel while she took him from behind, both of them watching their fractured reflections in its brushed surface.

Now it was 3:15 p.m., and she was hungry again.

Not just for pleasure. Not really. Pleasure was the excuse, the familiar doorway. What she craved was what waited on the other side: the obliteration of thought, the temporary amnesty of flesh, the weight of him inside her like an anchor in the sea that was trying to swallow her whole. She wanted to feel *held*. She wanted to feel *undeniable*. She wanted to fuck herself so deep into his memory that even if he left, even if Sara came, even if the entire world collapsed into its rightful order, some piece of her would remain, lodged in him like a splinter, impossible to extract.

Chapter 15

He was lying on the bed, still in the striped pyjamas he'd worn since morning. His arm was draped over his eyes, blocking the light, blocking her. He had not moved in an hour. His chest rose and fell with the shallow rhythm of a man conserving the last of his resources.

She stood at the foot of the bed and slipped out of what little she was wearing.

She always wore less in the apartment now. The armour of fabric had become unbearable; every seam felt like an accusation, every button a small betrayal of the vulnerability she could no longer contain. She had spent the day in nothing but his old dress shirt and a pair of black lace underwear, and now even those fell in a whisper at her feet.

She was beautiful. This was its own kind of cruelty. Her body had not yet learned to reflect the damage of her mind. The skin still luminous, the soft, rounded curves of her breasts still full and heavy with the architecture of desire. She stood in the afternoon light, naked and unashamed, a supplicant at an altar that had already stopped believing in prayer.

He didn't move. Didn't speak. His arm remained draped across his face. A white flag he was too tired to wave.

She climbed onto the bed, crawling toward him with the slow, deliberate grace of a tigress who had already decided: he was hers, and there was no escape.

The mattress dipped beneath her hands and knees.

She reached for his pyjama shirt buttons and worked them open, slowly, deliberately. The way one unwraps something fragile and precious. He didn't help. He didn't resist. His body accepted her ministrations with the mute compliance of a man who had learned that refusal required more energy than surrender.

She pushed the fabric from his shoulders with jarring force. Then his pants. Then the last thin barrier between them.

He was not hard. Of course he wasn't. He was hollowed out, spent. A vessel drained by the relentless tide of her need.

She looked at him, at the soft, vulnerable stillness of him, and felt something twist in her chest. Not pity. Not guilt. Just hunger: the kind that wanted to consume him whole, to crawl inside his skin and live there, to make herself so essential to his survival that leaving would mean tearing out a piece of himself.

She wrapped her fingers around him and began her ritual.

Her touch was practised, patient. She knew his desires better than she knew the contours of her own face. She worked him slowly, methodically, her gaze fixed on his face, waiting for the moment his body would betray him.

It always did.

He hardened beneath her hand, and the betrayal was not his alone, it was theirs. A shared, wordless conspiracy between flesh that refused to listen to reason. He was exhausted. He was depleted. He had nothing left to give. And yet his body rose to meet her touch like a flower turning toward a sun that would eventually scorch it.

She positioned herself above him.

"No." His voice was barely audible, a scratch, a ghost. "I can't. Please. I'm so tired."

She didn't stop. She couldn't. The hunger had moved beyond choice; it was reflex now, the desperate grasp of a drowning woman who has forgotten how to swim. She guided him to her entrance. She was already slick, already open, her body responding with a terrible fidelity to the proximity of his, and lowered herself in one slow, seamless motion.

He was inside her.

She closed her eyes. The world, for a moment, contracted to this single point of fusion. All the fear, all the accusations, and the futures that weren't guaranteed, it all dissolved in the wet, aching heat of their joining. She was not Anastasia, the refugee, the secret, the ghost. She was simply a woman containing the man she loved.

She began to move.

It was not just sex, in the ordinary sense. It was an act of reclamation. Each downward thrust pushed them deeper into the abyss, each upward withdrawal a promise of return. She rode him with her eyes closed and her hands pressed flat against his chest, pinning him to the mattress, anchoring herself to the rise and fall of his breath.

He said her name. Once. Twice. A plea, a prayer, a protest that crumbled on his tongue.

"Please. I can't — we can't —"

She didn't listen. She couldn't. His words reached her from a great distance, muffled by the roaring in her ears. She leaned forward, pressing his hands flat against his own chest, trapping them there beneath her palms. His fingers curled weakly against his sternum. Surrendering.

She rode him harder.

The rhythm grew frantic, uneven. She was chasing something now. Some shattering that would justify all this, some release that would scrub the slate clean. Her thighs burned. Her breath came in sharp, ragged gasps. Beneath her, his body had gone rigid, his hips rising involuntarily to meet hers, the betrayal complete.

"I'm coming," he gasped. "Get off — I'm coming —"

She didn't move.

His body had spoken. His release tore through him like a convulsion, violent and helpless. She felt it: the hot pulse of him inside her, the desperate, flooding surrender of a man who had lost the ability to say no. His body arched off the bed. A sound escaped him, something between a groan and a sob.

And she kept riding him.

The moment she came was the moment he was still spilling inside her. Her orgasm crashed over her like a wave striking another wave, collapsing without distinction. Her inner muscles clamped around him in long, slow contractions. Once, twice, three times — squeezing, demanding, *taking*. She did not stop until she had wrung from him the very last drop, until he was empty and she was full.

Only then did she still.

She remained seated on him, breathing hard, her forehead resting against his. The sweat cooled on their skin. His hands were still trapped beneath hers, pressed to his own chest, as if she had made him witness his own immolation.

He didn't speak. He didn't move. He simply lay there, beneath her, inside her, emptied of everything he had tried so desperately to hold back. His eyes were open now, fixed on the ceiling, and she saw in them something that seized her chest.

Defeat.

He had given her everything. Again. And again, it was not enough. It would never be enough. She could drain him dry a thousand times, wring from him every drop of seed and sweat and surrender, and still the hunger would return. Because the hunger was not for his body. It was for his *staying*. His choosing. His binding himself to her so completely that departure became anatomically impossible.

He had given her a nikah in secret: a bond invisible to the state, a vow spoken only before God.

But god was not the one she feared.

God forgave.

Sara's name on his papers did not.

He was tied with a chain she could neither break nor wear.

She wanted him to come inside her and stay. To lock him in her body the way she had locked herself in his life. To make the choice irreversible, biological, permanent.

He could not.

Or simply, would not.

She climbed off him slowly.

For a moment she just stood there, suspended between the bed and the rest of the apartment, her breath still uneven, her pulse refusing to settle. The air felt heavier now. Used.

She did not look at him.

She walked to the bathroom without hurrying, the floor cool beneath her feet. The mirror waited there, blank and impartial. She stood in front of it and stared at her own reflection: the flushed skin, the loosened hair, the faint tremor in her hands she had not noticed before.

A warm, viscous sentence ran down her thigh, his verdict, her evidence. She didn't wipe it away. She watched it trace a silver path toward her knee, and she thought:

This is all I get.
This is all I can take from him.

And it is never enough.

She did not wash. She stood there longer than necessary, as if the mirror might offer explanation.

It did not.

Chapter 16
The Territory of Mad Love

When she finally stepped into the kitchen, the clock above the wooden bench was ticking with exaggerated patience. Three-thirty. The ordinary persistence of time felt almost obscene. She sat on the bench and unlocked her phone. Her thumb moved without intention, scrolling, refreshing, searching for nothing in particular.

A few minutes later, Hassan appeared in the doorway.

He had dressed.

He stood there for a moment before speaking.

"Why didn't you listen to me?"

His voice was low, stripped of anger. That frightened her more than if he had shouted.

"I asked you to stop," he continued. "You didn't. You kept going. It was against my will. Why did you do that?"

She did not look up from her phone.

"Because I wanted to," she said, almost gently. "I was hungry."

The word sounded small. Childlike. As if that were explanation enough.

"We already did it twice today," he said. "I was exhausted. And you didn't even use protection."

She shrugged faintly. "I'm sorry. I lost control."

He stared at her, searching her face for something — remorse, understanding, fear. He found none he could trust.

Chapter 16

"You know you can get pregnant, right?" he said. The exhaustion in his voice hardened into something more brittle. "And I won't accept that child. I won't give my name. I won't bring a child into something this broken. We're not married. You know that."

The words landed heavily.

He believed he could refuse it. A child would carry his name anyway.

She finally looked up.

"Yes."

"Then why would you do it?" He opened his hands, helpless. "We can't have a child like this. Consent has to be mutual. Don't you think?"

Silence settled between them.

The clock kept ticking.

Her gaze drifted — not away from him, but through him, as if calculating something beyond the room. After a few moments:

"But we did nikah," she said at last. "You remember?"

He exhaled through his nose. "Yes. In secret. How am I supposed to explain that to my family? They don't know anything. We have to register it properly. And I can't do that while Sara is still under my name."

There it was. The real architecture.

"Then divorce her," Anastasia said quietly. "And put my name instead."

The words hung in the air.

He did not answer.

Silence clarified everything.

The change in Anastasia was slow at first. A hardening of her gaze, a sharper edge to her words. The soft respect she once held for him eroded, replaced by a brittle, watchful hostility. It wasn't that she stopped caring; it was that fear had begun to eclipse everything else. She watched him more closely now. Listened for tone. Measured pauses. Read judgement into silence. The terror of losing him, of being abandoned in a foreign country with nothing and no one, became a constant, humming dread in her veins. She felt herself shrinking under his gaze, convinced that every question was an evaluation, every concern a verdict. The more she feared it, the more she fought him. And the more she fought, the more she pushed him toward the very edge she was trying to keep him from.

For Hassan, it was a new kind of trauma. Her distrust became a mirror, reflecting his own anxieties back at him in a distorted, terrifying loop. He felt himself being watched too. Not for what he did, but for what she feared he might conclude. Innocent questions began to feel dangerous. Concern sounded like accusation. His nights were no longer for rest, but for long, circular arguments that left his mind raw and his body trembling with exhaustion. Arguments where he found himself defending intentions he hadn't known needed defending.

He'd lie awake long after she finally fell into a fitful sleep, watching the digital clock march toward 5 a.m., the hour he had to rise. Drag himself through the cold dark to the bus, the train, the metro. Another day of coding with a mind that felt like shattered glass. He was a battery, drained to zero, with no charger in sight.

Her fear fed his mistrust. His mistrust fed her fear.

A closed loop. A downward spiral.

And Anastasia, trapped in her own terror, was already planning for survival. She saw herself through the version of his eyes she feared most: reduced, disposable, already condemned for what she had done to survive. He was the one who could stay or leave. She was the one who would be left behind.

What will I do if he leaves? Where will I go? Who will protect me?

Fear, once planted, has a way of becoming real.

December 17th.

The spiral tightened until it snapped. The apartment felt claustrophobic, the air thick with all the words they'd already shouted and the ones they were too tired to say. Hassan, hollowed out and frayed beyond recognition, finally spoke the sentence that had been hovering between them for weeks.

"I can't do this anymore," he said quietly.

She froze.

"What do you mean?"

"I need space," he said. His voice wasn't angry, just empty. "We both do."

Her breathing quickened. "What are you saying?"

"It means…" He ran a hand over his face, the stubble scraping his palm. "I need space. You need space. We are destroying each other in this box."

The words landed exactly where she feared they would.

"You're throwing me out." Her voice was flat, a cold statement of fact.

"I'm not *throwing you out*," he said, the frustration seeping back in. "I will take you to the migration hostel myself. I will help you move your things. I will give you money, enough to be okay. This isn't… this isn't abandonment. It's a pause. A chance for both of us to breathe. To think about what we're doing to each other."

"A *pause?*" A harsh, disbelieving laugh escaped her. "You send me to a hostel with a handful of cash and call it a *pause?* That is the definition of abandonment, Hassan. I knew it."

"It's not! God, can't you see I'm trying to find a way that doesn't end with us hating each other?!"

"The only way that happens is if I stay!" she screamed, surging to her feet.

"I will NEVER leave you!" She pointed her finger at him.

Then suddenly she turned and rushed toward the bathroom, slamming the door shut behind her. He followed in urgency.

"Anastasia!" He was at the door instantly, his palm flat against the wood. "Open this door."

"I will *not* leave this apartment!" Her shout was muffled, ferocious, fraying at the edges.

Something in her voice terrified him.

"Anastasia," he said, knocking hard now. "Open the door. Don't do something stupid. Please."

There was no answer. Only a long, terrifying silence, punctured by a sharp, stifled *tsss.*

When she finally opened the door, her face was pale as chalk, eyes wide and glassy, tears streaking down her cheeks. She held her left arm cradled against her abdomen. A deliberate, terrible presentation, as if presenting a sacred, ruined object.

"This is the day I will NEVER forget," she said hoarsely, making it sound like a vow carved in stone. Eyes narrowed to slits, the muscles around them trembling with strain, it felt almost like a threat.

She extended her arm.

Chapter 16

On the tender skin of her inner wrist, carved with chilling, precise delicacy, were the letters: **HK 17 Dec.** The skin around it was raised and flushed, beads of blood welling along the crude inscription.

Hassan felt the world drop out from under him. Nausea rose in his throat. He reached for her arm.

"Why would you do this?" he whispered. "Why would you hurt yourself?"

"So, you know," she said, voice breaking. Her gaze locked on his, holding him accountable. "So, you remember. So, I remember."

"You wouldn't give me your name. So, I took it."

The fight, the frustration, drained from him instantly, obliterated by a cold, surgical panic. He rushed to the kitchen, snatched a clean cloth, and pressed it gently into her hand, guiding it to the wound.

"Hold this. Press."

He went into the bathroom, his own hands trembling as he tore through the cabinet, sending cotton pads and pill bottles clattering into the sink until he found the brown bottle of antiseptic. When he turned, she was standing exactly where he'd left her, a statue of shock. The cloth already blooming with a dark, rose-red stain.

The next minutes passed in a silent, focused ritual. He led her to the couch, gently pried the cloth away, and cleaned the inscription with a stinging solution. She didn't flinch. Her silence was worse than any scream. He dressed it with gauze and tape, his movements methodical, each piece of tape a feeble attempt to seal not just skin, but the rupture between them.

What followed was not a discussion, but a gradual collapse. The adrenaline bled away, leaving them both hollowed out. Words started, then crumbled into tears. Accusations melted into incoherent sobs. They slid from the couch to the floor, their backs against its solidity as if it were the only thing keeping them from dissolving completely.

After hours of endless talking, crying, breaking down, they made peace just because they were too exhausted to keep fighting.

She looked at him then, quieter, her head resting against the couch cushion on the floor.

"You know, if you had left me," she said softly, staring straight ahead at the blank television screen, "I would have gone to a bridge and jumped off from it."

He looked at her and simply knew. He had learned the shape of her despair as intimately as the shape of her body.

"And you know where I would jump off from," she added.

A faint, ghostly smile touched her lips. He nodded, tilting his head to the right side.

"Right from the middle," he said — just as she whispered it.
"Right from the middle."

Their voices merged in the quiet room, a chilling harmony.

Their eyes met.

Symmetry.
Precision.

The strange, meticulous way her mind worked. A person for whom even escape had to be balanced, centred, exact. It was the same precision that had once drawn him in: the way she folded laundry into perfect rectangles, aligned the spice jars by height, noticed when the two plants on either side of the TV were not perfectly aligned, adjusted them until the world obeyed her standards.

And he still loved it.

That severity. That immaculate control.

They were the same that way. Two perfectionists who had finally found something, someone, worth the effort of getting exactly right. And now they were getting it exactly wrong.

That was the truest tragedy of all. They had crossed into the territory of mad love.

She leaned into him, shaking, wrapping her arm around his. "I was so scared."

"I know," he said, the words heavy with a shared, terrible understanding. "I know."

Chapter 17

Demolition of the Pedestal

Something fundamental had shifted. Fear had crossed a line. And once crossed, it never fully goes back. It takes a seat somewhere deep in the mind and begins asking questions. Not to understand, but to be reassured. And reassurance, fear believes, must be absolute. Final. Unchanging.

The problem is that fear does not trust answers. It wants certainty where none can exist.

Once fear takes root, it demands proof from the other person. Proof of loyalty, proof of permanence, proof that tomorrow will not undo today. And so, the mind begins to dig. It peers into silences, reads meanings into pauses, interrogates glances, searches tone and timing as if truth were hidden there, waiting to be extracted.

But the answer fear seeks is not inside the other person at all.

Still, the digging continues.

And in the act of pushing, of demanding reassurance again and again, the other person is forced to confront questions they never asked themselves before. Doubts are planted where none existed. Possibilities are introduced simply because they are named. What was once imaginary begins to take shape, not because it was inevitable, but because it was insisted upon.

Fear, in this way, is not prophetic. It's creative. It manufactures the very reality it claims to foresee.

Just like hope.

Hassan's fear looked forward, toward what *might* happen, toward futures that threatened to collapse before they arrived.

Chapter 17

Anastasia's fear looked backward, toward what had already been lost, toward abandonment she had survived once and vowed never to survive again.

Both were responding to pain, but from opposite directions.

But fear does not want resolution.
It wants control.

It wants to be fed answers endlessly, even when those answers erode trust, intimacy, and peace. It convinces people that vigilance is protection, that suspicion is wisdom, that love must be monitored to survive.

But love cannot breathe under surveillance.

And once fear becomes the loudest voice, it stops being a warning and becomes a script. One both are forced to follow, even as they swear they don't want the ending it promises.

Fear never settles.

It only waits — for someone to believe it.

The tension between them had become a third presence in the apartment. Breathing when they breathed, thickening the air until every word felt strained. They fought daily. Not the loud, explosive battles of passion, but the grinding, corrosive attrition of two people trapped in a shared wound. Each argument left a residue, a thin film of resentment that built up over days, until the very space between them seemed to vibrate with a dissonant, painful frequency.

Hassan could feel his mind fraying. The clarity he once prized — the logical pathways of code, the clean architecture of solutions — was now a tangle of dread and hypervigilance. Sleep was a shallow, troubled pool. Food lost its taste. He moved through his workdays in a fog, his own thoughts echoing in a chamber of exhaustion. He watched himself deteriorating in the mirror. The shadows under his eyes, the tight set of his jaw, and with a cold, clinical horror, he saw the same unravelling in Anastasia.

Her fear had metastasised into a constant, quiet panic. Her eyes tracked him with a desperate forensic scrutiny. She was forever listening for the subtext in his silence, parsing his sighs for hidden meaning, digging for evidence of an exit strategy he did not have. He had said it once, in a moment of suffocated despair: *Maybe we need a break.* The words had hung in the air, and her reaction was not sadness, but a tectonic shift of terror. She had refused, utterly and absolutely. Yet, paradoxically, she seemed to be constructing the very scenario she feared. She picked at tiny flaws, magnified minor irritations into betrayals, as if she were trying to *force* him to leave. To make the invisible monster visible, to control the timing of a collapse she believed was inevitable.

He didn't want her to go. He wanted the opposite. He wanted the woman he'd fallen in love with, the one with soft eyes and gentle hands, to return. He wanted *peace.* He wanted her to stop trembling long enough to see that he was drowning, too. He wanted respect, not deference, but the basic, grounding respect that allows two people to face a storm without tearing each other apart.

Just behave, he'd think. Not in anger, not in judgement, but in quiet, desperate exhaustion. *Just be calm. I'll fix the rest. I always do.*

But Anastasia was a sea in a hurricane, and no promise of a future harbour could calm the present waves.

January 3rd, 22:17.

The bedroom was a capsule of dim light and heavy silence. Anastasia was beside him, her body a tense line under the duvet, the cold glow of her phone screen painting the walls in shades of blue.

He kept his back to her.

"Can you put the phone away?" he said quietly. "I'm trying to sleep."

"I'm just reading," she replied. "It's a book."

Chapter 17

"Can you read it in the living room?"

"You can go to the living room," she shot back, not looking up.

Something tightened low in his stomach, a thin wire pulled too hard.

"What are you doing?" he asked, turning towards her, the softness gone now.

Her fingers kept moving. Quick. Controlled. The slight downward angle of the screen. The way her shoulders curved around it.

He knew that posture.

It was the same one from months ago. The same shield of light, the same sealed-off silence that had once hidden conversations he wasn't meant to see.

"Nothing," she said.

Her answer was a reflex, too quick, too thin. "Nothing."

The word was a key turning in a lock he'd prayed was sealed forever.

He didn't plan his next move. His body acted. He sat up, his hand snatching the phone from her grip. She gasped, a short, sharp sound of protest.

The screen burned his eyes. Facebook. But not her profile. An account he didn't recognise. A man's profile photo filled the display. A stranger's face, smiling from some sun-drenched past.

"Who is this?" His voice was gravel.

She stared, her eyes wide pools of panic. "I don't know. When you grabbed it, it… it just opened. Somehow."

The absurdity of it was an insult in itself. It made no sense. Logic and pathways shattered. The lie was so flimsy, so insulting, that it wasn't just a denial, it was an erasure of his very intelligence, of all the pain they'd already endured.

The argument erupted, ugly and loud. It spilled out of the bedroom, their voices, raw, broken, furious, tearing through the quiet of the sleeping neighbourhood. Accusations flew like shrapnel. Old wounds were ripped open and salted with new fury. Hours bled together, a timeless stretch of mutual devastation.

1:07 a.m.

Somewhere in the back of his mind, a voice whispered: *You have to get up for work in five hours.*

Until Anastasia, backed against the wall of her own terror, let out a scream that was less sound and more rupture.

"WHAT ARE YOU DOING TO ME?!"

Her face was unrecognizable. Eyes bulging, veins standing out in her temples. And something in him, something fundamental — snapped.

It was not a decision. It was a systems failure. A total overload of a psyche pushed past its limits.

His hands grabbed her shoulders. He pushed her backward. She fell onto the bed with a soft, terrible thump. He was on top of her, his weight pinning her down, his knees locking both her arms. His vision tunnelled to her horrified face.

Then his right hand rose. It seemed to move in slow motion, detached from his will. A puppet of pure, unprocessed trauma. It descended.

It was a sound not of violence in a movie, but of violence in a home, in a bed, between two people who had once whispered promises there. He did not hit her once. He held her there, and with each word, a new, measured, monstrous blow fell, right to left.

"What." *Slap.*
"Are." *Slap.*
"You." *Slap.*
"Doing." *Slap.*
"To." *Slap.*
"Me?" *Slap.*

The slaps were punctuation. The pauses were the sentence. A cold, rhythmic tide of a man drowning on dry land.

Then, as suddenly as it began, it was over. The fury vanished, leaving a vacuum so absolute it sucked the soul out of the room. Hassan collapsed sideways onto the mattress beside her, the physical weight of what he had done crashing down upon him. A low moan escaped him, then broke into shuddering, violent sobs. He curled into himself, weeping uncontrollably. Heaving gasps that came from a place deeper than shame. A place of fundamental ruin.

He had hit a woman. He — Hassan, who had prided himself on his control, his kindness, his protection of the vulnerable. He had become the thing he despised. A woman-beater. The label branded itself onto his soul, one of the many yet to come, permanent and damning. In one uncontrollable, involuntary moment — a reaction born of a daily, grinding trauma — he had dragged himself from the light and into a shadow he could never escape.

The blade of dignity he had once carried found its mark.

For long minutes, there was only the sound of his broken crying. When he finally lifted his head, she was gone from the bed. He heard the bathroom door click shut. He got up and went to the living room, as far from her as he could, not trusting himself.

On some level, maybe this was what she had wanted. Not the pain, never the pain, but the demolition of the pedestal. He had been the "good man", the stable one, the judge upon the throne of his own moral certainty. She had been the exposed one, the flawed one, kneeling in the wreckage of her secrets.

Now, he was in the mud with her. Now, he was exposed too. As violent, as abusive, as capable of domination. The perfect balance of shame. No more judge and penitent. Now they were equals in the dock, both guilty, both broken, both staring at the ruins of the people they thought they were.

The dynamics were complete. A tragic, awful equilibrium. Love had not saved them. It had simply given them the deepest possible place to wound each other.

For a moment, there was nothing. No sound, no thought, no room. Just a white, silent void where a person had been. She lay where she had fallen, motionless, like a vessel struck at its centre, taken down not by a storm, but by a single, precise torpedo from the ship it thought was its escort.

Her mind was a flat, numb plane. The tears on her cheeks had already dried, leaving stiff, salty tracks. A single, vast thought slowly breached the surface of her shock:

Is this what my life is?

The question wasn't frantic. It was heavy, and final.

Are they all the same, underneath? Is the price for being in a weak position always violence?

A deeper, colder wave rose:

Is it a curse to be born a woman in this world? To be a canvas where men paint their rage? Is this what my parents raised me for?

This wasn't despair; it was a bleak, clear-eyed accounting of what her life had become.

I don't deserve to be treated like this.

Then the sensation rushed in to fill the void. A deep, throbbing heat bloomed along her jaw, a vivid, humiliating counterpoint to the numbness in her soul. It was this physical anchor, the pure, simple pain, that forced her to move.

She pushed herself up, her body operating on a silent autopilot, and walked to the bathroom. She closed the door, shutting out the sound of his weeping in the bedroom. The light was cruel and electric. At the sink, she ran the water cold, splashing it over her face, the shock of it a welcome distraction from the fire in her cheek.

Then she looked up.

In the mirror, a stranger stared back. The woman had her eyes, but they were older, harbouring a new, unforgiving knowledge. The left side of her face bore a faint, rosy imprint. A ghost of his palm that promised to bruise. It wasn't just a mark on skin; it was a brand on the story of her life. She saw the map of her future redrawn in that flush. A topography of shame, secrecy, and diminished expectations. This was her face now. The face of a woman who had been hit.

Meanwhile, in the living room, Hassan had collapsed into a different kind of ruin. He sat on the floor, his back against the couch, as far from the bedroom as he could get. He stared at the hand that had betrayed him, his own silent sobs shaking his frame. This was the shame that could not be washed off.

Anastasia walked back to the bedroom. She did not look at him as she passed the living room doorway. She simply returned to the bed, lowered herself onto the cold sheets, and lay on her back, staring at the ceiling. She did not curl up or seek comfort. She arranged herself like a body laid out for burial. Still, straight, utterly vacant. The fight was gone.

Hassan did not know whether he slept.

There were no dreams, only fragments. The ceiling. The dark. His own breathing, shallow and unfamiliar. When he rose, it felt mechanical, like a body moving without permission.

He dressed without looking at himself. Shirt. Jacket. Shoes. The apartment was silent in the way ruins are silent.

They did not speak.

He closed the door behind him and stepped into the morning as if nothing had happened. Yet everything inside him had collapsed.

On the train, his reflection stared back at him in the glass.

Who are you?

The question echoed, merciless.

And beneath it, another face — old, familiar, cruel: *Now you see. You're no better than me.*

He flinched. Turned away from the glass.

How could I do that?
What broke inside me?
What kind of man loses control like that?

He replayed the moment again and again, not to understand it, but to reject it. To prove it hadn't really been him.

I am not this person.
I don't hit.
I don't hurt.

But the memory did not argue. It simply existed.

These hands did that.

He stared at his hands. The same hands that had once held his honour. That had held hers during nikah. That had tended to her wound, trying to undo what could not be undone. Now they were the hands of a man he did not recognise.

The realisation was unbearable.

Chapter 17

All the identities he had clung to; a good man, patient man, righteous man, fell apart like paper soaked in water.

If I am capable of this, he thought, *then who am I really?*

Work passed without meaning. Screens blurred. Words floated past him unheard. Guilt pressed against his ribs until breathing felt like an effort.

And then the thought struck him, cold and sharp:

Maybe she'll leave.

He gripped the edge of his desk. The possibility hadn't occurred to him until now, that she might simply walk out, that this might be the end of everything he'd tried to hold together.

Perhaps it will be for the best.

But the thought brought no relief. Only a different kind of dread.

What if she goes out today and tells someone? What if she goes to the police?

His stomach clenched.

No. No, no, no. She can't do that. Could she?

He reached for his phone, then stopped himself.

Let's call her. No. It's too soon. Too soon.

By afternoon, shame had turned physical. Heavy, nauseating, corrosive.

He wanted to undo time.
To tear the night out of existence.
To disappear before becoming *someone* he despised.

For Anastasia, the morning arrived with a different weight.

She moved slowly. Carefully. As if the world might crack if she stepped wrong.

Violence was not new to her.

That was the worst part.

She had seen it before. In another life. Another man. Another country. She had learned the signs, the shifts, the moments where safety thinned.

But Hassan —

Hassan was not supposed to be that man. His hands were to be ones that built shelter, not walls.

She stayed in bed almost all day. Only when Hassan was due home did she collect herself.

She stood in the kitchen, kneading dough for *varenyky*, her hands working automatically, memory guiding motion when thought could not. Flour dusted her wrists like ash. With each fold and press, a single, primal thought pulsed through her: *Run. Just run. Leave this room, this man, this suffocating story behind.*

Her hands stilled, buried in the soft, yielding dough. *But where?* The question was a dead end, a locked door. She had no one. No family here, no friends, no country that felt like her own. In her utter aloneness, she was his perfect mirror. They were supposed to be each other's sanctuary. Two lost notes finding a single, resonant frequency. A harmony built from mutual fracture, not a dissonance to deepen it.

She just wanted to vanish without a trace. To have the courage to open the door and walk into the Stockholm cold and never look back. To let the freezing air scrub her clean of his touch, his voice, the memory of his hand landing on her face. The desire was a physical ache, a tightness in her lungs that begged for escape. *Make it stop. Just let everything stop.*

But beneath the urge to flee lay the deeper, more permanent wound: the knowledge that some things are indelible. The slap wasn't just a moment of pain; it was a fracture in time. She would see it in the slight narrowing of his eyes when he was tired, feel its echo in any raised voice, flinch at any sudden movement from his hands. The fear was no longer abstract; it had a home now. A specific memory to feed on, and it had rooted itself deep in her nervous system, whispering: *It can happen again.*

And as she stood there, the silence pressing in, she understood the most devastating truth of all. She could pretend. She could stay, for survival, for fear of the unknown cold. She could even say the words: *It's okay.*

But she would never, could never — forgive him.

Forgiveness meant erasure, and this was now a part of her geography. A ridge on the landscape of her life. To forgive would be to betray the woman lying numb on the bed that night.

A cold vault opened inside her, silent, precise, unyielding. She catalogued the facts without feeling: January 3rd. Trigger: the phone. Six measured blows. The words he spat before each one landed. These were not memories to haunt her. They were evidence. Contingency. In a country where she had no roots and no rights, proof was the only weapon that might one day buy her freedom, or at least a head start. She had no intention of using it yet. She only needed to know it existed. That knowledge alone was power, thin and lethal as a blade pressed to the throat.

She picked up the rolling pin. Flattened the dough with slow, deliberate strokes, jaw locked. She would set the table. She would look him in the eye. But inside, the vault stayed sealed, untouched, unforgiven. She was no longer trapped by walls alone. She was caged by the ruin of what they had been, and by the quiet, surgical certainty that what he had done could be done again.

And next time, she would be ready.

She told herself to breathe.
To stay present.
To not let fear rewrite everything.

The door opened in the evening.

Hassan entered like someone walking into judgement.

He dropped his bag on the floor. No care, no strength left to pretend. His eyes found her in the kitchen, standing there, sleeves rolled, hair loosely tied back.

Alive.
Present.
Still there.

Something inside him broke completely.

He crossed the room and suddenly fell to his knees before her. His forehead pressed against the top of her feet, his body folding inward like a confession.

"I'm so sorry," he said, his voice breaking as tears fell on her feet. "Please… please forgive me."

His words came apart.

"I don't know what happened to me. I have never, ever done anything like that in my life. I hate myself for it. I hate that I became someone you shouldn't have had to face."

Forgiver became the penitent.

He was on his knees. The ultimate altar of a man's shame. Every ounce of pride, every layer of masculine armour, was shed on the kitchen floor. This was not strategy. This was the raw, undefended core of a person witnessing his own moral bankruptcy.

He sobbed openly now, shame pouring out without dignity.

"I lost control. I'm so ashamed. I can't — I can't even look at myself."

For a long moment, there was only the sound of his crying at her feet and the soft sizzle of oil in the pan. Anastasia stood frozen, her breath shallow.

Then, slowly, she placed a hand on his shoulder.

"It's… okay," she said quietly.

Two words. Empty of tone. They were not absolution. They were a pressure bandage applied to a gushing wound. A desperate, temporary measure to stop the bleeding in the room.

It's okay.

It meant:

The noise must stop. The world must right itself. I cannot process your breakdown on top of my own.

Her voice carried no warmth, only the relief of a ceasefire.

He lifted his head, searching her face for the truth. Her eyes were dry, distant, looking through him to some point on the wall. She had not forgiven him. She had contained him.

And in that stark, silent moment, the asymmetry of their ruin became perfectly, tragically clear.

Chapter 18

A Monument to Guilt

Three days after the incident, they moved through the apartment like ghosts in a shared haunting. The silence was no longer empty; it had grown dense, almost solid, a weight they carried on their skin like the memory of what had happened there. They spoke in necessary monosyllables — *Yes. No. Tea?* — their voices carefully sanded of tone. The kitchen, where he had knelt and she had stood, became a neutral zone, a site of careful negotiation over sink space and cupboard doors.

Hassan slept on the couch. It was not discussed. On the night that followed, he simply took a pillow and a blanket to the couch while she lay stiffly in the bedroom. The arrangement became fact. His back ached from the springs, but the physical discomfort was a penance he welcomed, a concrete anchor for his abstract shame.

He watched his own hands with a forensic detachment. Hands that typed through code for hours. That held the railing on the metro. That unlocked the same door every night to silence. Ordinary hands. Yet every time he looked at Anastasia, he saw them anew, not as tools, but as weapons that had breached the one sanctuary he was supposed to uphold. The same hands that built now destroyed. The contradiction was a splinter lodged too deep to remove.

I am a man who builds. I am a man who destroys.

Both truths coexisted now, and the cognitive dissonance hummed beneath his skin, a low-grade fever of self-loathing.

Anastasia, for her part, had become a study in contained motion. She cleaned. She organized the spices by frequency of use. She folded laundry into perfect, sharp-cornered rectangles. Her efficiency was a silent rebuke and a fortress. She was building a world of perfect, controllable order within their four walls, a stark contrast to the uncontrollable chaos of their emotions.

She avoided his touch, not with drama, but with a subtle, instinctual reflex. When he passed in the hallway, she turned her body slightly, a quarter-turn that presented her shoulder, not her front. It was the body language of someone navigating a room with a dangerous, unpredictable animal. The fear he saw there was worse than any anger. Anger could be met, could be weathered. This quiet, operational caution erased him. It said he was no longer a person, but an anomaly. A risk to be managed.

In response, Hassan initiated a protocol of care. It was not just warmth; it was calibrated countermeasures. Flowers appeared on the table every few days — tulips, pale and straight — their vibrancy a stark contrast to the apartment's mood. His questions became a constant, low-frequency hum: "Do you need anything?" "Are you warm enough?" "Do you want me to do the dishes?" Outings were scheduled like diplomatic missions: dinners at quiet restaurants where they chewed in silence, shopping trips where he would hold up a dress "green, to match your eyes," he'd say, and she would nod, her smile a thin, perfunctory line.

It was a performance of normalcy so diligent it felt like grief.

His mission objective became her birthday. January 9th. Anastasia's twenty-fifth. A quarter-century, and the first she would spend orbiting the gravity well of his shame. He wanted it to be a surprise, a perfect breach in the cold war between them.

The evening before her birthday, he stopped at a confectionery on his way home — the best in town, known for their handmade cakes. He bought a *prinsesstårta* — the classic Swedish princess cake, a dome of whipped cream and marzipan — this one a soft pastel green. The bakery had a festive version: tiny, piped marzipan carrots on top, with even tinier green fronds. They looked like little bunnies. The sight pierced him with a sweet, painful ache. *Krolik.* Her name for him, Ukrainian for 'bear.' *Krylchika.* His for her, 'little bunny.' Names from a gentler season, now fossils in their language.

He also bought sparklers. Seven thin wands of potential light.

He entered the apartment with the stealth of a man planting a bomb of joy. She was in the living room.

"Don't look!" he called out, his voice strained with forced cheer. He hurried to the kitchen, shielding the cake box. He heard the soft shuffle of her retreat, not curious, but compliant.

He hid the cake in the fridge and waited for midnight, the minutes ticking by with the weight of condemned hours.

When it finally came, he moved. In the dark bedroom, he gently placed his palm over her eyes. She stiffened instantly beneath his touch. A full-body flinch she couldn't suppress. "Shh, it's a surprise," he whispered. He guided her, her steps hesitant, to the bright kitchen.

"Happy birthday, my love."

He lit the sparklers. They erupted in a furious, hissing spray of white-gold sparks — aggressive, beautiful, violent — illuminating her face in frantic flashes. In that light, what he saw was not wonder, but a startled emptiness. He presented the cake, the green dome with its whimsical carrots. "See? Bunnies," he said, his voice cracking slightly.

He cut a slice, the marzipan giving way with a soft tear. He offered her the first forkful.

Anastasia looked from the sparklers fizzling out in a saucer, to the cake, to his desperately hopeful face. A vast, hollow disappointment opened inside her, cold and silent. In Ukraine, a twenty-fifth birthday was a *pivnytsya* — a small jubilee. It marked a passage from youth into a new chapter of adulthood. There should be a gathering, however modest: toasting, laughter, *kalachi* bread, perhaps a ribboned gift of perfume or jewellery. Not this. Not a secret slice of cake in a silent kitchen after midnight, a gesture that felt less like celebration and more like a hasty, guilty sacrament.

Chapter 18

Her mood didn't just sink; it crystallized into something hard and clear. This was the sum of his effort. A hidden cake and pyrotechnics. The grand proof of his 'care'.

"Thank you," she said. The words were neutral, clean, and utterly devoid of the self he was trying to resurrect. She ate a few bites, the sweet cream cloying and heavy on her tongue. She was consuming his apology, and it was giving her no sustenance.

They slept back-to-back, the space between them charged with a fresh, bitter current.

It broke just after dawn.

"It was my twenty-fifth," she said to the ceiling, her voice flat.

"I know," he replied to the wall.

"A cake. Some sparklers."

He turned, propping himself on an elbow. "Anastasia, that was just the midnight surprise. I have the whole day. I took it off. We'll go to Duetto. Your favourite pizza. The one with the burrata. Then maybe a film. There's that tracksuit you wanted online, I ordered it. It's just late. I thought we could choose a gift together. A necklace, perhaps?"

He was listing his plans, his provisions, like a quartermaster reporting inventory. Each item was a brick he'd laid to build a path back to her, but she saw only a wall.

"You ordered the suit?" she asked, finally looking at him. Her eyes were not soft with gratitude, but sharp with a bleak calculus. "So you decided. A cake you decided. A suit you decided. A pizza you decided. Where is *my* day? Where is the thought that is about *me*, not about you fixing what you broke?"

"That's not fair," he said, sitting up, the helpless anger rising. "I *am* thinking of you! I planned everything to make you happy!"

"You planned everything to make *yourself* feel better!" she fired back, sitting up too, the duvet falling away. "The flowers, the dinners, this... this *schedule* of a birthday! It is all a monument to your guilt, Hassan! Not a gift for me! Do you even know what I wanted? I wanted one day where I didn't look at you and see the man who hit me! I wanted one day where you didn't look at me like a problem you need to solve with cake and sparklers! I wanted to feel like a person, not a... a project for your redemption!"

Her words, quiet and searing, landed with more force than any shout. They stripped the careful wrapping off all his gestures, exposing the raw, panicked need beneath.

He deflated. "I just... I wanted it to be perfect." "Nothing is perfect," she stated, the finality chilling. "Nothing here is even okay. A cake cannot fix that."

The plans for the day hung in the air, now spoiled, meaningless. The pizza, the cinema, the delayed gift, all were now symbols of his failure, not his devotion.

The bitterness of the night did not dissolve, but by the thin, hesitant light of morning, they performed the familiar, weary ritual of truce. They loved each other still, a fact that had become not a comfort, but the central knot of their suffering. It was a love twisted and rewired, its old pathways of joy now overgrown with the dense, thorny foliage of mutual fear. They were two planets locked in a decaying orbit, each pulling the other closer with the gravity of need, even as they silently, incrementally, pushed against the inevitable collapse.

They dressed for the day with a quiet, focused civility. The unspoken plans were reinstated, not with excitement, but as a necessary script to follow. To deviate would be to admit the fracture was too wide to bridge with pizza and a film.

At Duetto pizzeria, the aroma of baked dough and melted cheese was a tangible nostalgia. They were given their usual corner table. Anastasia ordered the Pizza alla Burrata — the one with sun-dried tomatoes and a cloud of creamy cheese in the centre.

Chapter 18

She smiled at the waitress, a soft, genuine curve of her lips that he hadn't seen in weeks. He watched that smile, and a fragile, desperate hope fluttered in his chest. *See? She is happy. We can be happy.*

He reached across the table, his fingers covering hers. Her hand did not jerk away, but neither did it turn to clasp his. It lay there, a neutral object beneath his touch, like a book he was permitted to rest his hand upon but not open. "I'm glad we came," he said, his voice thick with the effort of lightness.

"Me too," she replied, her eyes on the bustling kitchen, her smile now fading into something more pensive. "It smells like it used to."

They ate. She praised the crust. He refilled her water glass before she could ask. They looked, to anyone watching, like a stunning, intimate pair — the handsome, attentive man and his graceful, thoughtful companion, sharing a meal in easy silence.

A perfect couple.

The cinema was a cathedral of manufactured darkness. They chose a big, loud American action film where the problems were simple and solved with explosions. In the velvet black, shielded from the world, the performative ease of the restaurant softened into something that almost felt real. Her shoulder leaned against his arm. He let his head tilt to rest against hers, breathing in the scent of her shampoo, cherry and almond. For ninety-minute segments, they could be just two people in the dark, hearts synchronizing to the same soundtrack, their own complicated plot suspended. He bought her a bag of sweet, salty popcorn, and when their fingers brushed in the cardboard tub, it felt, for a fleeting second, like an accident between strangers, charged with innocent potential.

Walking home through the crisp January evening, the city lights shimmering on the canal, they were the picture of contented companionship. He had his arm around her shoulders; she had hers around his waist, her steps matching his. They pointed out a passing dog, commented on the unusual warmth of the evening. They looked like the very definition of *us*.

But inside their shared silhouette, the mechanisms whirred in opposite, silent directions.

In him: A frantic, analytical curation.

Remember this. Catalogue this: her laugh at the movie, the weight of her against you. This is the data. This proves the system can still function. This is the love you must protect. You must be better, softer, more careful. Do not trigger any fear. Manage the variables. Sustain this state.

In her: A cold, quiet audit.

This is nice. This is also a lie. These arms around you are the same arms that were raised. This voice making gentle jokes is the same voice that broke on the word "me." Do not let the pizza, the darkness, the walk, make you forget. Enjoy the performance, but do not invest in the play. Be happy now, but remember you are also afraid.

They wanted, with a desperate, parallel longing, for everything to be normal. The wish was a shared, shimmering mirage they both chose to walk toward, knowing it was made of air. They loved the idea of them, the ghost of the couple they had been at Midsummer, even as they became strangers to that ghost.

Chapter 19

Speaking in Skin and Silence

Anastasia didn't understand it herself, how the frozen vault could coexist with her flame for him. But they did. The same body that recoiled in the light craved him in the dark. Perhaps that was the cruellest mercy: the body kept its own accounts, indifferent to the soul's reckoning.

Finally, they reached their apartment door. He fumbled for the keys, metal scraping against the lock before it gave way with a sharp click. They stepped inside. He closed the door softly and turned, leaning back against it as the weight of the evening settled on his shoulders like wet concrete.

And then he saw her.

She was already looking at him. Leaning against the opposite wall of the narrow hallway, one knee slightly bent, her head tilted just enough that the hallway light carved a soft gold line along her cheekbone. The public calm was gone, stripped away by the privacy of their threshold. Her eyes darkened to something almost black in the low light, pupils blown wide, feral and unguarded, locked onto him with a focus so absolute it stole the air from his lungs. They were already inviting him, a look he knew too well.

A quiet storm brewed in them.

It wasn't an invitation; it was predation. A hungry stillness, dense and magnetic, radiating from her like heat off asphalt.

Pulling him forward before he was aware of moving. She was not the wounded girl from the kitchen. She was not careful. She was a woman poised on the edge of her own need, and she was starving.

Chapter 19

He had been waiting for this, for *her*, for what felt like an eternity of walking on glass.

He didn't speak. Words were useless now, the currency of a bankrupt nation. He pushed off the door and crossed the two steps between them in one fluid, decisive motion.

His hands found her, one cradling the nape of her neck, fingers tangling in the roots of her hair, possessing. The other arm banded around the narrow span of her waist, pulling her from the wall and into the solid length of his body. No gentleness, no tentative question. It was a reclamation.

She met his force with a surge of her own. A sharp, breathy gasp was swallowed by his mouth as it crashed down on hers.

It was not a kiss; it was a conflagration. Devouring air and reason in the same breath.

Her lips were shockingly soft, a silken contrast to the rough, bruising force of the kiss. They yielded and demanded, moving with a hungry, practised rhythm that shattered his last vestige of control. She tasted of red wine and the faint wild sweetness that was only her.

Her hands flew to his head, fingers combing through his hair, gripping, pulling him closer. One arm locked around his neck. Her body arching and pressing against him from chest to thigh, leaving no space for doubt, for fear, for anything but this.

The kiss was deep, searching, brutally honest. It spoke of lonely weeks, of bitter silences, of a need so profound it had curdled into anger and was now boiling over into this pure, physical language.

Clothes became obstacles in their desperate dialogue. His hands, trembling slightly with adrenaline, found the zip of her dress and yanked it down. The sleek material sighed open. She shrugged it off her shoulders without breaking the kiss, letting it fall in a whisper at their feet. He wrestled with his own clothes, trench coat already discarded, fingers fumbling with the buttons of his shirt in frantic haste.

She helped, impatient, nails grazing his skin as she shoved the fabric away. Not caring where it landed.

The heat between them was a palpable, aching force.

She took charge of the agony. Wrapping one long, sculpted leg high around his hip, she anchored herself. The thin lace barrier was a maddening tease. He groaned into her mouth, raw and animal, hands sliding down to clutch the backs of her thighs. With a heave born of pure adrenaline and need, he lifted her effortlessly. She locked both legs around his waist, her arms around his neck, their mouths still fused in a wet, searing kiss.

He carried her like that, a tangled, passionate cargo. Down the shorter side of the dark hall. They stumbled once, a bump against the wall only fuelling their urgency. He didn't navigate; he aimed for the bedroom.

He swung her onto the mattress. She landed with a sharp bounce, the mattress dipping under her weight, her hair fanning out across the duvet, her chest heaving.

She was revealed in lace the colour of crushed roses, a perfect match for the dark wine stain of her lipstick. Lingerie that hid nothing, only accentuated the breathtaking landscape of her body. The bra was more suggestion than barrier, delicate and intricate, its front a modest illusion of coverage that made everything beneath it more potent.

The matching panties completed the devastating ensemble, a delicate band of lace low on her hips.

In a sudden rush of joy, she rolled across the bed and back again, the motion playful and unguarded. As she turned, the lush, rounded hills of her hips rose into view, full and softly curved against the duvet, giving him a fleeting, breathtaking glimpse of every inch of her.

At the back, a small feminine ribbon rested just above a dramatic, open triangle that framed the elegant notch at the base of her spine, a detail of daring elegance, a secret she wore for herself, for nights like this.

He stood over her, wrenching his belt loose, shoving his trousers down in one frantic motion. The air was cold on his feverish skin. For a second, there was only the sound of their ragged breathing.

She lay before him, a vision of dishevelled perfection. Her beauty in that moment was not soft or romantic; it was elemental. Face flushed, lips swollen and berry-dark from his kiss, eyeliner smudged into a savage, beautiful mask. Hair a dark river across the pillow. The elegant line of her throat led down to the stunning, full curves of her breasts, rising and falling rapidly, constrained by daring red lace. Her waist was a sinuous dip, descending to the delicate arcs of her panties, where the lace framed the gentle, aroused swell of her mons pubis.

Her legs, long and powerfully elegant, were slightly parted, an unspoken challenge and invitation. Toned from years of quiet discipline, balanced from long walks across the western countryside, they possessed the poised, sculpted symmetry of someone who carried beauty without ever trying to.

He was stark contrast: broad, chest heaving, muscles corded with tension, body a map of taut strength and rigid need. Stubble dark against his jaw, eyes brown and depthless with desire that had long eclipsed guilt or thought.

Their eyes locked. No words, only a silent, screaming transmission that passed between them.

I need you. Now. All of you.

It was a fierce, mutual ingestion of the other's presence. A frantic attempt to inhale the essence of what they were losing. To feel, in the most visceral way possible, that they still existed for one another. Passion forged in the furnace of fear: a doomed, beautiful attempt to bridge the chasm with the only language that hadn't yet completely failed them.

He came over her like a storm front, blotting out the dim ceiling light, his shadow swallowing her whole. He didn't claim her mouth again. Not yet. Instead, he began a slow, reverent descent, a pilgrimage across skin he had once believed he had lost the right to touch. His lips hovered a hair's breadth away, trailing warmth like a whisper of flame across her cheek, her throat, the frantic hollow where her pulse hammered. Down the sternum. Over the ribs. Across the gentle curve of her belly. Every exhalation a promise, every pause a tease. Raising every fine hair on her body without leaving a single mark.

She shuddered, arching into air, chasing a contact he refused to give. By the time his hovering lips reached her toes, she was trembling, wet, desperate — set ablaze by nothing but the ghost of his kiss.

Then he began kissing her at her feet. Lips pressed against the high arch of one instep, then the other. His mouth travelled the elegant line of her calf, tasting salt on her skin, feeling the fine tremor in her muscle. He kissed the sensitive hollow behind her knee; she gasped, toes curling into the duvet. He moved up her thigh, stubble a delicious abrasion against silken skin, path relentless.

His lips pressed to her belly, skin warm, slick with anticipation. Tongue traced the delicate bowl of her navel, dipping briefly, circling, before planting a warm, open-mouthed kiss that made her abdomen clench. He moved higher, to the centre of her chest, just between her breasts, breath hot through the lace. He lingered, as if listening to the frantic drumbeat of her heart.

Then the side of her neck, below her ear. He didn't just kiss, he bit. A sharp, precise pressure that was more possession than pain. She cried out, her hands flying back to his hair. He soothed the spot with a slow, wet stroke, then sucked her earlobe into his mouth, nibbling, breath ragged and hot. "Hassan," she pleaded, the word fragmented.

Finally, he returned to her lips, kissing her with a depth that felt like drowning and salvation. All the while, his hands on her breasts, palming their full, heavy weight through the lace, thumbs circling hardened peaks in firm, maddening rhythm.

His hand slid to her back. She arched, helping his fingers find the clasp of the bra. With a swift, practised flick, the bra released. Straps slid down her arms. The fabric fell away.

Her breasts were revealed, full, lush, breathtakingly perfect. Nipples erect, deep dusky rose-pink, crinkled tight with arousal. He bent his head, mouth suddenly devastatingly tender. He didn't just suck; he adored. He took one peak into the warm, wet cavern of his mouth, tongue swirling around the rigid flesh in a torturous rhythm. He alternated soft drawing pulls with the lightest graze of teeth, each motion pulling sharp, involuntary sounds from her throat. He lavished the same devoted attention to the other, free hand continuing its maddening, rhythmic work on the first. The sensation was electric, a direct, thrumming cord of pleasure that ran straight from her nipples to the molten core of her.

She arched off the bed, back a tense bow, one hand clenched in the sheets, the other anchored in his hair, holding him to her.

Then his mouth moved lower, to the waistband of her panties. He didn't use hands. He caught the fragile lace with his teeth, eyes locked on hers, burning with primal intent. He tugged, gently at first, then insistent. She raised her hips; with teeth and one guiding hand, he pulled them down her legs, discarding the last scrap of fabric.

He didn't move between her legs immediately. He kissed the inside of one knee, then the other, hands spreading her thighs with firm, undeniable pressure. His mouth began a devastatingly slow ascent up the silken skin of her inner thighs, kissing, nipping, licking. Each touch was a promise, each stroke of his tongue bringing him closer to the aching, soaked heart of her.

She was utterly exposed, utterly wet, air cool against feverish heat. The scent of her arousal, musky, sweet, intensely feminine. It filled the space between them.

Finally, his breath ghosted over her intricate, soaked flesh. She shuddered violently.

His first touch on her was not his tongue, but his lips, a soft, closed-mouth kiss on her swollen folds. A high, desperate whimper broke from her. Then he parted her with his fingers, and his tongue found the dark, blooming flower of her desire. A single devastating stroke from bottom to top, gathering every drop of her wetness. Salt and summer rain.

She was ravenous.

Not just for touch, not just for release. Ravenous for him, for proof that he still existed in the way she remembered. For certainty that the fracture hadn't yet swallowed the animal part of their connection.

He groaned against her, the vibration sending a shockwave of pure sensation through her. Focus narrowed to the taut, aching bud of her clit, circling with exquisitely torturous precision. She surged toward him, back lifting off the mattress as if trying to meet his tongue halfway. Fingers twisted in his hair, not guiding but demanding. Pulling him deeper, harder, faster, as if she could consume him through the contact.

His tongue plunged deeper, tasting her fully. She moaned, a low, raw sound that tore from her chest, shameless and trembling, rising in broken waves that filled the room. To him it was music, the most beautiful, filthy symphony he had always craved, the sound of a woman being devoured and loving every second of it. Proof that in this one sacred way she still belonged to him.

Every plunge of his tongue was answered with a buck of her hips, every slow stroke with a fresh, shattered cry. She didn't whisper "don't stop" — she snarled it, voice frayed and fierce, hand pressing him deeper, thighs clamping around his head like she might never let him go. Eyes rolled back, lower lip caught between her teeth. Her body was a live wire, trembling, slick, greedy, taking everything he gave and still wanting more. Always more, as though no amount of pleasure could ever fill the hollow that fear had carved inside her.

Plunging and retreating. A rhythm that mirrored the act to come. He was feasting on her with hunger born of too many silences, hands holding her hips down as she bucked helplessly against his mouth.

He was relentless.

She seemed lost in a vortex where thought and fear could not follow. A spinning, weightless realm of pure sensation. Every touch, every ragged breath he took against her skin, every deep, claiming stroke was a counter-spell against the silence that had plagued them.

It was an exorcism by pleasure, a frantic, wordless prayer to feel something other than broken.

He moved above her, within her, with ferocious intensity, passion sharpened into conquest. Hands that had once struck now cradled her face with tenderness. Lips that had spoken cold apologies now traced the shell of her ear, her jaw, the frantic pulse at her throat, whispering shattered words in a language of need. "*Ty… moya…*" You're… mine… The possession was not cruel, but desperate, a plea for her to be irrevocably his again.

She met his desperate claim not just with submission, but with a worship of her own. As he whispered the words into her skin, she gently pushed against his chest, guiding him to sit back on the edge of the bed. Her eyes, dark and unblinking, held his as she knelt before him on the floor.

With slow, deliberate motion, she gathered her tousled hair, twisting it into a loose, messy bun that exposed the elegant line of her neck. Never breaking eye contact, she leaned forward and pressed a warm, open-mouthed kiss to the flat plane of his abdomen. He shuddered. Her lips travelled down, a trail of fire, following the faint trail of hair that led from his navel to the base of his shaft.

There she paused, breath hot against him. She pressed another kiss, more deliberate, just at the root. Then her tongue followed, a slow, wet, agonizingly tender lick from the very base all the way to the tip, where a glistening bead of his arousal had already waited. A low groan tore from his throat. She inhaled deeply, taking in the musky, clean, utterly *him* scent she secretly craved, a primal perfume that bypassed all thought.

Then she took him into her mouth. It was not an act of service, but devotion. She took him slowly, deeply, savouring the weight and texture of him, the silken heat. Her world narrowed: the sound of his broken breathing, the taste of his skin, the feeling of him filling her senses. She moved with a rhythmic, deep reverence, her hand cradling him at the base.

His hands flew to her head, fingers tangling in the loose strands of her bun, not to force, but to feel the reality of her. He looked down, gaze drowning in hers. In her eyes, he saw no cunning or manipulation, but a raw, awestruck hunger, a mirror of his own need. From this angle, he could see the beautiful, heavy curve of her breasts, swaying gently with her motion, nipples desperate for attention.

Just as tension threatened to become unbearable, she released him and rose, climbing onto the bed to straddle his lap. She kissed him deeply, letting him taste himself on her tongue. An intimacy more profound than any word. The aching head of him brushed the soaked, delicate petals between her thighs, her bare, slick folds. She was so impossibly wet that with a slight, rocking shift of her hips, he simply, slipped inside. No force. No struggle. Just a yielding so perfect it stole his breath.

She took all of him, a gentle, gasping sigh escaping her as she settled fully onto his lap. The inside of her was a breathtaking, velvety heat. A tight, clinging softness that embraced him utterly. She began to move, not with frantic haste, but with a rolling, hypnotic rhythm of her hips, each deep undulation drawing a mutual groan. With each rock forward, the sensitive bud of her clit rubbed against the coarse hair at the base of him, dual sensation making her eyes flutter shut in a cresting wave of pleasure. She rode him with a natural, perfect grace, head tipped back, breasts bouncing gently, hands braced on his chest.

He could take no more. With a growl his hands gripped her waist, then slid around to clutch her back. In one powerful, fluid motion he rolled her over, pinning her beneath him without ever slipping out of that heavenly warmth. The sudden shift drew a sharp cry of surprise and desire from her.

Now he drove into her, deeper, more urgent.

They were not making love.
They were not reconciling.

They were feeding their addiction of each other.

This was the mutual administration of a vital, toxic dose.

She met him thrust for thrust, body arcing off the bed, fingers digging into the hard planes of his back, anchoring herself to this fleeting, perfect unity. The universe contracted to the points where they were joined: searing heat, sweat-slick slide of skin on skin, tangled press of mouths. It was a furious, beautiful race toward oblivion they both needed.

When the climax tore through them like a shared seismic rupture, it struck her first, a white-hot detonation igniting deep in her core. Something ancient and involuntary awakened: rhythmic pulses of tightening and release that seized him, not as invasion but as sublime invitation. For a suspended, breathless second, time locked. Beneath the breaking of her breath, the words escaped — *don't stop* — fractured, pleading, dissolving into sound.

Her core drew tight around him, then loosened, then gathered him again. Each silken contraction deliberate and majestic, pulling him deeper as if her body were absorbing him, insisting he belong there. Every brutal thrust became a wet collision, stealing the air from her lungs. What had drawn him in now claimed him fully, a pulsing, silken vise born from a molten core, gripping him deep, pulling his very soul in. The heat turned convulsive, overwhelming, shattering her awareness into brilliant fragments.

A choked, sobbing cry tore from her throat, part pleasure, part profound relief. The sound of a woman coming violently apart. He felt it immediately, that heavenly spasm around him, an electric signal his body could not deny. Control vaporized. A ragged "Oh God" tore from him as he was swept away in her wake. Her body pulsed not just around him but through him, forcing him to feel every ripple of her release as it mingled with his own. He surrendered to that sacred rhythm, a profound dialogue of flesh where every contraction was a whispered testament to her pleasure, every thrust a silent plea for forgiveness.

His release followed instantly, a shuddering echo of hers: wave after wave of exquisite pressure claiming and milking him in a primal, wordless exchange. Their bodies locked into one synchronized pulse, breath aligned, as if suspended beyond time. His groan tore from the depths of his being, drowned by the sound of her breaking beneath him. His body buckled, every muscle locking then going liquid as he poured himself into her, into this fragile, temporary wholeness forged in the heart of their mutual ruin. His forehead dropped to her shoulder, final thrusts a desperate, trembling surrender.

For long minutes afterward, they simply existed in the wreckage of sensation. The frantic energy dissolved, leaving their bodies heavy and spent, slick with sweat. Breathing slowed, syncing in the dark room. He shifted but did not pull away, remaining buried inside her, face nestled in the curve of her neck. One hand stroked her hair with a hypnotic rhythm.

This was the truce their bodies could broker that their minds could not. The physical release had been profound, a necessary reset. The dose had been administered.

Hassan, mind clearing from the blissful haze, felt a wave of complex tenderness. Holding her like this, feeling her heart slow against his, he wanted to believe this was the reset button. That from this point, they could rebuild. But a colder part whispered that this was just another peak in the cycle, soon to be followed by another valley of mistrust and pain.

He pressed a soft, final kiss to her shoulder and slowly withdrew, rolling onto his back beside her.

The cold space he left was instantly filled. Anastasia turned into him, her body seeking his warmth with a frantic, clinging need. She threw an arm across his chest, hooked a leg over his thighs, and buried her face against the damp heat of his shoulder. It was less an embrace than a claim staked, a physical manifesto: *You are mine. This is mine.*

In the sanctuary of his warmth and the steady rhythm of his heart, she found a fleeting solitude from the screaming fear in her mind. She wanted him with a desperation that felt cellular, as if her atoms had been arranged to orbit his. This skin-to-skin quiet was the only proof she could trust: that on this fundamental, animal level, they were meant for each other. It crossed every boundary of logic and pain. They were mad for each other. It was the one truth that hadn't yet bent.

For Hassan, lying in the dark with her wrapped around him, there was a profound peace. The gnawing guilt, the spectre of Sara, the exhausting calculations: all of it receded. In this moment, he was not a failure or a liar. He was a man whose very presence was a sanctuary. He would have given anything, his career, his future, his very soul, to fossilise this instant. To live forever in the quiet, post-storm harbour of her limbs.

He felt powerful. Invincible. She had handed him a throne built from her own submission, and seated upon it, he felt like a king. Her need was his validation; her surrender, his strength. A man clings to such a feeling with everything he has. He will wage wars to keep it. He will build empires upon it. He will, in his darkest hours, mistake it for love.

But thrones built on fault lines do not stand.

They wait to fall.

Chapter 20

Blueprint of Abandonment

Within days, the fragile peace crumbled. The fear, like a toxic vine, grew back faster and thicker around Anastasia's heart. Her watchfulness returned, sharpened now by the memory of his recent, potent kingship. *If he is so powerful, what stops him from leaving?* Hassan, for his part, was sinking under a weight that no amount of physical reassurance could lift. The messages from Sara's family were polite, persistent daggers. Sara herself, sensing his paralysis, had shifted from accusation to a cloying, worried concern that was somehow worse.

"You sound unwell, Hassan. Let me come and take care of you."

The pressure clamped around his skull like a cold vise. The exhaustion was no longer just emotional; it was a physical ache in his bones, a tremor in his hands, a constant, dull roar behind his eyes.

Anastasia watched him deteriorate, and her own fear sharpened into a silent, constant calculation. Her eyes tracked him, not just for emotional clues, but for practical ones. She noted the times he checked his messages from Pakistan, the duration of the calls he took in the bedroom. She started, almost unconsciously, to keep a mental log. Her own name wasn't on the lease. Her residency permit was temporary protection that could expire. Her "marriage" existed in a religious limbo, invisible to the system.

In this state, anything out of the ordinary, any deviation from Hassan's exhausted, predictable routine, felt like a potential threat. A sudden errand. An unannounced purchase. A shift in his sleeping pattern. Each had to be scrutinised, dissected for the hidden damage it might bring to her fragile existence. His life was no longer just his own; it was the unstable ground upon which she stood, and she had to scan it daily for fissures.

Her love for him was a frantic, clinging thing, but beneath it a colder engine hummed: *If he collapses, where do I stand? If he leaves, who do I call? If he chooses her, what evidence do I have that I was ever here?* She hated these thoughts. They felt like a betrayal of the midsummer dream. Survival had taught her that dreams burn first — but ashes can still be evidence.

Hassan knew he was breaking. So he did the only rational thing he could think of as a last resort: he sought a professional. He booked an appointment at the *Vårdcentral* for January 15th. A silent, desperate white flag waved at his own crumbling mind.

To Anastasia, the appointment was not a cry for help. It was a tribunal.

What if he tells the doctor about me? What if he describes the fights, the carving, my past… and the doctor — a rational Swedish authority — tells him the obvious: 'She is the problem. She is unstable. For your own health, you must leave her.'

The logic felt inevitable. He would be medically absolved. He could leave on a higher note, his conscience clean, prescribed serenity in a little bottle. She would be pathologized, discarded, the crazy woman who ruined a good man's peace.

She could not allow that narrative to be written without her in the room.

"I want to go with you to the doctor," she announced, her voice carefully neutral, belying the panic beneath.

"You can't," he said, rubbing his temples. "It's a private appointment."

"I'll sit in the waiting hall. Just to be there for you. For support." The words "support" and "surveillance" hung between them, indistinguishable.

Too tired to wage the war this would become, he agreed. "Fine. You'll have to wait outside."

On the morning of the 15th, they walked the five minutes to the clinic in a tense, shared silence. The Vårdcentral was a study in Scandinavian calm — soft lighting, pale wood, the faint smell of coffee and disinfectant. Anastasia took a seat in the waiting hall, a plastic chair that felt like a dock. She watched him go to the reception and then disappear behind a door, and for forty minutes she dissected every possible sentence he could be uttering on the other side.

Inside the consultation room, Hassan sat under the gentle, probing gaze of a Middle Eastern doctor in his fifties. He unspooled a carefully edited version of his truth. He spoke of his wife in Pakistan, of the years of waiting, of the vicious, unexpected accusations from her family that had shattered his reputation and his peace. He described the insomnia, the crushing fatigue, the inability to focus, the constant, low-grade anxiety that felt like a hum in his wiring. He painted a portrait of a man betrayed and abandoned by the person he'd sacrificed everything for.

He did not say a single word about Anastasia. Not one. She was the locked chamber within the vault of his troubles. To mention her was to make her real to the Swedish system, to ink her name into a journal that could be subpoenaed, to risk a chain of events he could not control. He contained the spreading fire by denying one of its largest flames even existed.

The doctor nodded, his fingers tapping softly on the keyboard. The diagnosis appeared on the screen, a clinical translation of Hassan's ruin: **Adjustment Disorder with Mixed Anxiety and Depressed Mood. Severe Stress Reaction. Somatic Symptoms (fatigue, tension headaches, psychomotor agitation).**

"Your body is shouting what your mind is trying to process," the doctor said kindly. "The betrayal, the isolation — it's a profound trauma. We need to lower your stress load dramatically."

He suggested a course of SSRIs. Hassan refused, a flicker of his old aversion to chemical dependence. The alternative was time.

"I am signing you off work for thirty days," the doctor said. "Complete rest. No dealing with these family pressures. If, after a month, there is no improvement, we revisit medication and a referral to a psychiatrist."

Hassan took the slip of paper, a medical pardon from the front lines of his own life. He felt both relief and a deeper shame. He was now officially a broken thing, with a doctor's note to prove it.

When he emerged, Anastasia searched his face like a seismograph. She saw the profound sadness in his eyes, the new lines of defeat around his mouth. Her heart plummeted. *This is it. He looks devastated. The doctor confirmed I am the sickness.*

"What did he say?" she asked, rising, her voice tight.

"Let's go outside. I'll explain."

He explained wearily: the stress. The trauma from Sara. The thirty-day sick leave. The possible medication.

She listened, but her mind was a filter, catching only what it feared. *Where is the part about me? It must be there, hidden. He is just not saying it.*

"So…" she pressed, her tone sharpening. "What will you do for thirty days? Just sit in the apartment? With me?"

He was exhausted, his guard down, his thoughts already spiralling toward the insoluble problem of Sara. The words left him without strategy, a simple, terrible expression of a fantasy of escape.

"Maybe," he sighed, looking past her, "I'll go to Pakistan."

The words landed not as a possibility, but as a sentence.

Pakistan.

The word was a master key that unlocked every dungeon of her terror. He would go. He would be nursed by his rightful wife, surrounded by his family, his narrative cleansed. She would be left in the Stockholm winter, in an apartment tied to his name, with no money, no status, no reason to stay, thrown out like garbage while he healed in the sun.

The five-minute walk home was a silent battleground. The fight didn't erupt in shouts; it seeped out in hissed accusations, in bitter silences that spoke volumes, in the wide, frigid space they left between their bodies as they moved. He walked with the heavy tread of a condemned man. She walked with the brittle, furious energy of someone who has just seen the blueprint of her own abandonment. The clinic's clean, hopeful air was far behind them. They were back in the familiar, toxic atmosphere of their making, carrying home not a cure, but a fresh, potent strain of the same disease.

The words hadn't been a plan. They'd been a pressure-release valve, twisted open under the relentless force of her interrogation: *What will you do for thirty days?* A demand for a blueprint he didn't have, for a future he couldn't envision. Trapped and exhausted, yearning for any solution on the horizon, he grasped at the most distant geography he could name: *Maybe I'll go to Pakistan.* It was less a statement of intent than a confession of helplessness, a verbal shrug thrown into the void of their conflict. If he had glimpsed even a hint of the cataclysm quietly assembling itself just two days ahead, he would have swallowed the sentence whole and chosen any other words, in any language.

The next morning, his last before the sick leave began, a hollowed-out version of himself went to work. The medical certificate was a slip of crisp, official paper that felt like a verdict in his hands. He sat across from his manager in a glass-walled meeting room, the bright, orderly world of code and quarterly goals feeling like a diorama of a life that no longer belonged to him.

Chapter 20

"I need to take some time off," Hassan said, his voice steady but devoid of its usual undercurrent of certainty. He slid the form across the table. "My… personal circumstances. They've become untenable. My doctor believes it's affecting my health."

His manager, a pragmatic Swede in his forties, scanned the document. His expression shifted from professional curiosity to a flash of genuine concern. The clinical terms: *severe stress reaction, adjustment disorder*, translated into a universal language of human collapse.

"Hassan," he said, setting the paper down. "We've noticed you haven't been yourself. Of course. Your health is the only priority."

The company's response was a model of supportive, detached efficiency. The leave was approved without a moment's hesitation.

"Take all the time you need. Use the company's support resources if they'd help. Just let us know if there's anything at all we can do."

It was kindness, but it felt like a dismissal. He was being gently, compassionately removed from the machinery of normal life. As he gathered his laptop and a few personal items from his desk under the quietly concerned glances of his colleagues, the finality of it settled upon him.

For the next thirty days, he would have no structure, no external mandate, no escape into the logic of work. He was being sent back full-time, to the bomb he could no longer defuse. To the silent apartment, to the watchful, fearful eyes of Anastasia, and to the ghost of Sara that now haunted every phone notification.

The company's understanding was a door closing, leaving him alone in a room with all the problems he could no longer outrun.

Chapter 21

The Deposition

Hassan left the Microsoft campus not with the relief of a reprieve, but with the dread of a prisoner being granted an empty, endless yard. He couldn't face the apartment. Not yet. Not with the spectre of thirty vacant days looming, and the echo of his own reckless words — *Maybe I'll go to Pakistan* — hanging in the air between them.

Instead of turning towards home, he drove to an acquaintance's place, Ali, a fellow Pakistani from his previous job. They weren't close friends, but they shared the unspoken bond of displacement and the polite, surface-level camaraderie of countrymen abroad.

Ali opened the door, surprise softening into concern. "Hassan? Is everything okay?"

"Yes, yes. All good," he said, the lie automatic and thin. "Just… had a long day. Would it be possible to crash here for the night?"

The question was unusual, but Ali, reading the exhaustion etched into Hassan's face, simply nodded and stepped aside. "Of course. You know where the spare room is."

That evening, and through the next long, stagnant day, Hassan hid. He lay on Ali's guest bed, staring at the ceiling, his phone buzzing intermittently on the nightstand like a trapped insect. He didn't need to look to see the messages stacking up.

Anastasia (17:07): *Where are you?*
Anastasia (22:47): *Please tell me where you are? Don't you care about me?*
Anastasia (23:12): *Are you coming home tonight?*
Anastasia (00:31): *I am worried about you.*

Chapter 21

Anastasia (01:18): *Why are you ignoring me? Who are you with?*
Anastasia (07:05): *I couldn't sleep all night.*
Anastasia (09:41): *I am going crazy. Please come back to me.*
Anastasia (10:15): *Hello?*

He let them accumulate, a digital monument to her anxiety. Each notification was a tug on a leash he was desperately trying to ignore. To answer was to re-enter the labyrinth. He needed the silence, even if it was borrowed and cowardly.

In the morning, Ali knocked softly, then left a cup of coffee on the nightstand without asking questions. Hassan pretended to be asleep. By the time he emerged, Ali had already left for work, leaving a single note on the table: *Lock up when you leave. Hope you're okay.*

Finally, late the next morning, the guilt and the pressure grew too great. He typed a single, deflective line:

Hassan: *I am okay. Just spent some time with a friend at his place.*

The reply was instantaneous, a volley of suspicion:

Anastasia: *What friend? You don't have any friends here.*

Hassan: *A colleague from Pakistan. From my old job.*

Anastasia: *Why have you never mentioned him before? Who is he? What's his name? Where does he live?*

Hassan: *I'll come back and explain everything soon.*

He silenced the phone. The inquisition was a familiar script, and he was too tired to perform his lines.

Later that afternoon, with a heaviness in his limbs, he drove back home. The clock on the dashboard read 4:00 p.m. He parked, swiped his tag at the building's main door, and climbed the stairs, each step a reluctant return to the arena. He turned the key in the lock, bracing for the tension, the tears, the accusatory silence.

He was not prepared for what he saw.

Anastasia stood in the centre of the living room, transformed into something almost otherworldly.

She wore a dress of liquid silk the colour of sunlit honey, its glossy sheen catching every stray beam of light and turning it to molten gold across her skin. Sleeveless, it clung and flowed in perfect obedience to the elegant architecture of her body, skimming her collarbones, tracing the gentle swell of her curves, nipping at her waist before spilling into a long, fluid skirt. A high slit parted the silk on the left side, rising daringly above the ankle with each subtle shift of weight, revealing the long, sculpted line of her leg like a secret offered and immediately withdrawn.

A small clutch of sparkling gold rested in her hand, its surface alive with tiny prisms. Matching heels, strappy and impossibly delicate, lifted her already graceful posture into something regal, elongating her calves in that unconsciously seductive way that had always undone him.

Her hair was swept up in a loose, intricate knot, soft tendrils escaping to curl against her neck. The makeup was masterful in its restraint: skin luminous, cheeks kissed with the faintest flush, eyes dramatically enlarged by the precise, velvet-black wing of eyeliner he had always craved, the one that turned her gaze into something magnetic, almost predatory in its clarity. And her lips, that signature deep, dark red, the one he could never look away from, were painted in a perfect satin finish, a quiet declaration against the softer gold of the dress.

She was no longer the fearful, track-suited ghost of the past weeks. She was elegance distilled, deliberate beauty weaponised with taste and care, every choice, from the teasing slit to the glittering clutch, chosen to remind him exactly who she could be.

Hassan stopped dead in the doorway, his bag slipping from his fingers to thud on the floor. All his worry, his resentment, his exhaustion evaporated in a single, disarming shock of pure aesthetic awe. She was a balm to his frayed senses.

Chapter 21

Before he could speak, she moved. She crossed the room in a few quick strides and launched herself into his arms. He caught her instinctively, her weight a welcome familiarity. She wrapped her legs around his waist, her arms around his neck, and kissed him. It was a kiss of reunion, deep and passionate, laced with a desperate, performative sweetness. He kissed her back, losing himself in the scent of her perfume, something new, floral and expensive, and the overwhelming relief of her not being angry.

He broke the kiss, breathing heavily. "You look… ravishing."

A small, victorious smile touched her lips. "Thank you." She unwrapped her legs and slid down his body.

"What's the occasion?"

"No occasion," she said, smoothing his rumpled shirt. "I just wanted to be ready for you. To make you feel good."

It worked. His worries dissolved. This was the woman he had fallen for: the graceful, feminine, attentive partner. This was the version he craved, the one that made him feel not like a jailer or a patient, but like a man. He loved her fiercely in that moment.

"Let's go out," she said, her eyes bright.

"Sure," he agreed, eager to cement this fragile, perfect bubble.

She took charge, as she often did with his wardrobe. "Wear the cashmere sweater in camel," she instructed, "and the cream trousers. The ones that fit you perfectly here." Her fingers brushed his hip, a possessive, intimate gesture.

You're mine. You look like mine.

She chose his shoes, his watch. He complied without question, savouring her attention. He loved wearing what she chose; it felt like being cared for, being curated. It was a silent language of belonging.

They were a stunning pair. Him, tall and sharp in the warm camel she'd chosen, the soft knit easing the tension he carried in his shoulders. Her, a vision in honeyed gold, every movement graceful.

They went to her favourite sushi restaurant, Sio Sushi — an upscale place with dark wood and the quiet hum of contentment. She ate delicate maki rolls topped with roasted onion, silky slices of salmon, the creamy bite of avocado, each piece touched with just a hint of wasabi's sting. She laughed at his jokes, her hand resting on his arm. She was the perfect girlfriend. He was the doting, admiring boyfriend. For two hours, they were the couple they'd always pretended they could be, beautiful, harmonious, in love.

On the drive back, lulled by the warm glow of sake and temporary peace, Hassan mentioned an errand. "I need to swing by the furniture store on *Kungsgatan*. Just to pick up a sideboard I ordered. It's on the way."

He felt her posture shift beside him. The relaxed warmth vanished, replaced by a subtle rigidity.

"A sideboard?" she asked, her voice carefully neutral. "The apartment already has one."

"I know. This one was on a steep discount. I've wanted something like it for a long time." He'd seen the mid-century modern piece weeks ago and, on a whim during his lunch break, bought it as a treat for himself. He needed something solid. Something that wouldn't argue back.

But in the fertile soil of her fear, the simple statement sprouted monstrous implications. *Why is he buying furniture now? He's on sick leave, he's talking of Pakistan, and now he's redecorating. Is he preparing the space? Is he making it nice... for her?* The questions coiled, silent and venomous, in her mind.

The pick-up was quick. The sideboard, flat-packed, was heavy and bulky. He wrestled it into the back of the car with some effort. She stood watching, arms crossed, not offering to help. The silent car ride home was a different silence from the one they'd driven out in. This one was thick, pressurised, humming with her unspoken accusations.

"Why did you need this?" The question finally erupted as they turned onto their street, sharp as broken glass.

"I told you. It was on sale, and I liked it."

"You're rearranging things," she stated, the real question screaming beneath the words.

"I'm not rearranging anything. I'm just adding a piece of furniture, Anastasia." His patience, worn thin by the emotional whiplash of the day, began to fray.

He looked at her, and for a moment the anger had nowhere to go. She wasn't looking at him anymore, but past him — already placing it in the room. Measuring. Imagining hands that weren't hers opening its drawers.

She said nothing else.
The silence was a verdict.

Liar.

Back at the apartment, the performative harmony was in shreds. He struggled to get the large box through the door. With a resentful sigh, she stepped forward and grabbed a corner, her movements stiff. Together, they manoeuvred it into the living room. As they set it down, she winced, a hand flying to the small of her back. The gesture was both genuine and weaponised.

In the bedroom, the tension sought a physical outlet. He looked at her, her beautiful dress now a symbol of the evening's failed artifice. He watched her straighten slowly, one hand still at her back. The room felt smaller now, stripped of pretence. A raw, frustrated energy coursed through him. "Do you wanna fuck?" he asked, the coarseness of the word a challenge, an attempt to reclaim the earlier passion through sheer force.

She met his gaze, her eyes hard. "Yes."

It wasn't lovemaking. It was a collision, a furious, wordless battle for dominance and release, a way to scream without making a sound. It was hard, fast, and left them both breathless and strangely empty, lying side by-side in the dark as the sweat cooled on their skin.

The fragile ceasefire lasted only as long as their heartbeats took to slow.

As the reality of the room seeped back in, so did her rage. She sat up abruptly.

"Why did you make me carry it?" she accused, her voice trembling. "You know I have back pain now."

"I'm sorry, my love. It was heavy. There wasn't anyone else I could ask for help," he replied genuinely.

"Do you really think I don't know who this is for?" she hissed, turning to face him, her beautiful features twisted with hurt and suspicion. "Huh? You're making a nice home, aren't you?"

"You are thinking completely wrong," he shot back, pushing himself up on his elbows. The exhaustion was back, a tidal wave. "Can we please just talk about this tomorrow?"

He said it as a plea for postponement, a desperate grab for a few hours of quiet. He had no way of knowing that the *tomorrow* he was hoping for, a day of calm, of explanation, of slow repair, would not exist. The clock was already ticking down to a different kind of morning altogether.

"You just used me," she spat, the words final. She flung herself off the bed, pulled on her burgundy silk nightdress, picked up her phone, and stormed out of the room, slamming the bedroom door behind her with a force that shook the wall. The bang was not just a sound; it was a punctuation mark, a period at the end of a sentence he hadn't finished reading.

Chapter 21

He lay there for a minute, stunned, the echo of the slam vibrating in his bones.

God, I'm so tired.

He fought the urge to chase her, to escalate.

Keep your cool. Do not follow. Let it breathe. This can't be our whole lives, this constant detonation. It's exhausting. We can't keep living like this.

He stared at the ceiling, the white paint blurring.

We'll ask her tomorrow to leave for good. When we've both slept, when the air is clear. Tomorrow. It has to be tomorrow.

The thought felt like a life raft. But the sound of her muffled sobs from the kitchen drilled through his resolve.

Don't. Don't you dare get up. Stick to the plan. One more night of this, then you get out. Just don't act recklessly today. But he was already giving in.

He rose in the dark, the echoes of the slammed door still vibrating in the quiet. He pulled on his striped pyjama pants and matching shirt, the soft cotton feeling absurd against the tension coiling in his muscles. The hallway was a tunnel of shadows leading to the wedge of light spilling from the kitchen.

What are you doing? Get back in bed. Stick. To. The. Plan.

His bare feet were cold on the hardwood, each step a betrayal of the promise he'd just made to himself.

I'm not going to talk, he lied to the voice in his head. *Just need water. That's all. Just need to see if she's… if she's okay enough to be left alone.*

The sobs had quieted to wet, shuddering breaths now, and the sound of it — that awful, choked silence — pulled him forward more surely than any scream ever could.

Tomorrow. We'll still do it tomorrow. I'm just… I'm just checking. Then I go back to bed.

He reached the threshold, his hand gripping the doorframe. He took in the scene with slow, dreadful clarity, knowing full well he was walking into the blast zone anyway.

The kitchen was a still life of domesticity turned cold, and his eyes swept it like a searchlight. To his left, the refrigerator hummed, the room's only pulse, beside a narrow shelf stacked with the sleek, unused shapes of the air fryer and microwave. Above them, storage cabinets.

Then the empty wooden bench: the place he'd expected to find her, now an accusation of vacant space.

In the centre of the room, dominating everything, sat the heavy wooden table: tired roses, salt, pepper, a bowl of apples and oranges. Some birthday roses had dried where they stood, like forgotten props on a stage. In the far-left corner, a small side table bore the whimsical red popcorn machine, a relic of simpler nights. Still no trace of her.

He turned his gaze right. A curtained window. A tall cabinet in the corner, closed over electronics boxes and quiet dust. The overhead cupboards ran into the extractor hood above the stove. The old green glass lamp shade above the table was dark; a single under-cabinet light bled muted gold across everything else.

His eyes searched everywhere. She was nowhere.

Until the space beyond the table stopped him.

Across the room, the balcony door was shut. Its salmon-coloured curtain bulged outward, pressed by the shape behind it. She was wedged between glass and fabric, hiding in the thin membrane between the apartment and the outside world. Sitting. Forehead against the cold door. Her body outlined by a faint, sickly streetlamp glow filtering through the weave. The nightdress drank the light, making her look like a phantom caught in a shroud.

Chapter 21

He stood frozen in the kitchen doorway, a spectator to a tragedy. The geometry of the room felt like a trap. She was as far from him as she could physically be without leaving, a deliberate, eloquent distance.

He didn't know what to say. *I'm sorry* was a currency that had hyper-inflated into worthlessness between them. *I love you* felt like a lie woven from half-truths and desperate need. So, he just stood there in the dim kitchen, watching the woman he loved, and feared, dissolve into the architecture of their shared unhappiness. The ghost of the unassembled sideboard waited in the living room, a monument to his misguided attempts at normalcy.

A minute passed. Two. The curtain shifted with each breath she took.

His voice, when it finally came, was low and rough, scraping against the quiet.

"Can you please come out of there?"

She didn't move. Silence stretched, thin and taut, until it was severed by her voice from behind the curtain: sharp, clear, crackling with anger.

"Yes. I can."

The fabric stirred. She emerged not like someone stepping into the light, but like a soldier leaving a trench. She didn't look at him. With stiff, deliberate steps, her bare feet whispering against the light brown wooden panels, she brushed past the heavy central table and lowered herself onto the middle of the wooden bench, her back straight.

She placed her phone on the table with a definitive tap, then folded her arms over its surface, resting her weight on them. She stared straight ahead at the sink counter across from her, offering only her side profile to him in the doorway. The scene had shifted, but the tragedy of it remained, now framed by the stark geometry of the kitchen.

She was a statue of beautiful, furious misery, and the space between them felt wider than the entire apartment.

The silence after his plea for her to come out was a vacuum, and she filled it with a torrent that had been dammed for months.

"You have just used me," she said, her voice low and venomous. Her fingers traced the grain of the wooden table. "For so long. I have felt it." She pressed a fist to her sternum. "You took everything from me. My safety. My peace. My —"

"Anastasia, please," Hassan began, his hands held out in a placating gesture. "Can you please calm down —"

"Calm down?!" she exploded, whipping her head to face him, her eyes blazing. "You haven't even married me!" The word was a shriek that bounced off the cabinets. "There is no proof. No paper. No one who knows, not your family, not the state — just God! Huh. I am just a ghost in your life. A dirty secret you keep in a box!" Her voice broke into a sob, but fury quickly staunched it. "You made me believe, and then you made me nothing. No one has ever treated me like you did."

That did it. The thread of his patience, already frayed to a filament, snapped. His calm façade crumbled, revealing the raw, wounded righteousness beneath.

"I tried to help you and this is what I get in return — that I used you?" His voice rose, cutting through her sobs, still standing in the doorway. "Look around! You are the one living here! Eating my food, wearing the clothes I buy, sleeping in the bed I pay for! I am the one providing everything! And for what? To get my brain fucked every single day by your accusations? I had to take sick leave from work because I couldn't bear the stress you create — your constant, endless nagging! You're blaming me for every shadow in your head!"

"So, you are not the problem?" she fired back, still sitting, leaning over the table towards him. "You are exactly the problem! You couldn't handle a woman with a past! You couldn't handle that I was scared! You just wanted a quiet, stupid doll to dress up and fuck! I cook for you. I clean for you. I do everything you ask of me!"

"I wanted a partner! Not a paranoid ghost who interrogates every receipt and sees a conspiracy in a piece of furniture!" he roared. "I asked you to leave!" The memory of that night flooded back. "I begged you for space, to just stop, and you refused! Instead, you carved my name onto your skin to manipulate me!"

"I wanted to fix things!" she cried, tears streaming freely now, her beautiful face contorted in anguish.

"I was perfectly fine living with that old man," she spat, the words designed to maim, "until you dragged me out of there and promised me a life!"

The air left the room. Hassan stared at her, a cold, disbelieving horror dawning on his face. Then it twisted into something darker.

"We were in love," he said, each word a hammer strike, his voice trembling with fury and betrayal. "And you were hiding a whole other life from me. Have you forgotten everything? You begged me. On your knees. You wept and asked me to rescue you. Was that a lie, too?"

She met his gaze, and in her eyes he saw a terrifying, absolute nihilism.

"Yes," she whispered. "I deeply regret that. It was a mistake. I should have never left that place."

The admission was a nuclear blast in the confined space. It vaporized the last remnants of their shared narrative.

"You see…" she continued, her voice regaining a chilling, analytical steadiness as she watched him unravel. "You see me as a slut. I can see it in your eyes. You judge me every day. I live in fear of what you think of me — of how sick and damaged I am."

"I NEVER thought like that!" he bellowed, slamming his palm on the doorway. "I accepted you! As you were! It was your own fears, your own sick, consuming insecurities, that poisoned everything! Not mine!"

They were bleeding their history onto the light-brown wooden floor — a toxic spill of regret, shame, and shattered pride. It was a summary of their entire catastrophic union: her terror of abandonment, his suffocating sense of obligation, their mutual, spectacular failure to be what the other needed.

Then she went for the kill shot, the one truth he could never escape, the indelible stain on his soul.

"And you..." she said, her voice dropping to a razor's edge of contempt. "You even hit me. You are a sick man, Hassan. A violent, sick man."

The words hung in the air, stark and undeniable.

Something inside Hassan didn't just break; it crystallised. In that suspended, agonising second, his gaze, feverish with hurt and rage, darted from her accusing face to her phone, lying screen-down on the table where she had placed it with such deliberate finality.

His mind, the logical, problem-solving engineer's mind, made a terrifying, instantaneous connection: the way she had positioned herself, the way she was steering the conversation toward words like *used me*, *hit me*, *sick man*.

It wasn't just a fight anymore.

It felt like a deposition.

Chapter 22

Three Heartbeats Behind

A cold, sick understanding washed over him, cutting through the red haze of anger. His voice, when it came, was suddenly, frighteningly, calm. Low. Detached.

"Anastasia," he said, his eyes locked on the black slab of the phone. "Are you recording me?"

The effect was instantaneous. All the colour drained from her face. The furious, tragic mask she wore shattered into pure, unguarded shock. Her mouth opened slightly, but no sound came out. Her eyes, wide with a deer-in-headlights terror, flicked instinctively, guiltily, toward the phone on the table.

That flicker was all the confirmation he needed. The battlefield had just transformed. This was no longer a fight between lovers. It was a trap, and he was already in the cage.

The silence after his question was a held breath, thick enough to choke on. Then she shattered it, her voice a weapon of scorn.

"Of course not," she hissed, the words dripping with theatrical disbelief. "This is how you think? You see? You are sick. Even in this moment, you think I am recording you?" She threw her hands up, a pantomime of wounded innocence that rang utterly false in the charged air.

Hassan didn't blink. The storm in him, the hurricane of guilt, righteousness, and exhaustion, had condensed into a single laser-point of cold clarity.

"I asked you a simple question." His voice was low, a controlled burn. "Are. You. Recording. Yes. Or no."

Each word was a block of ice dropped between them, definitive and heavy.

Chapter 22

"You have no right to ask me that!" she fired back, recoiling as if the question itself were a physical advance. Her body twisted away, a study in performed violation. "You are diverting! You have hit me, Hassan. Many times, in the past. I remember that. I will never forgive you for that."

She was stitching the narrative back together with practised, desperate hands, threading the undeniable fact of his violence with a broader, more usable tapestry of blame.

His voice dropped further, becoming dangerously calm, the eerie eye of the hurricane.

"Anastasia." His use of her full name was a chasm. "Please. Tell me if you are recording. I will not even touch your phone. Just… please delete it."

Her eyes, wide and glistening with rehearsed tears, darted, a skittering, trapped-animal movement he now recognised as calculation, not fear. Then she moved. It was a subtle, furtive dip of her shoulder. She grabbed the phone from the table and, in one fluid motion, brought it down into the shadowed space of her lap beneath the solid wooden ledge of the tabletop. Her thumbs moved in a frantic, hidden dance under the table, her gaze locked on his, defiant, but the slight tremor in her forearms betrayed her.

She was deleting evidence.

The confirmation was a silent, devastating detonation in Hassan's chest. Trust didn't just break; it vaporised, leaving a vacuum filled with icy, strategic dread.

Since when? The whole fight — or even before? From the moment she hid behind the curtain? What is her plan? To collect proof? To play it for the police?

The calculations were a dizzying vortex of dread in his mind. This wasn't an emotional meltdown; it was a tactical operation. She wasn't just hurting; she was archiving.

"You can't do this," she blurted, seeing the terrible understanding harden in his eyes like frost on a window. "You have no right to see my phone!"

He moved. Not with the earlier hot rage, but with a grim, determined purpose that was far more frightening. He pushed off from the doorway, his body uncoiling. He didn't run; he lurched across the short distance, his hand a claw, reaching for the phone clenched in her white-knuckled fingers.

What happened next was not a sob, not a shout. A shrill, wire-tight scream ripped from her throat, a sound so sharp it seemed to crystallise the air. It was involuntary in its pitch, utterly deliberate in its purpose. A tactical siren. It hit him like a physical blow, stunning him for a fraction of a second.

That fraction was all she needed.

She exploded from the bench like a sprung coil. Instead of darting past him toward the kitchen door and the hall, the logical escape, she reversed direction, scrambling away from him, deeper into the room's trap. She was a blur of burgundy silk against the salmon-coloured tiles, rushing not for freedom, but for the balcony door.

He shoved past the heavy round table, thighs brushing at its edge in the tight space, adrenaline burning through the momentary stun. He caught her wrist just as her fingertips brushed the cool metal of the balcony door handle. His grip was iron, born of a primal, panicking need to contain the catastrophe.

"Give it to me," he gritted out, voice raw, extending his hand, trying to pry the phone from her grip.

But she was liquid, desperate, her bones seeming to dissolve in his grasp. With a twist of pure, feral instinct, she yanked her arm free, wrist slithering through his grip. In the same continuous motion, she twisted the handle and flung the balcony door open.

The world rushed in.

Chapter 22

A gush of cold, damp Stockholm night air invaded the kitchen's stifling heat, carrying the distant scent of wet concrete and dormant earth. It was a shocking slap against their feverish skin.

And then she screamed into the void.

"HELP! HELP!"

The words weren't a plea; they were a weaponisation of the night itself. They tore through the domestic hum of the refrigerator, through the thin plaster walls, crafted for unknown ears in the sleeping, indifferent building. It was the sound of their private, shameful ruin being blasted into the public domain.

Hassan's mind didn't go blank; it went white. Pure, undiluted panic, cold and electric, surged up his spine.

What the fuck is she doing?

He shoved past the heavy round table to reach the gaping balcony door, in a desperate attempt to close it. He stumbled, thrown off-balance by his own frantic momentum, and his shoulder collided with the wall near the hinges. A bright flare of pain lit up his joint, instantly ignored. He slammed the balcony door shut with a force that rattled the glass panes in their seals. He had just severed her broadcast.

This was no longer about a secret recording, a bitter fight, a misunderstood piece of furniture. This was a cliff-edge, and she had just jumped, dragging them both into a social abyss. The delicate glass sphere of their contained life had been hurled onto the concrete of reality.

While he fought to seal the balcony, she had already ducked low, a phantom flowing around the opposite side of the heavy wooden table. In the economy of chaos, she had traded a scream for a head start.

When he turned, breathing hard, the kitchen doorway was empty. She was already a fleeting shadow disappearing into the darkness of the hallway.

His body reacted before his mind could formulate a thought. The imperative was singular:

Contain the sound. Contain her.

He spun back toward the kitchen doorway, launching himself off the door.

What followed was a symphony of small, devastating sounds: the frantic slap of her bare feet on the hall tiles; then a pause, a muffled shuffle; the distinct, quiet thump of the sleek shoe rack being disturbed. She was at the rack by the front door. Putting on her slippers.

She wasn't just fleeing in blind panic; she was equipping herself to flee properly. This was planned, or instinct had, in its brilliance, mimicked planning.

He heard the sound of the door being slammed open as she sprinted out.

He burst out of the kitchen into the hallway just as the apartment's front door drifted back toward its frame, recoiling from a violent impact he had been too late to see.

Breath tearing at his chest, the cold, rocky-textured off-white tiles biting into his bare soles, he crossed the hallway stretch. His left hand grabbed the closet door just before the front entrance, using it as a hinge to pivot sharply left toward the exit. He pulled the ajar door open quickly but carefully, not letting it slam against the inner wall.

He saw her descending the stairs, their eyes meeting briefly, for a searing instant, before her head and shoulders vanished around the dwell of the stairwell.

Chapter 22

He knew it then, with a sinking certainty as she disappeared completely:

He was already three heartbeats behind.

Chapter 23
The Fatal Step

Anastasia didn't look back. She couldn't. Looking back meant admitting this was real, that the man she had loved was now a predator at her heels. Her lungs burned. The burgundy silk of her nightdress clung to her thighs. *If I could just reach the main door, I could disappear, I could find another home, another life —*

Hassan acted with the certainty that their private life had already spilled into the hallway and there was no sealing it back in, yet some feral part of him believed that if he caught her fast enough, it might still be contained. But it was too late.

The hallway became a courtroom.

The flickering fluorescent lights blinked like an indifferent jury. The air itself, stale, Scandinavian, heavy with the faint smell of other people's peace, hung as the prosecution. And Hassan, a wrong man in a wrong place, terror flooding his eyes and desperation driving his stride, was the defendant.

The sentence had been written long before he ever set foot in their land.

You are a brown man.
You are chasing a white woman.
She is running.
Therefore, you are a monster.

The logic was brutal, woven so deep into the fabric of the Western world that it no longer required explanation. It lived in the way security guards' eyes lingered on him in department stores; in the polite, frozen smiles of shopkeepers who subtly rechecked his groceries; in the tightening grip of women's hands around their purses in elevators.

Chapter 23

He was a shadow in a society built for light.

Tolerated. Sometimes even praised. Never fully seen as human.

A third-class citizen in a first-class world, his worth contingent on silence and gratitude. Like everywhere else. Success, when it came, was merely a longer leash.

And Sweden, the progressive, egalitarian paradise, was the most sophisticated machine of them all. It did not discriminate with slurs. It did it with silence: bureaucracy polished to chilly courtesy, prejudice refined enough to call itself culture. A woman-driven society where the narrative was sacred: woman, victim; man — especially one like him — aggressor. Always.

Truth was irrelevant. Nuance was a luxury reserved for people with the right passports, the right skin, the right history.

He had felt the invisible wall a thousand times. The condescension dressed as compassion. The way his anger was "concerning", while theirs was "righteous". The way his passion was "volatile", while theirs was "passionate". He was from the East. He carried the dust of Lahore in his soul, the heat of conflict in his blood. To them, he was a potential problem to be managed, a statistic of integration.

He knew white supremacy here wasn't shouted; it was breathed in the air like winter chill that seeped through the concrete. It was the assumption of chaos at his origin, of inherent patriarchal violence in his bones. They had saved him from himself by letting him in, and the unspoken contract demanded his perpetual atonement.

And now Anastasia — pale, beautiful, European Anastasia — was tearing down the hallway the embodiment of perfect victimhood. She was the picture their newspapers loved. The story their courts understood. All she had to do was scream once more, into the right ear, and his life, the one he had built from nothing, over thirty-two years of relentless effort, would be erased.

He would be the migrant who snapped.
The husband who hid a mistress.

The violent Pakistani.

The headline wrote itself. They would dissect his life with clinical disgust. Blame his culture. Pity her for being ensnared by his exotic, toxic charm. Deportation would be mercy. A cell would be more likely. She would emerge as the traumatised survivor, her story worth more than his ever was.

This wasn't just about stopping her. This was about stopping the avalanche of a narrative that had been gathering momentum since the day he was born with the wrong name in the wrong part of the world. His degree, his job, his clean record — they were tissue paper against the hurricane of her one, credible sob.

All his life had funnelled into this stairwell. Every slight, every masked insult, every time he bit his tongue and smiled, every time he made himself smaller to fit their world, it all coalesced into a pure, survivalist terror.

He wasn't just running after a woman.

He was running to plug a hole in a dam holding back an ocean of their prejudice.

He ran not with the hope of winning, but with the desperation of preventing total annihilation. His bare feet slapped the speckled concrete, a frantic, hollow drumbeat against the building's indifferent heart. His breath sawed in his throat, raw and burning. Each pulse in his ears shouted the same truth:

If she gets away, you lose everything.
They will believe her.
They will always believe her.

Catch her.
Contain the situation.

Get control.

Chapter 23

The green metal railings blurred into a cage. The patterned leaves on the wall smeared into a mocking verdant streak. The staircase yawned below, a concrete throat waiting to swallow him whole.

He was a brown ghost chasing a white phantom down into the bowels of a system that had already tried and convicted him. And he ran, because the only thing more terrifying than catching her was the certainty of what would happen if he didn't.

Hassan's body, still thrumming from the slam of the balcony door, registered the empty threshold not as an absence but as a vector. His eyes, wide and dark with a hunter's clarity sharpened by fear, traced the invisible line she had drawn through the air: out the door, an immediate, desperate pivot left. His mind did not process the decision. His muscles executed the algorithm of her escape.

He sank his centre of gravity instinctively, folding forward into acceleration. His body followed the path she had carved. His left hand shot out and struck the doorframe where hers had been moments earlier, fingers spreading wide as they bit into the painted frame. The contact was not for balance. It was for force. He loaded his shoulder and core against the resistance, twisted sharply, and tore himself left in a single, brutal motion. Muscle groups locked together — lat, oblique, spine, turning his torso into a driven lever that snapped him into the corridor.

Bare feet slapped concrete, skidded, then traction caught. He surged forward at full commitment. Arms drove hard and tight, elbows cutting back through stale air. He was not running through the hallway; he was compressing it, demanding it shorten beneath him.

The space narrowed into a single vector. Doors dissolved into peripheral smears. Everything collapsed into one fixed point ahead — her.

He reached it without slowing.

His right hand closed around the rail exactly where hers had been, fingers wrapping fully, thumb locking, wrist aligning as his grip tightened to its limit. The metal was cold and unyielding. There was no pause. No adjustment. Forward momentum translated instantly into a 180° rotation. He pulled hard with his arm while pivoting on the ball of his right foot, snapping his trajectory from horizontal corridor into vertical descent in one continuous motion. The railing took his weight and his urgency, groaning faintly in its brackets as his body swung through.

She was already below.

By the time his eyes registered her position, she was nearly at the middle of the staircase, pressed to the right side, one hand clamped to the rail, her body drawn inward and braced. Almost in the middle. Still moving.

Urgency flooded him, complete and blinding. Thought never formed. Panic and adrenaline burned through muscle and nerve, erasing calculation. His grip locked harder, forearm and shoulder contracting to their limit, and he used the full strength of his right arm to thrust himself downward.

It was not a step — it was a launch.

He pushed off with his legs while pulling with his arm, committing his entire mass into the stairwell. The first three steps vanished beneath him. His body went headfirst into the descent, chest angled forward, spine extended, arms already spreading as if to claim her.

For an instant, he was almost airborne.

The air tore past his skin. Time stretched thin. His world narrowed to the burgundy silk just ahead of him.

His left foot came down first.

It struck the fourth step flat enough to hold, the impact driving sharply upward through ankle, shin, knee, and into the hip. The leg absorbed it, muscles locking under load, stabilising him just long enough to carry the motion forward. He was still advancing. Still closing the gap. Still reaching.

His right foot followed.

It landed on the eighth step, the same reckless geometry of skipped stairs. The step directly behind her. Too fast. Too close. The ball of his foot met not the tread but the rounded concrete lip at the edge, where the surface curved away into empty space. There was no purchase. His future slid away with it. Weight arrived where footing could not.

His arms remained wide, fingers stretched toward her back, his body still committed to the belief that forward motion would continue. The illusion held for a fraction of a second longer as the edge slid beneath him and his ankle folded inward under the crushing momentum.

Balance disappeared without announcement.

Oh fuck —

The staircase tilted. Support fell away.

He was still reaching when gravity took full possession, his centre of mass tipping past recovery, his body pitching forward into the descent he could no longer stop — silent, relentless, already falling one step behind the woman he was trying to catch.

The impact was absolute.

His right palm struck the back of her right shoulder blade with the blind, unchecked violence of a body that had already surrendered to momentum. It was not a shove, but a collision, mass meeting mass with nowhere left to dissipate.

It drove the air from her lungs in a single, silent gasp, wrenching her grip from the railing as if her fingers were made of paper. She was falling, but not down, forward, into the void he had become. Her body twisted, a ragdoll in a nightmare.

The last point of stability vanished, and with it any remaining illusion of control.

She was propelled.

Hassan was fully airborne now, a horizontal projectile of panic, the decision to catch her still firing through his muscles even after the ground had withdrawn its consent. The blow to her shoulder became a brutal pivot point. Her body twisted under the torque, torso rotating as her legs lagged behind, silk flaring as gravity seized unevenly. The staircase ceased to function as structure. It became vertical space.

They turned toward each other as they dropped.

For a suspended, breathless instant, gravity seemed to hesitate, not stopping, only tightening its hold. Her rotation brought her face toward his as their falling arcs collapsed into one. His arms continued the reach he had begun on the stairs. His mind had not yet accepted the verdict of gravity, now stripped of control, almost enclosing her as momentum overruled intention.

Their eyes met.

And what flashed in their terrified eyes was not accusation, not forgiveness, only the terrible clarity that neither of them had ever truly been in control.

In that suspended second, they finally saw each other without the story.

It lasted no more than a heartbeat.

Long enough for two lives to flash behind their eyes.
Short enough to untangle nothing.

They were no longer separate forces, but components of a single catastrophe, bound by the same failing arc.

Then the fall asserted itself.

Chapter 23

They dropped past the remaining half of the stairs in a tangled collapse of limbs and velocity. The geometry of the staircase imposed its first punishment as they neared the landing.

His arms closed further around her as gravity finished collapsing their distance, not in protection, not in intent, but as a consequence of converging mass. There was no time left to separate.

Her left ankle struck first.

It smashed into the inner edge of the final concrete step with brutal precision, bone met stone at an unforgiving angle. The joint compressed violently, absorbing the full weight of her downward momentum before her foot could clear. Almost simultaneously, her right ankle clipped the outer edge of the same step, the impact glancing, duller, but enough to twist the leg outward as the rest of her body continued to fall.

The force snapped her upper body down.

She hit first, her right shoulder slamming into the concrete with a concussive thud that drove the air from her lungs and spun her sideways. A fraction of a second later, his left shoulder struck hard beside her, the impact dispersing through muscle and bone as his body followed her down. The force did not stop them. It converted cleanly into motion.

They slid.

Across the smooth, dust-filmed concrete of the landing, they skidded toward the elevator doors at ground level. He rolled partially onto his left side, friction tearing at fabric and skin, his mass bleeding speed evenly. She slid mostly on her right side, momentum concentrating unevenly through her shoulder and hip, silk offering no protection as her body failed to realign in time.

Their paths diverged by inches.

His slide ended first. His momentum died as the back of his head tipped and brushed the flat metal of the elevator door, a muted, hollow contact, barely registering.

Hers did not.

Her slide carried her just beyond the door's edge, toward the structural protrusion of the wall. The right side of her head snapped sideways and struck the sharp corner of the floor skirting beside the elevator frame, the rigid ninety-degree edge where concrete met metal.

The impact was dense.

When everything finally stopped, there was no immediate marker of damage. No dramatic spill. No instant confirmation. Just stillness, bodies at rest where motion had exhausted itself. On the outside, he was unscathed.

He was upright almost immediately, the pause between impact and motion so brief it barely existed. Pain registered only as interference, background noise to a singular, overriding impulse:

Get her inside.

Away.
Out of sight.

Back into the apartment.

He dropped to his knees beside her almost instantly. His hands were already on her, fingers digging into fabric and flesh as he tried to haul her upright. He spoke her name once, a thin, hoarse sound that felt unreal, disconnected from the body that produced it.

She did not rise.

Her legs buckled the moment he tried to lift her, joints trembling violently, bone and muscle refusing all command. She sagged against him, dead weight collapsing inward. He shifted, dragged her closer, wrestled her right arm up and around his neck. With his other hand, he grabbed her waist, hauling her against him with brute insistence.

A sound escaped her then, low and guttural at first: a wounded, bottom-of-the-lungs *aaaah* that caught on the air. It climbed unbidden, tightening with terror, thinning into a higher, wavering pitch as it left her lips, straining toward a word it could not quite form:

"— Hel — p —"

It was less a word than a fractured exhalation, frayed and swallowed by the pounding rush of her own heart.

He didn't hear it as language. Only as noise to be quelled. His hand trembled against her skin. He pressed harder.

He began dragging her toward the stairs, half lifting, half pulling, her feet scraping uselessly over the concrete. Each step was a negotiation her body kept losing. She slipped; he yanked her back. She faltered, her legs folding, her full weight sagging into his grasp.

Her head lolled forward. Something warm and wet streaked down her temple and cheek.

He did not see it yet.

She tried to cry out again, another thin, broken sound, and his right hand came up automatically, pressing over her mouth, fingers clamping tight against her jaw. Not violent. Not gentle. Just immediate, a reflex born of the need to stop this horror from leaking into the world.

She resisted weakly, a faint struggle against his palm, then went still.

Her body gave in to the motion. She tried to walk because he forced her to. One foot, then another. Each movement was dragged from her, her knees trembling, her balance shattered.

They climbed the stairs in a grotesque, fragmented dance, Hassan hauling, bracing, pulling, his breathing a raw gasp that echoed through the quiet stairwell.

By the time they reached the top, her blood had begun to spread with vicious insistence.

It ran from her hairline in a steady rivulet, down her temple, soaking her nightdress. The dark stain spread across the burgundy silk, gleaming wetly in the hallway light. Impossible to miss.

He saw it then.

The sight landed without context or hierarchy, just another overwhelming signal crashing into an already overloaded system. There was no reckoning. Only the primal command, louder now:

Inside.
Inside.

He shoved the apartment door open with his shoulder.

She collapsed forward immediately, falling hard onto the threshold. She lay half in, half out, her body twisted so her face was turned toward him. He grabbed her again, his hands sliding on blood-slick fabric, and pushed her backward into the apartment.

She crawled.

Palms dragging, legs trailing uselessly behind her, she pulled herself forward inch by inch, leaving a smeared crimson trail across the floor. And there, under the bedroom light spilling into the hallway where she lay, the full damage unveiled itself.

Too much blood.

It streaked her face and pooled into a growing, dark halo beneath her head.

This wasn't the blood of a scrape or a stumble.

Chapter 23

It belonged to a fall you don't walk away from.

Something in him fractured, a final internal seam giving way. In that splinter of time, his entire life collapsed inward, compressing into a single, screaming truth:

he was already guilty.

The copper smell, the heat of her skin, the echo of the chase, it all arrived at once. Too much. Too fast. His mind could not sequence it.

He slammed the door shut behind them.

The lock clicked into place with a sound both sharp and absolute.

Chapter 24

The Bargain in Blood

Driven by a spike of paranoid instinct, Hassan leaned forward, pressing his eye to the cold metal of the peephole. The empty, indifferent hallway stared back.

No one.

The world outside vanished.

Inside the sealed apartment, the aftermath descended, its terrible weight finally catching up to the velocity of their ruin.

"Oh my God — no. No, no, no." He turned from the door abruptly, hands flying to his head before dropping uselessly to his sides. His eyes flicked over her body, the blood, the way she lay twisted on the floor. "Why did you run? Why would you do that?" he whispered, his voice hysterical.

He crossed to her again, panic making his movements sharp, inefficient. "Don't move. Anastasia, don't — just stay still."

She tried anyway.

Her palms pressed to the floor, arms trembling as she attempted to push herself upright. The moment her weight shifted, pain ripped through her skull and down her spine. A sound tore out of her throat, raw, frightened.

"Don't touch me," she said, breathless and shaking. "Don't touch me at all."

He froze for half a second, hands hovering inches from her shoulders. His gaze darted behind him, toward the hallway, the door, the sealed world outside.

Chapter 24

What if someone heard?
What if someone saw?
What if they called the police?

Against her protest, he slid an arm under her, another around her back, lifting her with clumsy urgency. Her body sagged, legs barely cooperating, every movement dragging a low, involuntary moan from her mouth.

"I'm trying to help you. You're hurt. Just — let me help you."

They staggered into the hallway.

The mirror beside the bedroom door caught her first.

She saw it all at once.

Her face streaked with dark, uneven trails. Blood running from her hairline, down her temple, along her jaw and neck, soaking the front of her nightdress, burgundy silk indistinguishable now from the darker red spreading across it. She raised a hand to her scalp, fingers probing shakily through her hair.

They came away wet.
Sticky.

Red — wrapping her fingers like a verdict.

A cut on her scalp, just above the hairline, bled like it had been opened with a knife. It looked fatal because the head doesn't know how to bleed quietly.

Her breath hitched sharply. Panic surged, sudden and overwhelming. "Oh my God —" Her voice climbed. "Oh my God, leave me alone."

She shoved away from him and lurched toward the bathroom.

He followed immediately, close enough that his chest almost brushed her back. Moving when she moved, stopping when she stopped, her shadow, unavoidable.

"Let me clean it," he said quickly. "Just water. I'll clean it with water."

He reached for her arm, trying to turn her away from the bathroom mirror, away from her own reflection.

"Don't touch!" she snapped. "I'll do it myself."

She leaned over the sink, turning the tap on with shaking hands. Water splashed white and loud against porcelain as she bent her head forward, guiding the stream toward the cut. Blood thinned, ran faster, spiralled pink and then red into the drain.

He stood behind her, useless and vibrating.

"I'll get something," he said. "A cloth. You need pressure."

He rushed to the kitchen, yanked open a cupboard, grabbed a small cleaning cloth — folded, untouched. Then more. Kitchen napkins, tearing them free in thick wads. He ran back, breath loud in his ears.

By the time he returned, she had shut off the tap. Her hands were braced on the sink. Her shoulders sagged.

"I need to lie down," she muttered. Her voice was thinner now. Distant.

She turned unsteadily toward the bedroom.

He scooped up the scattered napkins, the cloth, followed her again as she crossed the hallway. Her steps dragged. He put a hand lightly at her elbow, then firmer when she nearly stumbled.

"Sit," he said once they reached the bed. "Don't lie down. Sitting's better. Less pressure. Just — sit."

She obeyed, sinking onto the edge of the mattress.

He knelt in front of her and began wiping her face and neck with the napkins, careful but frantic, dabbing rather than dragging. She flinched with each touch.

Chapter 24

"Ah —!" Her breath shuddered. "Be careful."

"I am," he said too quickly. "I am."

He unfolded the cloth and pressed it against her hairline, firm, direct.

She hissed through her teeth, hands clenching in the bedspread.

The blood soaked through almost immediately.

"Hold this," he said, thrusting the cloth toward her hands. "I'll get water."

He went back to the kitchen, grabbed a bowl, filled it at the sink. As he headed back toward the bedroom, his eyes caught the hallway floor.

The streaks.

Drops.

His stomach lurched.

"Oh my God," he whispered. "There's blood out there."

He rushed back to her, dipped the cloth into the bowl, wrung it out, pressed it back to her wound, cleaning again. The blood kept coming, dark and steady.

"Press harder," he said.

She looked at him, eyes glassy, frightened. "Call an ambulance."

"Wait," he said instantly, too fast. "Just wait. It'll stop."

He fled again to the kitchen for more napkins, more, always more, then stopped short at the door. Hands pressed flat against the wood as he leaned into the peephole.

The hallway stared back.

Empty.

He cracked the door open and slipped out, dropping to his knees near the right side, close to the green rails that had just witnessed the horror. The blood drops there had already begun to dry, darker, tacky. He scrubbed at it with a napkin.

It smeared.

"Fuck," he muttered.

He spat onto the stains, wetting them, then scrubbed again, harder. The stains didn't let go; they faded, but not enough to pass. He didn't wait.

He rushed back toward the bedroom, plunged the napkins into the water bowl he'd filled earlier until they were heavy and dripping. She was still upright then, slumped on the edge of the bed, one hand pressed to her head, the other slick and shaking.

He dipped the cloth again, wrung it out, replaced it against her wound with more force than care.

"Press," he said. "Harder."

Then he was gone again.

The door opened. Closed. Opened.

This time he moved faster, more efficiently. Knees to concrete, wet napkins scrubbing hard. The water loosened what had dried. Blood lifted, diluted, erased in seconds. A drop here. Another there. Gone. Gone. Gone.

He didn't linger.

Back inside. Lock. Click. Peephole.

While he was out there, she had reached for her phone in her pocket.

Chapter 24

Her fingers slid on the glass, smeared red. She squinted at the screen, breath shallow, chest fluttering.

1. 1. 2.

The numbers swam.

She pressed call.

The ringing hadn't even begun when she heard his footsteps.

Panic spiked.

She stabbed the screen, cut the call, dropped the phone onto the side table as if it had burned her. When he entered the bedroom to wet the napkins in the bowl, she stared at him, wild-eyed, breathless, shaking. In that moment, she knew with a quiet, sinking certainty:

He is not going to call them.

Later, when he came back from the hallway the second time, she was no longer sitting.

She lay back on the bed, head propped awkwardly on a pillow, hair matted and dark with blood. Her voice was weaker now, thinner.

"It puts less pressure if I lie down," she said.

He didn't answer. He was already sitting next to her again, hands moving, cleaning, replacing the cloth that refused to stay clean.

"Please, call an ambulance."

There was no command in it anymore. Just need.

"I can't." His voice cracked with something close to hysteria. "You just ran out of the apartment. I can't trust you."

She swallowed hard. "Please. I beg you. Please call them."

Her breath hitched, panic climbing again. "Otherwise, you'll have a corpse lying in your bed tonight."

He recoiled as if struck.

"Then it's God's will," he snapped. "I can't do that. I have no trust in you anymore. I don't know what you'll say to them. Maybe you'll say I did it."

"Hassan." Her right hand lifted, her left elbow sinking into the bed to support her weight, trembling. She caught his chin, turning his face toward hers, forcing him to look. "Hassan — look at me —"

Her eyes were glassy, wet, terrified.

"I swear," she said, dragging the words out as if binding them in blood, "I won't say anything. I promise. After that I'll disappear from your life forever. Just please call them."

"You recorded me," he said suddenly, eyes blazing. "You were probably planning this. They're going to arrest me."

"No — look, look," she said, crossing her heart clumsily with her right index finger, the gesture childish and desperate. "I swear. I won't do that. Please trust me."

"I cannot," he said. The words came out sharp, absolute. Fear had eaten everything else.

"This needs to be stitched," she said, anger bleeding into her voice despite the weakness. "Otherwise, I'll bleed to death."

"Then I'll stitch it," he shot back.

Her breath broke into a sob. Panic flooded her face.

"I will scream. I swear."

His jaw tightened.

"Then I'll kill you myself."

The words landed wrong, too big, too final. *Not her. Never her.* What he meant clawed uselessly behind them: his life, his future, everything that would end the moment anyone heard. The words just hung in the air. He didn't take them back. He couldn't. He just pressed the cloth harder.

The threat collapsed something inside her.

She turned her face slightly to the side, tears spilling freely now, soaking into the pillow, mixing with blood. Her body shook with quiet, helpless sobs.

Is this how I die?
My parents won't even know what happened to me.
Is this how my life ends?

"I beg you," she whispered, over and over. "I beg you. Call them."

He didn't.

He cleaned the wound again, hands methodical now, pressing the cloth hard against her hairline, jaw clenched, breath ragged. They spoke while he worked, words spilling out fractured, defensive, desperate; half to her, half to himself.

"You shouldn't have run. You did this to yourself."

The blood kept coming. Dark. Steady. Too much.

It's not stopping.

The thought arrived clean, clinical, detached from the panic screaming beneath it. He looked at her face, pale, eyes half-closed, lips moving in whispers he couldn't hear. The cloth in his hand was already soaked through.

I need to call.

He stood without a word. Didn't tell her where he was going. Didn't want to raise hope he might shatter. His legs moved automatically, carrying him out of the bedroom, through the hallway, into the living room.

Where's my phone?

He patted his pockets. Empty. His mind scrabbled backward through the chaos — the sideboard, the driveway, the sushi restaurant. He'd had it in his hand when they came home. He'd placed it somewhere. *On the console. By the TV. No.*

Then he saw it — on the small table by the window, where he'd set it down an hour ago, a lifetime ago, while they wrestled the flat-pack box through the door.

He grabbed it. Thumb stabbed at the screen.

1. 1. 2. 2.

The line crackled. A recorded message. In Swedish. The call dropped off almost instantly.

No. No, no, no.

He stared at the screen. His thumb was shaking so hard he could barely steady it.

The phone slipped from his fingers onto the couch. He picked it up and turned back to check on her.

When he came into the bedroom, she was still on the bed, still bleeding, still waiting. He sat down beside her without a word, picked up the cloth, and dabbed it back against her hairline.

Then —

Something shifted.

Not a sound. Not exactly.

A feeling.

His body reacted before his mind did. His shoulders stiffened. His hand froze mid-press. Every nerve sharpened at once.

He sensed someone was at the door.

Chapter 25

The Arrival of Blue

Hassan rose slowly. Not abruptly, not with the panic still tearing through his chest, but with the deliberate caution of someone moving through a minefield he could already feel detonating beneath his skin. He lifted his weight off the bed inch by inch, careful not to disturb the floor.

"Wait," he said, voice low, stripped of warmth. "Don't talk."

From the bed, Anastasia shifted weakly. "What is it?"

"Shhh," he whispered, sharper now. "I said — quiet."

His bare feet met the floor with deliberate softness. Each step was placed, not walked. Heel suspended. Ball of foot lowering with reverence, like a prayer offered to silence. His pulse roared so loud in his ears that it felt impossible that the apartment itself couldn't hear it.

He reached the door.

Paused.

Then leaned forward and pressed his eye to the peephole. The world outside snapped into focus.

Blue.

Uniform blue.

Two figures stood just beyond the doorframe's immediate edge, four, maybe five feet back. Perfectly positioned. Not knocking. Not pacing. Just standing. Hands resting near belts heavy with devices, radios clipped high on their shoulders. The word *Vakter* gleamed white across their chests.

Chapter 25

Waiting.

His stomach dropped through the floor.

"Oh my God," he breathed, barely a sound at all. "They put them out there."

His hands trembled against the door.

From the bedroom, her voice floated out, thin but alert now. "Who put who where?"

He didn't turn. Couldn't. "Someone called security," he said. "They're just standing there. Not moving. Just waiting."

The words tasted like metal.

She pushed herself upright.

He felt her before he saw her, her movement dragging out of the bedroom toward the hallway, uneven footsteps closing the distance. Panic surged, flooding every channel at once.

She reached the door.

"Let me take a look."

"No," he said immediately. Too loud. He softened it. "Please. Don't."

Her eye went to the peephole.

She inhaled sharply.

Relief broke across her face in a way that made something inside him tear cleanly in two. Her shoulders dropped. Her mouth parted. Tears welled, not from fear now, but from release.

Someone had come.

For her.

"They're here," she whispered, almost reverent. Her knees trembled as the fear started draining out of her.

He moved fast then. Too fast.

His left elbow pressed into her front, trying to block, to steer, to pull her backward from the door. "No — Anastasia — please—"

"Don't," she said, and there was steel in it now. Confidence blooming, sudden and dangerous. She reached for the handle.

Her fingers slipped on the metal, slick with blood. She clawed at it, nails scraping loudly, desperately, leaving faint red streaks behind.

"Stop," he hissed. "Stop — don't open it."

She twisted against him, weak but frantic, her body driven by a singular instinct now: escape. Her mouth opened, breath filling for a scream.

He saw the future collapse inward.

If he stopped her, she would yell.

If he didn't, they would arrest him.

There was no third option.

"Help me," he prayed. "Please. Just — help me."

He clasped his hands together tightly, fingers interlocked in a childlike gesture of supplication, as if placing himself entirely at her mercy. Roles flipped.

The words tore out of him raw, unplanned, obscene in their desperation. *Please — help me — don't say anything. Don't ruin me.*

She didn't hear him.

Or she did, and chose not to.

Her hand closed around the handle.

He released her.

The door swung open.

Light spilled in first — hallway light, harsh and public. Then the air. Cold. Neutral. Official.

They stood there together, framed in the doorway.

Exposed.

Two security guards straightened instantly, eyes flicking from her blood-soaked nightdress, her matted hair, her trembling body, then to him. Barefoot. Breathing too fast. Standing too close.

The narrative assembled itself without effort.

Victim.
Culprit.

Labels snapping into place like magnets finding their poles.

Her knees buckled slightly. One of the guards stepped forward at once.

"Ma'am," he said calmly. "Are you hurt?"

She nodded. Once. Hard.

"Yes," she said.

The word echoed like a verdict.

Hassan felt the floor tilt beneath him, not falling, not yet, but shifting, rearranging itself into something he would never climb out of. The private war was over.

This was public now.

And there would be witnesses.

She didn't scream.

She didn't need to.

While Hassan stood frozen in the doorway — his body exposed, his mind lagging behind the speed of consequence — she lifted her eyes and met the gaze of the guard on the left. Just for a second. Then again. A small, precise movement. Not frantic. Not theatrical.

A signal.

Her pupils widened. Her lower lip trembled. She gave the faintest shake of her head.

I'm in danger.

Hassan saw none of it. His mind was still back in the kitchen, on the stairs, drowning in the blood and the chase.

The future was already happening without him.

The guard registered it instantly. His posture shifted, professional, predatory, decisive. His shoulders squared. His body angled between her and Hassan without theatrics, without escalation. Protection without permission.

The other guard had already turned away, hand lifted to his radio.

His Swedish poured out fast, efficient, professional, too fast for Hassan to fully track.

"— kvinnlig… vit… ungefär fem sju… tidiga tjugoårsåldern…"
White female. Five-seven. Early twenties.

Hassan flinched internally.

"— blöder från huvudet… extremt panikslagen…"
Bleeding from the head. Extremely panicked.

The guard's eyes flicked back at Hassan briefly, then away again as he continued.

"— manlig… brun… cirka fem elva… tidiga trettio… oskadd…"
Brown male. Five-eleven. Early thirties. Unharmed.

Each descriptor landed like a nail.

"— verkar ha slagit henne…"
Seems to have hit her.

Hassan's chest constricted violently.

"No —" he whispered, but the word never made it past his teeth; he didn't understand exactly what had been said.

"— hon är rädd för honom… ambulans tillkallad —"
She is afraid of him. Ambulance requested.

The radio crackled back with affirmation. The chain locked into place.

The first guard turned fully to Anastasia now, voice low, steady, rehearsed for moments like this.

"Ma'am," he said gently. "You're going to be fine."

She nodded again, tears spilling freely now, her body shaking in full permission.

"Just come out of the apartment," he continued, extending a hand but not touching her. "Stand here. Sit by the stairs."

Hassan surged forward half a step, panic detonating through him.

"We both fell," he blurted. "Tell them — we both fell."

The guard snapped his head toward him immediately.

"You are not allowed to speak to her," he said flatly.

The sentence severed any illusion of participation.

Hassan stopped breathing properly. His mouth opened, then closed. His hands curled uselessly at his sides.

Already guilty.
Already managed.

Anastasia said nothing.

She didn't look back.

She obeyed.

She stepped past Hassan, past the threshold he had tried to seal shut, and into the hallway. Her legs trembled as she lowered herself onto the stair edge where the guard indicated. Blood continued to slide down her temple, dripping silently onto the concrete between her bare feet.

Hassan stood alone in the doorway now.

"I was trying to help her," he said desperately, words spilling faster, louder. "She fell. She hit her head. I tried to call the ambulance but the number didn't go through."

The guard nodded, calm, neutral.

"Don't worry," he said. "Everything is going to be fine."

The words did not reach Hassan as comfort.

"Can you please bring a chair?" she asked Hassan. He didn't hear her over the drumbeat of his heart.

"They're on their way," the guard added. "The ambulance."

Hassan swallowed hard. "But — you said something about the police."

"Yes," the guard replied evenly. "They are also on their way. To investigate what happened."

Chapter 25

The hallway tilted.

This is it.

The thought arrived fully formed, cold and absolute.

It's happening.

The machinery had engaged. Reports logged. Descriptions transmitted. Roles assigned. No clarifying sentence. No nuance that could survive the visual truth of blood, fear, and proximity.

They are going to arrest me.
Seeing this, how could they not?

His heart hammered against his ribs, each beat loud enough to feel incriminating. His mind scrambled, grasping for the last fragments of control.

Act cool.
Nothing you did is wrong.
Just go inside.
Get dressed.
You're going to the hospital.

He nodded stiffly, unsure why.

"I — I'll just…" He gestured vaguely toward the apartment. "I'll get dressed."

No one stopped him. No one even acknowledged he'd spoken.

That, more than anything, terrified him.

Behind him, the apartment door stood open — wide, violated — its private darkness now bleeding into the public corridor. The bedroom light still burned inside, harsh and accusatory, illuminating a space that no longer belonged to him. And as he turned back inside, every step felt like retreating into a room that would soon be searched, catalogued, and stripped of all its excuses.

Already condemned.

He turned back inside mechanically.

He dressed himself with hands that no longer felt attached, shirt tugged on crooked, buttons missed and redone, black jeans pulled up with jerking movements.

"Can you please pick my phone and the keys? They are in the bedroom on the side table," Anastasia shouted from outside.

He obeyed mechanically. Everything in that apartment felt radioactive now.

He picked up her keys — and his own — slipped them into his pocket, then he picked up her phone.

A sudden, sharp thought cut through the fog: *the recording.*

He opened the phone to check, thumb swiping to her recording app. Nothing. The audio file was gone.

Deleted? In the kitchen, or after. Or maybe she was never recording.

Shit.

Maybe I should reset the phone. No. Then I am definitely guilty. Just give it to her.

Then he went to the living room and picked up his own phone from the couch.

When he stepped back out, the lock clicked shut behind him.

He turned the key once.

Then again.

As if repetition could reverse time.

Too late.

Far too late.

He gave the phone back to her.

Footsteps were already rising in the stairwell.
Heavy. Purposeful. Multiple.

The sound alone tightened something around his throat.

They came into view as he finished locking the door, ascending in formation. A woman first. Then men. Three — no, four — behind her. Dark navy uniforms swallowing the light, bodies armoured in gear that looked designed not to protect, but to dominate.

The policewoman moved with cold authority. A body camera sat squarely at her chest, its small lens already alive, already recording. Her utility belt was dense with equipment, radio, restraints, baton, gloves clipped and ready. An earpiece curved into her ear, wire disappearing beneath her collar. Shoulder patches bore insignia and crossed keys. Her cap shadowed her eyes, but not enough to hide the judgement burning there.

The men behind her looked impossibly tall, broader, heavier, faces set into neutral lines practised into permanence. Their boots struck concrete in unison. A sound of ownership.

Hassan felt his pulse jump erratically, slamming against his ribs.

Stay calm. Act normal. Nothing you did was wrong.

The policewoman's gaze cut to him first.
Hard. Measuring.

Then to Anastasia.

It softened.

Not sympathy exactly, but recognition. Pity sharpened into purpose.

She turned to the security guards and spoke rapidly in Swedish.

The hallway filled with a language Hassan couldn't penetrate, clipped consonants, professional cadence, words firing back and forth like data packets. He caught nothing except tone.

Condemnation.

The guard gestured once, subtle but unmistakable, toward Anastasia. Then toward him.

The policewoman nodded.

She stepped closer, eyes never leaving them, and switched to English.

"What happened?"

Hassan jumped at the question; words spilling out before she even forms it. "She fell."

The policewoman tilted her head slightly. "Where did she fall?"

His mouth went dry.

He could not say the truth. He could not describe the chase, the stairs, the collision. That story sounded insane. Guilty.

"In the bedroom," he said, then faltered. "Or the bathroom. I — I don't know."

Anastasia remained silent. Not a word. Not a sound.

The policewoman's eyes sharpened. "How did she fall in the bedroom?"

"I don't know — she stumbled? Maybe she hit her head on the bed frame," he said quickly. "Or the floor."

The words felt stupid the moment they left him.

"Did you call the ambulance?" she asked.

"Yes," he said immediately. "I did. But it didn't go through."

The policewoman nodded once.

"Okay," she said. Then, turning slightly: "I will ask her some questions now."

She spoke again in Swedish, short, directive.

Before Hassan could process it, two of the male officers stepped toward him.

"Wait," he said. "What—"

One of them took his arm.

Firm.

They started guiding him toward the stairs.

From behind, Anastasia's voice finally broke the silence. "Where are you taking him?" she said, still concerned about him.

No one answered her.

"Where are you taking me?" Hassan asked, panic cracking through his attempt at control.

Hands closed around both his arms now. Grip tightening.

"What are you doing?" His voice rose despite himself.

As they turned him away, a shadow passed him; he caught a brief glimpse of someone entering the apartment across from his, a woman in civilian clothes, a dark hoodie pulled up, moving with quiet purpose. She didn't hesitate. Didn't look around. She slipped inside as if she had been there before.

The door swung inward behind her.

For a fraction of a second, the nameplate beside the frame caught the hallway light, metallic, plain, unremarkable:

M. Karlsson

Then the door closed.

He didn't pay much attention. He couldn't. The pressure on his arms tightened, the stairs pulling him downward, the moment already dissolving under the weight of what was happening to him.

Down they took him.

As they passed the first landing, he saw them, blood drops scattered on the steps like questions he couldn't answer: one here, then there, then nothing for so long.

Fuck. I didn't even think about these.

Then past the grey slippers.

Past the ground floor. Past the familiar. Into the basement, where the air turned colder and smelled faintly of damp concrete and machinery.

They stopped near the elevator doors.

He was positioned with his back to the metal, the chill seeping through his shirt. One officer stood directly in front of him, three steps up the stairs, elevated just enough to dominate the space.

The others flanked behind.

Boxed in.
Caged.

His heart hammered violently now, each beat a countdown he couldn't see.

"Am I under arrest?" Hassan asked.

The question hung in the air.

Unanswered.

Chapter 26
The Seven Drops

Anastasia waited until his footsteps were gone. Not just faded — *gone.* Until the sound of him was no longer anywhere her body could track. Even then, she didn't relax. Her shoulders stayed high. Her jaw stayed clenched. Her eyes kept flicking toward the stairwell as if he might reappear through sheer force of will.

A minute passed.

Maybe more.

Time had stopped behaving normally.

The policewoman stood a few feet away, angled toward her but not crowding her. The guards had shifted position, creating space — space that felt enormous and fragile all at once.

"What is your name?" the policewoman asked.

"Anastasia," she said. Her voice came out thin, scraped raw by fear and blood loss.

The woman nodded once, recording it somewhere — either in memory or in the small black lens blinking steadily at her chest.

"Tell me what happened."

Anastasia swallowed. Her tongue felt thick. Useless.

"I'm afraid of him," she said instead. "Let him leave first. Maybe he can hear me."

The policewoman glanced toward the stairwell, then back to her. "He can't hear you now."

Chapter 26

Anastasia shook her head faintly. "He said he'll kill me. He'll kill my family."

The words dropped between them, heavy and absolute. Not shouted. Not embellished. Just stated.

Her hands trembled in her lap. Blood had dried in places now, tight and pulling at her skin. Her head throbbed in waves — pressure, release, pressure again. The hallway smelled like metal and disinfectant and something faintly electrical from the guards' equipment.

The policewoman watched her for a moment without speaking.

Not staring. Assessing.

Then, gently, almost conversationally, she asked, "Do you know someone here?"

Anastasia looked up, confused. "Here?"

"In the city," the woman clarified. "A friend. Family. Someone we can call to be with you."

The question landed deeper than it should have.

Someone to witness her.
Someone to anchor her.

Someone who made her *not alone.*

"I—" Her voice caught. She swallowed and tried again. "I don't have family here."

The policewoman nodded, unsurprised.

"But," Anastasia added quickly, as if silence might be misread, "I have a friend. From Ukraine. We've met a few times."

"That's fine," the officer said. "Would you like us to call her?"

Anastasia shook her head, then stopped herself. Control mattered now. Agency mattered.

"I can," she said. "I'll call her."

Her fingers fumbled for her phone. The screen lit too brightly, making her wince.

She scrolled through her contacts slowly, deliberately, as if speed might betray desperation. Found the name. Hesitated just long enough to feel the weight of the decision — then pressed call.

It rang once.

Twice.

"Hello?" A woman's voice answered in Ukrainian, warm and startled.

"Hi," Anastasia said in the same language. The word came out wrong — too normal. She adjusted. "I… I had an accident."

Silence stretched on the other end, immediate concern rushing in.

"What kind of accident?"

"I fell," Anastasia said, true enough. "I'm bleeding. The police are here. Can you… can you come? Please."

There was no hesitation this time.

"Yes," her friend said immediately. "Where are you?"

Anastasia gave the address, stumbling slightly over the words, grounding herself by the act of saying them aloud.

"I'll come right now," the woman said. "I'm on my way."

"Thank you," Anastasia whispered, and meant it in a way that felt almost painful.

Chapter 26

She ended the call and lowered the phone to her lap.

The policewoman had not moved.

"Someone is coming," Anastasia said quietly.

"Good," the officer replied. "That's good."

And it was.

Not because it changed what had happened.
Not because it softened anything.

But because, from this moment on, Anastasia would not be the only body in the room who mattered.

She would have a witness.

A reference point.
A second voice that did not belong to him.

Finally, something inside her gave way.

She spoke.

"We had a fight," she said, staring at the floor because it was easier than looking at anyone's face. "In the kitchen. I started recording. He found out."

Her breath hitched.

"I thought he was going to hit me," she continued. "So, I ran. And he ran after me. To stop me."

The policewoman didn't interrupt. Didn't nod. Didn't reassure. She let the words come out at their own pace.

"In the middle of the stairs, I fell," Anastasia said, her voice shaking now. "That's when I got this." She touched the air near her head, a weak, trembling gesture. The movement sent another sharp pulse of pain through her skull.

"Did he push you down?" the policewoman asked, already framing the sequence.

"I think," Anastasia said after a small pause.

The uncertainty slipped in uninvited. It scared her more than any clear answer could have.

"You think?" the officer asked gently.

"I… I don't know," she said quickly. "Everything was too fast. I just know I was falling. Then I hit my head. My legs. My shoulder. My arm." She paused, breathing shallow. "I think my foot is broken."

Her eyes burned.

"Can you please call the ambulance?" she asked suddenly, panic spiking again. "Please."

"It's already on its way," the policewoman said. "Are you sure he pushed you on the stairs?"

"I don't know, I told you," Anastasia said again.

"Did he also hit you?" the officer asked.

Anastasia hesitated.

The truth was complicated. The truth felt dangerous.

"No," she said finally. The word came out reluctantly, like it resisted being spoken. "No."

The policewoman still didn't write anything down.

The sound of sirens cut through the building moments later, muffled but unmistakable. Relief surged through her so suddenly that it made her dizzy.

Yellow vests flooded the hallway, bright and jarring against the concrete and blood. Paramedics moved with practised efficiency, equipment already in motion, an oxygen tank rolling softly, a folded stretcher appearing as if from nowhere, bags unzipped and laid open.

One of them knelt in front of her immediately.

"Hi, my name is Pontus," he said, calm, grounding. "We're going to take care of you."

They cleaned the wound first. Cool antiseptic bit into her scalp, making her gasp. Gauze followed, firm hands pressing where everything screamed not to be touched. One of them leaned closer, studying the injury: a horizontal laceration just above the hairline, maybe five centimetres long. Still bleeding. Enough to scare anyone.

"Scalp wounds bleed a lot," Pontus said, almost casually, "but we still need to close this."

"Press here," one of them said, guiding her fingers. "Tight."

She obeyed, jaw clenched, breath shaking.

"Can you move?" another asked.

She nodded weakly. The world tilted but stayed upright.

"Would you like to get on the stretcher, or can you walk?"

"I can walk," she said. She needed to. The stretcher felt too final.

They helped her to her feet, arms steadying her on both sides as her injured foot protested sharply. She hissed, but didn't stop.

The policewoman stepped forward just before the doors closed.

"I'll meet you at the hospital," she said.

Anastasia nodded.

She didn't know what would happen next.

She only knew she was still alive.

For now.

They guided her toward the elevator. Her gaze dropped before she could stop it. Blood drops where she'd been waiting for the ambulance, spilled in the time she'd spent sitting too still, trying to keep the shaking contained. Not a pool. Not a spectacle. Just evidence in small, uneven punctuation: round beads, a few dragged marks where something had shifted under her, where she'd had to brace and couldn't do it cleanly.

Hands came in on either side. They helped her up. Her weight moved reluctantly, as if her body didn't trust the idea of standing yet. The moment her feet took her again, the space narrowed. Walking became a series of decisions her body made, one step at a time.

She started toward the elevator.

The doors were open. Inside, on the upper half of the mirrored wall, her reflection waited, cropped by angle and height the way it always was. That mirror. The one she used to steal herself in whenever she had a second: quick selfies when no one was watching, hair adjusted; the same mirror she passed on laundry days with a basket biting into her arms.

Now it held a different inventory.

Her skin looked too pale under the light. The gauze at her head looked careless, temporary, like a bad solution on someone else's body. Her eyes were too large, unfocused, but awake in the wrong way. Her mouth hung slightly open, as if she'd forgotten it belonged to her. The woman in the mirror looked familiar only in structure, like a version of her assembled from memory and stress.

Two paramedics stepped in behind her. Their presence filled the small space without touching her. The doors hesitated, then began to close.

Chapter 26

She turned to face the front of the elevator, and through the narrowing gap she saw the stains again, up there on the stairs where she'd been sitting, where she'd waited, as if stillness could be mistaken for control. The marks weren't dramatic. They were mundane, physical, and therefore impossible to argue with.

The doors sealed. The elevator moved.
Down.

The hum of descent pressed into her bones. The building continued doing what it always did, as if nothing inside it had changed.

Then the doors opened.

Ground floor.

In front of the elevator door, in the middle of the landing: seven drops — maybe eight. Different sizes. One elongated, pulled slightly, as if whatever had fallen there had tried to move and gravity had followed late. Her eyes fixed on them with a clarity that made her stomach go cold. That spot. The place she had met the floor an hour ago and stayed there long enough for time to gather around it.

The paramedics guided her gently, like they were moving her through a scene that no longer belonged to her.

And then she saw the grey slippers.

Grey. Soft. Domestic in a way that felt obscene against the concrete. One lay overturned on the second-to-last step, sole facing upward like a question no one intended to answer. The other rested closer to the landing, nearer the blood than she was comfortable admitting. They weren't flung apart. Just separated enough to suggest disruption without chaos.

Something in her reached for them on reflex, the same automatic impulse that reached for a dropped phone or a slipped strap. But her hand didn't move.

She didn't touch them.

She didn't ask anyone to take them.

Touching them felt wrong. Not because she was afraid of what they meant, but because moving them would rearrange something that needed to stay exactly as it had happened. As if the truth was fragile and would shift if she laid a finger on it.

She kept walking.

And with a strange, steady awareness that sat just behind her ribs, she thought: *They'll photograph this. They'll record it. Someone will want the floor to speak in clean, comprehensible shapes. Someone will want the objects to explain the sequence.* If she moved the slippers now, she would be breaking the pattern, giving the future a neater story than it deserved.

She left them where they were.

They passed through the hallway door and continued toward the main entrance. Five more steps down. The automatic doors slid open with a mechanical sigh, indifferent to what they were releasing.

Cold air rushed in.

She walked barefoot.

Concrete first, hard, unforgiving, embedded with tiny pebbles that pressed sharply into her soles. Then the paving stones outside, uneven and damp, each step grounding and painful in a way that made her acutely aware of the body she still had. Finally, asphalt — flat, dark, faintly warm from the day, an unsettling contrast to the night air.

She didn't flinch. The pain was already there. It was simple. It didn't ask questions. It didn't reinterpret. It didn't negotiate.

The ambulance waited at the curb, doors already open, white interior light spilling onto the street. Yellow vests moved toward her. Hands appeared, ready to steady if she tilted or folded. Ready to make her a patient instead of a problem.

She climbed inside.

Only then did her knees begin to shake, small, involuntary tremors, as if her body had been holding itself together on borrowed attention and the debt had finally come due.

Chapter 27

The Handing Over of Keys

From the basement, Hassan heard everything. Not clearly, but enough. Boots pounding up. The sharp, efficient clatter of equipment. Voices layered over one another in Swedish, clipped and fast, the cadence unmistakable even if the words weren't. Radios chirping. Orders given and acknowledged. The building, which had always been quiet, now sounded alive with authority.

He stood where they had told him to stand. Back to the elevator doors, cold metal pressing through his shirt. His palms were damp. He wiped them on his trousers without realising he'd done it.

Then a pause.

A long one.

Muffled sounds followed. Voices lowered. The kind of quiet that wasn't calm, but procedural. Time stretched thin. His mind filled the silence with images he couldn't see, her on the floor again, blood, accusations spoken without him present to contradict them.

The elevator doors slid open somewhere above.

Closed again.

He heard footsteps on the ground floor. The main entrance. The heavy exterior door opening, the cold air rushing in. Someone speaking louder, directing. Then movement outward, taking her outside the building.

Away from him.

His chest tightened painfully.

Chapter 27

An officer standing a few steps up from him shifted his weight.

"I am a software engineer at Microsoft," Hassan said suddenly.

The words came out of nowhere, launched by panic rather than strategy. He needed to say something, needed to assert shape, legitimacy, a version of himself that didn't end in handcuffs.

The officer didn't look impressed.

"Mm-hm," he replied, noncommittal.

He didn't write anything down. Just let the words fall.

"What is your name?"

"Hassan," he said.

"And where are you from?"

"Pakistan." The word hung longer than it should have.

The air seemed to change immediately. Subtly. The officer's eyes flicked over him again, slower this time.

"Do you have family here?"

The question felt less like curiosity and more like an assessment. A quiet calculation. *How anchored are you? How alone?*

"No," Hassan said quickly. "No one here. They all live in Lahore. I am alone."

The truth made his voice shake.

When Hassan tried to take his phone out of his pocket, the officer's tone sharpened.

"You can't use the phone."

He felt small, alone.

"I have to inform my family," he said.

"You can't do that. You can't talk to anyone," the officer replied.

"Please," Hassan added, unable to stop himself. "Please tell me what is going to happen to me."

The officer ignored the plea.

"Who is she?"

"She is my wife — girlfriend," Hassan said, stumbling. "It's complicated."

The officer's eyebrow lifted slightly.

"Ah. Wife," he said, as if testing the word for fit. "How old is she?"

The question landed sharp and invasive, slicing straight into his fear.

"She is twenty-five," Hassan said. "She just looks younger."

The officer nodded once. Not agreement. Just acknowledgment.

"And how did you two meet?"

The implication was unmistakable: *Why you, how her, what's the justification.*

Hassan swallowed. His throat felt raw.

He explained, too quickly, too much. Where they met. How long they'd known each other. How things progressed. He talked as if volume and specificity might build a shield around him. It was exactly the opposite.

"I am an immigrant here," he said finally, as if confessing. "I hold a work visa."

The officer let the silence stretch after that.

Chapter 27

Hassan stood there, heart pounding, surrounded by concrete and metal and the invisible weight of a system that now knew his name, his face, his origin, and was deciding, quietly, what to do with him.

Footsteps came down the stairs again.

More uniforms.

Another policeman reappeared, his presence tightening the space instantly. He exchanged a few words with the officer in front of Hassan, rapid Swedish, low but efficient. He caught none of it, only the rhythm of authority passing seamlessly between them.

Then the officer turned to him and extended his hand.

"We need your apartment keys."

The words hit harder than a shove.

Hassan stared at the outstretched hand. The keys hung from his fingers on the Microsoft lanyard — blue, corporate, absurdly clean against the grime of the basement. Proof of a life he had built carefully, obediently.

"You don't have the right to do that," he said, voice trembling but defiant. "Do you have a warrant?"

The officer's expression didn't change.

"We don't need one," he said flatly. "Now hand them over."

Something cold slid through Hassan's chest.

"What if I don't want to give them to you?" he asked, the question cracking at the end. Trust had already burned away. There was nothing left to offer voluntarily.

The officer stepped closer.

"Then we'll have to take them by force."

That was it.

The last illusion dissolved.

Hassan's face crumpled before he could stop it. A sob tore out of him — humiliating and loud — his body betraying him completely. He wasn't violent. He had never been violent. He knew absolutely that resistance would only confirm whatever story was already being written about him.

With shaking hands, he took the lanyard with keys out of his pocket and placed the keys into the officer's palm. The metal was cold, already not his.

It felt like handing over a piece of himself.

The officer took them without comment, passed them to a colleague, who immediately turned and headed up the stairs.

Up into his life.

Time stretched.

Minutes crawled, viscous and heavy. The basement seemed to close in, the air thick with the smell of oil and damp concrete. Hassan stood frozen, imagining hands rifling through drawers, opening closets, scanning shelves. His laptop. His clothes. The traces of Anastasia, her things, her presence, the secret he had tried so hard to keep contained.

They were seeing everything now.

Judging everything.

Thirty minutes felt like an hour. Maybe more.

His thoughts spiralled violently.

What if they arrest me?
What if they call my family?
What if she tells them everything?
What if I lose my job because of this?

Chapter 27

His chest hurt. His vision blurred at the edges. He could barely feel his legs.

The radio on the officer's shoulder crackled to life. Swedish spilled out — final, clipped, decisive. The policewoman's voice, distant but unmistakable, issued instructions from above. The officer listened, his face a blank slate. He lifted his own radio, responded with a single flat syllable, and clipped it back onto his vest.

He turned to Hassan. His expression hadn't changed. That was the most frightening part.

"You are under arrest."

The words detonated.

Hassan cried out as his body gave up its last pretence of control. He slid backward until his spine struck the cold metal of the elevator doors, then sank down, knees buckling, hands clawing uselessly at the concrete. Sobs tore out of him, violent and humiliating, air shredding his throat. For a moment, black dots swarmed his vision, and he almost hoped he would pass out.

The irony was brutal: nothing on him showed what had happened. On her, everything did.

The private terror was over.

The system had spoken.

Writer's Coda

By morning, the stairwell was clean.

The concrete had been scrubbed until it held no evidence. No blood. No mark. Water carried everything away into drains that did not care what they erased. The railing was cold again. The steps were dry. Later, people passed with keys in their hands and places to be. No one slowed.

It is tempting to search for the exact moment everything went wrong. To believe there was a single decision, one word, one movement, that sealed the outcome.

But nothing breaks that cleanly.

Damage accumulates.

It gathers weight.

By the time it collapses, it has already been rehearsed.

Was it when she ran?

Or when he followed?

Or when fear replaced trust, and survival became louder than truth?

Later, others will impose order. They will draw lines between moments and call them causes. Systems require sequence. They do not wait for understanding.

Once the situation took a familiar shape, it no longer belonged to either of them.

A man.

A woman.

Injury. Fear. Proximity.

Stories that require footnotes do not survive first contact with authority.

Stories that collapse into a single line do.

Fear simplifies.

Institutions reward simplicity.

Survival is rarely interested in fairness.

Hassan will replay every second, searching for the moment things could have turned. Anastasia will not. She will move forward with what remains usable. And the system, faceless, procedural, perfectly calm, will close its files believing it has done its job. Because everyone followed the rules. Because nothing here was anomalous. Because this is how it works.

No monsters. No saints. Only momentum.

And momentum does not care who it crushes. Only that it continues.

This is how cycles are born. Not from cruelty alone, but from pain changing hands without ever being examined. The one who once begged learns the shape of desperation and, in time, learns to wield it. The one who once judged learns the cost of judgement and begins to pay it.

Some readers will close this book and ask: Was he guilty?

It seems simple. The law has answers. Public opinion has louder ones. But this novel was not written to be a courtroom. It was written to be a mirror.

How far back do you want to go?

Do you place guilt at the moment his foot slipped on the staircase? At the impact? At the fall? Or do you go further, to the chase that made the fall possible? To the terror that made her run? To the fight upstairs, where his hands first became something she feared?

Further still.

To the phone. To the stranger's profile. To the messages she hid. To the wound that never healed because his forgiveness was a cage, not absolution. Was she already guilty then? Of betrayal? Of seeding the mistrust that would bloom into violence?

Before that.

To her past. The war she fled. The men who hurt her. The fear she carried in her bones like a second skeleton. Fear that expects betrayal. Fear that sometimes, tragically, invites it just to confirm what it already knows.

To his past. The boy growing up brown in a world that saw him as threat before he ever spoke. The man who learned that control was survival, that proving himself was never enough, that the sentence had been written long before he ever set foot in their land.

If you go back far enough, everyone is innocent.

A child in Lahore. A child in Ukraine. Neither chose their skin, their history, their trauma.

If you go back far enough, everyone is guilty.

The world made them. And they made each other. And now she is bleeding on the floor.

This book does not answer the question. It only holds it up and says: Look.

What would you have done?

If you were him, terrified, cornered, knowing the world already believed you were a monster, would you have called for help? Or would you have done exactly what he did, desperate to contain a horror you knew would be read as proof?

If you were her, carrying old wounds, afraid of being abandoned, convinced that love always turns, would you have stayed? Would you have trusted? Or would you have run too?

There is no right answer.

There is only the question, waiting for each reader to answer it differently.

This novel is not an argument. It is an autopsy.

Power in love is never stable.

It does not belong to the strong or the righteous.

It flows to the one who needs the other less.

It does not defend him. It does not condemn her. It does not absolve the world. It simply traces the lines of force, historical, psychological, systemic, that converged on a staircase in Stockholm on a night that should have been ordinary.

They found each other in the gap between worlds.

And then they lost each other there too.

If you close this book with a verdict, you have read it differently from how it was written. If you close this book haunted, by the impossibility of answering cleanly, by the recognition that you might have done the same, by the ache of two people who should have been each other's salvation and became each other's destruction, then you have read it as it was meant to be read.

There is no single breaking point.

There is only the steady collapse.

And the silence after.

—*From the author*

Author's Note

This novel was written in response to a world that too often confuses power with worth and control with strength. In such a landscape, vulnerability is treated as liability, and those who struggle are not only overlooked but quietly blamed.

Destructive Resonance is not only an examination of a toxic relationship, but of the conditions that allow such dynamics to flourish — systems and mindsets that prize dominance over dignity, acquisition over authenticity. Trauma does not occur in isolation. It is shaped, reinforced, and sometimes normalized by the environments we inhabit.

I wrote this story from a place of witnessing, both inward and outward. The characters are not monsters; they are people shaped by fear, unmet needs, and a world that teaches us to mistake endurance for strength and possession for love.

If this book leaves you unsettled, I hope it also leaves you reflective. Perhaps it invites a pause — a moment to question what we call success, what we call strength, and what we are truly running toward.

Thank you for reading.

About the Author

F.R. Kriegler writes at the intersection of psychology, power, and intimacy. With a background rooted in the study of history and human patterns, he has long been an observer of the quiet mechanisms that shape behaviour — particularly trauma, dependency, and control.

Destructive Resonance is his debut novel, a work of psychological fiction informed by close witnessing rather than autobiography. It explores emotional dynamics that feel lived-in without claiming a single, literal source.

Kriegler lives and writes in a small town in Denmark. He is currently working on the second instalment of this story, which follows Hassan's psychological unravelling in prison, where memory, fear, and reality begin to blur.

www.ingramcontent.com/pod-product-compliance
Lightning Source LLC
LaVergne TN
LVHW030918080826
845145LV00013B/2951

* 9 7 8 8 7 9 7 7 0 1 1 7 1 *